BEGIN
AGAIN

KIMBERLY ELLEN DREDGER

BEGIN AGAIN

Dedicated to my Golden Sky, my sweet husband, Jim.
Without you the world would be a dark place, indeed.

Many thanks to my family,
to my Writers' Group, and to Reedsy,
for all the help in getting this book off the ground.

Prologue

The disintegration had been slow and insidious.

First, the single vitamin bottle in the cabinet was replaced by prescription bottles, which multiplied, spilling onto the counter.

Soon, Logan's nightly three fingers of scotch ended. The chemo pumped into his body made that luxury impossible. June's glass of wine ended, too, for awhile. Later a couple felt like a tonic.

The jeans he used to wear, boot-cut and faded from his work at the paper mill, were replaced with sweats—loose in the crotch and left leg, because that's where the catheter and bag had to be.

The green tufted leather chair they splurged on for their fifth anniversary, big enough to make love in, was taken out to make room for a recliner, because Logan couldn't sleep in bed, needed to sit up. Sleep was still elusive, but at least he could rest. And it was easier to access the cath bag, which June emptied several times a day. She only spilled it once. God, what a mess. Frustration, raised voices, tears. June knew Logan was afraid the house smelled bad, people would know just by walking in. But she always cleaned carefully, took out the trash immediately.

His work buddies came often at first. They'd stop by after their shift, have coffee or a beer and tell him the mill news. Bitch about the manager. Swap fishing stories. Brag about the big bull elk they got or whine about the one they missed. Their work clothes carried the stink of the paper mill—like rotten eggs—and Logan smiled to have it in the house again.

They'd bring packages of venison and their wives sent casseroles until June had to ask them to stop. Logan couldn't eat much anymore. Nothing tasted good to him and when he threw up, real food was worse than a cup of Campbell's or a glass of Ensure.

Then the recliner was replaced by a hospital bed.

The trips to the doctor became harder then. Logan had been a big man, was still tall, and though June was strong, there were times she felt she couldn't hold him up, guide him to the wheelchair, lift the damned chair one more blessed time into the back of the van.

The disintegration of the happy home they once had was slow and insidious. Then it was gone.

Now Logan McPherson was nine months in his grave in the hillside cemetery. Windswept. Clean. Cold.

1

Who will I be when I live there?

Montana June McPherson stared into the darkness over their bed—her bed. Another restless night. She groaned and rubbed muscles sore from packing to move. Couldn't rub away the ache in the broken heart; her pillow was sodden. While she watched, the crack across the ceiling plaster became visible as the spring day dawned.

Long strands of hair had escaped her braid and were tear-stuck across her cheek. She thumbed them back and wiped the tears, then rolled over to look at the collection on her bedside table. The letter. The box. The key to what would soon be her new house.

Who will I be when I move?

She'd come to this old farmhouse as a bride eleven years ago. Here, she'd been a lover and wife, teacher, daughter-in-law. And now—a widow. Nine months of widowhood seemed longer than ten years of marriage. The farmhouse and land near the Metcalf Wildlife Preserve had been heaven for June and Logan their whole married life. They planned to farm the fertile land themselves someday, but while Logan worked at the mill, they leased acreage to a neighbor.

June's godfather, Max England, had left the bungalow in Missoula to June in his will. When Logan became ill with the cancer that would kill him, they decided June should move there. The bungalow didn't have a mortgage nor acreage, two heavy burdens of the farm. Simply made sense. But leaving the farmhouse would continue breaking her heart. *This is home.*

Accenting that thought, she heard Ranger, her big yellow Labrador, groan and roll over as he started his waking process. Light coming in through the windows strengthened. The crack in the ceiling faded as the shadows disappeared. Day had begun.

She grasped the letter—precious last letter—and the box. They'd been on the shelf in Logan's side of the closet. She'd delayed emptying it as long as possible because she liked having his clothes there, retaining his own special scent. Not cologne. He hadn't worn any; rather the deep, earthy, what-had-been healthy male smell. His work clothes, jeans, flannel shirts: all that remained of Logan.

But yesterday the chore had to be faced. She folded his clothes into boxes for Goodwill, pausing when memories became too hard. *This shirt he wore when he proposed—he'd kept it all these years?* Later, *Never even got to wear this belt I gave him last birthday.* The final task was dusting the top shelf. She pulled over a chair, stood on it, and with her rag reached back. Way in the corner was a box she hadn't seen earlier. It was small, wrapped in Christmas paper. Taped to the bottom was an envelope, her name written on it in Logan's distinctive handwriting. In her shock she almost fell from the chair, diving onto their bed clutching the package. A cry of anguish, flood of tears. Ranger padded in and curled up on the oval rug, his simple presence bringing comfort.

Eventually June sat up and wiped her face. She inhaled deeply, rubbing the shiny paper of the little box. Had Logan forgotten it some previous year, or was he hoping to give it to her this past Christmas, the one he didn't make? He often bought presents or cards far in advance of a celebration, sometimes misplacing them and spending frantic minutes trying to find whatever it was. It'd always tickled June, but she was one who liked the anticipation before opening a gift. Wrapped presents under the Christmas tree were never a temptation to her, even when she was little. But this wasn't that Christmas morning feeling; this was bigger, more important. The last present.

June had caressed the envelope. She'd imagined Logan's long fingers as he put the letter inside. She remembered the feel of his tongue as she thought of him sealing the envelope's flap. With infinite care, she had removed the letter.

My precious Montana June.
I hope you'll find this letter and gift after you've had a chance to heal some.
Mom's going to put the box way back
in my closet—perhaps you'll find it when you start packing to move.
With luck, you'll be past the first most desperate time.
My darling wife, we believed we'd have all of our lives to love each other—
well, I guess I did.
I loved all of my life with you and cherished every day. Turns out that it
just wasn't the fifty years
we hoped for. But we took advantage of the time we had—

we never lost a chance to say 'I love you'
and I leave you with no regrets other than the big one.
I want more time.
You'll find that this present is pricier than what I've given you before, even
your wedding ring. Mom saved money over the years for our kids' college
fund, and well, that won't be necessary. She gave it to me and took me to
Missoula (remember the day?) so we could buy this. I was glad to have the
time with her, though it was hard to leave you even for a couple hours.
I was happy you were going out with your girlfriends—hoped you'd laugh
and have some fun.
SO, my dear one. Open the package.
I hope you'll wear this with the same love that you've worn your wedding ring.
But June, you need to make me a different sort of vow.
You'll grieve. Wouldn't be healthy not to.
But then, my sweet Montana June, please go on with your life.
You're too good a woman to be alone.
I want you to find some good man to love, and marry the son-of-a-bitch.
Oh, hell, I mean marry the lucky guy. Promise me.
None of us knows now what happens when we pass over the great divide,
but by the time you read this, I'll know. I hope I'll be there, watching you
read these words,
loving you as I have for years. I want you to feel me putting my arms
around you.
Remember how much I love you.
Logan"

It had taken time for June's sobbing to stop. When she was able, she wiped away her tears. She'd allowed her breathing to settle, then lifted each piece of tape and removed the gold paper. Inside was a glossed wooden box from the upper-end jewelry designer in town. She opened the lid. There, nestled in white satin, lay a gold bracelet. She lifted it out and looked inside the heavy band. Inscribed were Logan's last words to her:

To My Montana June. Begin Again.

Now, after a sleepless night thinking about the letter, she took off the bracelet and kissed it; reread his message to her; slipped it back on her wrist where it fit as if made for her. She wasn't sure she was able to do it—begin again. But if Logan wanted it, she'd try.

She picked up the third item she'd brought with her to bed last night and bounced it in her hand. The key to the little bungalow in Missoula. She got up to face the work ahead.

THERE WAS WORK to be done at Grandpa Max's bungalow before she could finally move in. She settled Ranger in his kennel, then drove the thirty miles to Missoula.

Maxwell England's house had been packed to the gills with a decade's worth of stuff—piles of mail, old newspapers and pure junk, like the bundles of used milkshake straws June had already thrown out. What'd he saved those for? But there were treasures, too, things she'd take time going over later, the sweet effluvia of life with Sarah. Each box had to be examined, almost like triage—what's precious, what to keep to examine later, what can go into the garbage now.

Grandpa Max wasn't a blood relation, rather her godfather. She and Logan used to visit the old couple as often as possible. June cooked meals and stocked the freezer while Logan mowed the lawn or shoveled the walks, depending on the season. At six foot four and well-muscled, Logan knocked out almost any job in short order.

This house was a jewel while Sarah was alive. She and Max had designed the smallish brick bungalow, making each square inch count with built-ins all over. The focus of the place was the large great room, as big as the bedroom, sitting room, and kitchen combined. When Sarah died, Grandpa Max lost the heart to keep it neat. He started hoarding anything that reminded him of Sarah. And he wouldn't let June tidy. "You move it, how the hell will I know where to find anything? Leave it alone, Juney."

Grandpa Max died three months before Logan's diagnosis.

Now, the main floor was empty, the junk gone, the large picture windows scrubbed. The kitchen to the right and sitting room beyond were also empty of furniture and the stuff of a lifetime. Through the sitting room was the bedroom with its long, high window looking onto Mount Jumbo to the east.

June'd emptied the basement too, so the morning's jobs included scrubbing the concrete floor, washing away decades of dust and cobwebs, dislodging one old mouse nest in the far back corner. Her nostrils flared with the odor of wet concrete, a smell that brought memories of spring rain in the city. After the floor, she tackled the empty shelves, using "Mrs. Meyer's All-Purpose Cleaning Soap" in basil scent. All morning she hauled heavy buckets of hot soapy water down the stairs; scrubbed with heavy brushes or big mops; sopping and squeezing, then hauling dirty water back up to dump in the alley. She was soaked and tired, but eventually the basement was no longer stuffy. The place was fresh again.

Fresh.

Clean.

A fresh, clean start.

Damn it. She didn't want a fresh, clean start for herself. She wanted her old life, with Grandpa Max to visit, Logan to love, work and laughter and happiness.

Not this pain.

The tears came. No stopping them. June dumped the last bucket and let emotion flood.

Minutes later, cried out, Montana June wiped her eyes. She just didn't have the intestinal fortitude, as Grandpa Max would say, to work anymore today. Now she was dirty, sad, and empty. Time to go back to the house that soon wouldn't be home.

THE EVENING SKY pinked up as Montana June turned onto the long dirt road to the farmhouse. Through her open window she heard the liquid trill of a meadowlark. Slowing in front of the old garage, she had a perfect view of the sun lowering behind the mountains. The long, low sunbeams highlighted the fire lookout at the summit and the tops of the Chinese elms surrounding the farmhouse. The old house needed a new roof. The leased hayfield to the south brought in a little money, but not enough to cover taxes and the never-ending upkeep that a century-old house required. Once, she and Logan thought they'd sell Max's house, use that money for repairs. But the man who leased the hayfield had always wanted the farmhouse too, and asked if they'd be willing to sell. Though at first they turned down his offer, when it became obvious Logan was dying they realized it was the right choice.

June parked the Jeep—a CJ5 1950s vintage hard-top—in front of the garage, jumped down from the seat, and let Ranger out of his kennel.

"Hey, old boy. How you doing?" June ruffled the old yellow lab's neck and scrubbed behind his ears. He placed his big, flat head against her legs and leaned in. She kneeled down to hug him.

"Come on. Let's get some dog cookies and a drink, sit out on the porch while the sun goes down."

The screen door squeaked open then banged shut behind them, and the floor creaked, all sounds of an old house in need of repairs she now wouldn't have to pay for. The living room looked good, though. Logan had refinished the hardwood floor the summer before he got sick. The only things out of place were Logan's work boots and dirty socks, left by his chair after his last shift at the mill. He'd always done that. It drove June crazy that the stinky things'd sit there until he got ready for his next shift. Then, finally, he'd put the socks in the hamper. Every work shift. But that last time, there hadn't been another work shift. During the illness, she'd left them there hoping life might go back to normal. Now, she left them there because they were part of Logan.

Dog cookies and booze were kept in the same cabinet, an old breakfront near the wood stove in the kitchen. June poured herself a glass of wine, grabbed two cookies for Ranger, then stepped out to the back porch. She sat on the second step as usual and put her arm around her dog. She closed her eyes, breathing in the clean scent of spring. Growing things. Warm earth. The meadowlark trilled again and some of the stress in June's heart relaxed. She fantasized that pretty soon Logan'd come out with his scotch and sit on the step behind her, his knees on either side, and wrap his strong arms around her as he had so many evenings. Sunset was a favorite time.

June's cell phone rang in her pocket with her mother-in-law's ring-tone.

"Hi, Mom."

"Darling girl. You sound tired. Tell me about your day."

June told Maura what she'd accomplished, going into some detail about the stress of making so many decisions. Eventually, she wound down. "So, I came home and poured myself some wine. I'm out on the porch with the big guy. Oh, there it goes—last rays of sun just slipped behind the mountain. How're you, Mom?"

"My day's been good. I did my volunteer stint, then came home and took care of Nanny and Kid. I've got my own glass of wine here, and Mr. Mouser on my lap. Been a full day." Maura's little household on the mountain consisted of her goats and her cat, gardens and books. She'd lived alone ever since Logan's father died twenty years before.

While Maura chatted, June gave silent thanks for the older woman. Maura McPherson had been a mainstay and June's best friend since they'd both lost the person most precious to them. There was nothing she couldn't share—they'd already gone through the worst together. From the beginning of June's marriage to Logan, Maura'd been a real mother to her.

June's parents died when June was fifteen. They'd been on an extended anniversary trip to Spokane staying at the fancy Davenport Hotel. On the way home, Lookout Pass was icy. A car coming from the Montana side and going too fast down into Idaho couldn't handle one of the curves, over-corrected and slammed into the MacKenzies' car. Both parents had died on impact. Max and Sarah, June's godparents, would've taken care of her, but were living in Europe at the time. June's sister Helena, who was twenty-five and working in Missoula, returned home to stay with June as she finished high school. That'd worked out fine. When June started college and moved into the dorm, Helena left to continue her own life. When June and Logan fell in love, Maura filled a niche that'd been an empty hole in June's heart.

Maura finished. "So that's it. A good day."

"Mom, your call was perfectly timed. I was hoping Ranger and I could come visit you soon. I miss you, and I found something I need to talk to you about. But you know what? I'm getting chilled, my glass is empty, I need a bath and Ranger needs his dinner."

"Of course. Why don't you come for dinner, day after tomorrow, about five. Now, you go run that bath. I'm gonna sit here a while longer and soak up this gorgeous view."

June said goodbye and clicked the phone off, tucked it into her pocket, then picked up her glass, saying, "Come on, big guy. Let's make your dinner."

June waited while Ranger took his time getting his hips into position so he could stand. Back in the warm kitchen, June filled his dish then went into the bathroom and turned on the spigots of the old clawfoot tub. She added some lavender bath oil Logan had given her his last Christmas, tested the water temperature and turned it up a notch. This was a night for a good hot soak.

Montana June returned to the kitchen and rubbed Ranger's head as she reached into the breakfront. She gave him another cookie and was about to pour more wine, then changed her mind. If this was a night for a hot soak, it might also be a night for a stronger drink. She chose Logan's favorite rocks glass, then poured a large slug of scotch.

Back in the bathroom, June put her drink on the tiny tub-side table and turned off her phone. She stripped off her grungy work clothes and dumped them in the hamper. Looking in the mirror, she brushed her long blond hair and tied it in a knot on top of her head. She leaned in toward the speckled glass. The freckles on her short nose hadn't faded. She stepped back and looked at her body. Tall enough to carry her extra weight, but she knew she'd need to do something about the pounds soon. Then, as she stepped toward the tub, she was surprised by something she should've expected.

"Oh, hell," she mumbled. "Just great. As if I need my period on top of everything else."

She wiped up, then put one foot, by centimeters, into the almost-too-hot water. Then the other foot. Bit by bit she sank into the fragrant, steaming bath. Her last reserves of strength ebbed away as the heat worked its magic on her stress. She took a drink of scotch, rubbed her head, and moaned. Tears again. Ranger came into the bathroom and collapsed on the mat.

June's period had always been so regular she planned around it. That it came now, when she wasn't thinking of it, brought her right back to that day, more than a year ago, when they'd had the first sign that something was wrong.

One blessing of married life for Logan and June was the physical part. Maura had stitched a sampler—as a gag bridal shower present—with the old saying, "Never go to bed angry" then under that, "(Just go to bed horny)." Even when they had one of their infrequent arguments, they'd look at that sampler over their bed and chuckle. Often they'd dive right in.

One late winter morning, Logan lifted himself off her warm, moist body and smiled.

"Hmmm, darlin'. Remind me again why I gotta work today? How 'bout I stay home and we keep this up all weekend?" Logan stretched his arms to allow June to move from under him. June watched Logan; her favorite sight in the world was her husband's face after they made love—dark brown hair all mussed, blue eyes glowing. But now, his expression of joyful fulfillment turned to puzzlement.

"Hey, Junebug…um, wasn't your time of the month just last week? What's this?"

June looked down at her thighs and saw the slick moisture between her legs was stained with blood.

"Oh, jeez, Logan. Thought I was all done. I'll clean up and we'll see about some breakfast."

Later that day, though, June noticed there was no further sign of her "friend," as her mother used to call it. In fact, there was nothing until the next time they made love. Perhaps June should go see a doctor.

The next day after Logan's post-work shower, he came to her looking pale. "Junebug, I guess it isn't you that needs to see the doc. It's me."

Logan was young. Only thirty-five. Prostate cancer doesn't often strike young men, but blood in the ejaculate is a warning sign. By the time they saw Logan's doctor and then a urologist, cancer had spread throughout his body.

June, in the now-cooling tub, finished her drink and put the glass back on the tiny table. Tears mixed with beads of sweat on her face from the hot water. Standing up, she wrapped the towel around her, then grabbed the towel bar as the alcohol, hot water, and stressful day hit. Ranger moaned as water dripped on him as she stumbled to the bedroom and fell into bed, towel and all.

2

A warm tongue and a quiet, almost apologetic whine woke Montana June the next morning as Ranger licked her hand and put his cold nose into her palm.

"Oh, jeez," June said, coming out of a deep sleep. "Ranger, you poor guy. Dang me!" She untangled her legs from the blanket, swung her feet to the floor, and sat up. "Hang on, let me get my head on straight. You'll be out soon."

June stood and grabbed her robe off the bedpost, then headed to the back door. Ranger brushed past her and loped down the old porch steps, rushing to the grass before lifting his leg. He looked over his shoulder and grinned at June.

"Well, big guy, I guess a hot bath and alcohol instead of dinner isn't the best idea I've had all week." June rubbed her head. "At least you got some dinner before I collapsed. Come on, I'll refill your bowl. Then I need some coffee."

The sun peeked over the Sapphire Range as June bumped open the front door with her hip, holding her mug of strong coffee in both hands. She leaned against the sill, one bare foot on top of the other. The fresh scent of plowed fields mixed with the rich smell of coffee. Meadowlarks and blackbirds added a symphony of sound.

"Ranger, 'member how your dad used to love all this?" Talking to Ranger wasn't a new thing, but it'd helped her through some bad times lately; might be crazy to talk to yourself but talking to your dog seemed quite acceptable. Friends are important, no matter how many legs they have.

June followed Ranger onto the lawn. As she walked, she plucked a handful of hard green dandelion buds. *These'll make a fine breakfast.*

Back in the kitchen, she got eggs from the fridge, poured olive oil in the omelet pan, and washed the dandelion buds. When the oil shimmered, she tossed the buds into the pan and watched them bloom as if by magic. June added the eggs and seasoning, and stirred. Mmmm… hot, soft-cooked eggs with fresh spring buds. She slid them onto a plate, poured another cup of coffee. A breakfast meant for the gods.

She'd learned about using weeds and native plants from Logan, who'd gotten it from his folks. His parents had been what he called old hippies. Maura and Logan's dad had lived at Bass Creek Commune where they learned many things about sustainable living. Logan was born at the commune. He took the best of their knowledge and used it the rest of his life. It was sad irony that Logan's healthy lifestyle, learned from his parents, couldn't save him from the cancer that killed him. Early-onset prostate cancer has a hereditary component. This, too, he got from his dad.

June finished her eggs and put the plate on the floor for Ranger to do the pre-wash.

"Hey, big guy, wanna come to Grandpa Max's today? Maybe go to the river for a quick swim?" She massaged his neck and he repaid her with his doggy smile.

While June dressed, she decided to wear a necklace her sister Helena had beaded for her years ago. But where was it? Not in her jewelry box. Perhaps in the nightstand? Looking there, she found something else. Crammed in back was her journal she'd made at a workshop years ago. She had color-washed the heavy pages and sewn them into the purple leather cover, but hadn't ever written in it. Until. Until it became the receptacle for the deepest grief. The entries weren't dated, rather were stream-of-consciousness writing. Right after Logan died, the practice became a lifesaver. But then, she stopped writing. Finding it now, nine months after his death, was a balm. Perhaps over time she'd dip into it, reading bits as she felt she could handle it. She placed it on the table, and, abandoning the search for the necklace, continued to dress for a day cleaning what would soon be her new house.

EARLY IN THEIR marriage, Logan solved a mystery for Montana June, figuring out a possible answer to a question June always wished she would've asked her dad. It was late August. Their wedding, held in the yard of the farmhouse, had been a month earlier, and now their lives were settling down to normal. Logan returned to the mill, and Montana June was gearing up for another year of teaching the kindergartners of Victor School. But classes wouldn't start until after Labor Day and this was Sunday. Logan and June were enjoying a day of rest.

The morning sun glowed through the white lace curtains of the bedroom. Logan lay on his back with his arms stretched up behind him, head resting in his hands. His dark brown hair was mussed, and he had a shadow of red whiskers on his chin. June, lying on her side next to him, ran her finger up his bicep, enjoying the solid muscle and musky scent. Through the open window came the sounds of birds, even the buzz of hummingbirds at the feeder. Logan wiggled as June's finger tickled.

"Hmmmm. Sunday morning's maybe my favorite time of the week. We can lounge in bed with our coffee while I take my time enjoying those sweet buns and strawberries of yours." Logan raised an eyebrow. "I kinda like this married stuff. What say we keep on doing it for about a hundred years or so, huh?" He reached over and tickled one of June's nipples, chuckling as it jumped to strawberry form.

"A hundred years? That's all you'll want me?" June's bare breasts pressed as she leaned in for a kiss; she lay her head on his shoulder. "Damn. I thought we'd always be together. Isn't that what you vowed? Remember you said 'I, Logan Donald McPherson, take you, Montana June MacKenzie, to have and to hold from this day forward....' Forever."

"Hey, Junebug. I always wondered. How come you're named Montana June? I get the Montana part. But your birthday's in March, not June."

"Mm-hmm. I don't know. Helena's named after the state capital, which I think is where she was conceived. Our folks honeymooned there and nine months later, bingo, Helena showed up. My dad named me, and he never called me just 'June,' always said the whole thing. That's all I know."

"Well, hell. Let's give it some thought. Bet we can figure this out." Logan went quiet for a moment. "Hoo-boy, bet I got it." His chest quaked with laughter; his eyes sparkled.

June picked up her pillow and hit him. "What? You solved it already?"

"What we've been doing just now must've put me in mind of it, Junebug. I can't believe you never saw this. You told me once your mom didn't want another baby, but your dad really did."

June frowned in concentration. "Yeah? So?"

"So, count back from March."

"March. February. January." June ticked off her fingers as she counted back. "Oh no, I don't believe I never saw that." She collapsed back on the bed laughing, her face warm with embarrassment.

"I think I'd've liked your dad. Wish I'd known him. Hey, Junebug? Sweet strawberry girl? Let's practice that thing he enjoyed so much. Practice makes perfect, they say. I think I might be ready again, see?"

(excerpt from Montana June's journal)
No more making love with that wonderful sexy man whose big body I know so well. My hands and entire body remember how he feels. I can explore him in my mind. I know where each mole was, how each inch of his body tasted, where he was hard and masculine and where his skin was soft as a baby's. No more. Never, never again. These are things I can't talk of with anyone. No one knows how desolate life is without Logan.

MONTANA JUNE SPENT the morning finishing boxes from Grandpa Max's basement. The last one she'd brought up was packed full of old letters from the 1940s, and another box contained only records from Sarah's club, the Matrix Table. These were keepers June would carry back downstairs. But all the others had to be examined carefully, to not miss anything. Memorabilia important only to the dear old couple, like napkins and matchbooks, were all put into a black trash bag. Some items, the dried corsages and old dance cards from their college years were problematic. Love seemed to emanate from them like perfume. But how could she keep them? Perhaps The Historical Museum at Fort Missoula would take the dance cards, at least. The crumbling corsages went into the trash. Each item required a decision, and it was an emotional drain. Ranger could do nothing but offer a heartfelt sigh at regular intervals.

"Okay, big guy, I hear you. I've worked long enough. Let's go for a walk. We both need to move."

The day was pleasantly cloudy. Greenough Park across the street was named after the people who'd donated it to the city decades ago. Part was park-like and groomed, but by law most was kept in a natural state, with trails leading through ponderosa and cottonwoods. This was Ranger's favorite. June frowned to see he didn't run straight to Rattlesnake Creek as he would've a year ago. Her friend was aging. Another worry, another sadness. Ranger took his time sniffing and marking, making his way to the stream for a drink. He walked all the way in, getting his belly and chest wet, instead of bending his neck to the water.

"Hey, Ranger, when you're done drinking all the water in the creek, let's walk around the park, stretch the legs, okay?" Ranger climbed out, looked at June as if to say, "Well, whatcha waiting for?" and took off down the path.

June pulled out the gather-bag she carried in her jacket pocket, and as she walked, picked lamb's quarters for her dinner, remembering Logan's lesson. The greens, weeds to most people, had leaves about an inch long, shaped like an elongated diamond or the hind-quarters of a butchered lamb. She picked whole stems, gathering bunches. Ranger kept close, smelling each tree on the way. Both were so involved that they didn't hear the footfalls of a runner on the curving path.

"Hey, look out!"

Too late. The man slammed right into June, knocking her down. Her bag of greens went flying.

"Oh, man, sorry. You okay?" he said.

"Uh, yeah. I think so. Hang on, let me get up." Ranger barked at the runner, protecting June after the fact. "Ranger, be quiet, now. Stop that noise!" To the man she said, "I guess I'm okay. That was kinda my fault, too. I wasn't paying attention." She reached for her gather-bag. "Looks like I didn't lose much." June brushed dirt from her legs, straightened, and wiggled her shoulders.

The runner was about June's height, with a lean body. He had a strange shock of white through his dark blond hair, just above his left ear. His face was sweaty, and he brushed it with his hands. "Uh…listen, really sorry. Hey, not to be rude, but if you're okay, on a time-trial… gotta be running." The man hesitated for June's tentative smile, turned and took off.

June stared after him.

"Really? Not much of a gentleman, is he, Ranger? Okay, let's get back. That's enough excitement for one day, I guess."

They made their way to the house, June walking gingerly after her fall. At the front door, she gulped as a wave of nostalgia struck her.

How many times had she and Logan come up this path on a Friday night? They'd have a bag of take-out food—stuffed baked potatoes or pasties—and through the windows they'd see Sarah puttering in the kitchen, getting glasses out for drinks, while Grandpa Max would be in the great room setting up the record player. Longing flooded June's heart. Tears clogged her throat.

She felt drained. Done in. She nested the empty boxes, took the black bags out to the garage for the trash. Picking up the lamb's quarters and grabbing a Diet Coke from the fridge, she loaded Ranger into the Jeep and headed home, across Missoula and up the Bitterroot Valley, to the little white farmhouse that was still, for a while, home.

(excerpt from Montana June's journal)
"Is this raw agony never going to end?
Will these bleeding stubs of my soul
ever heal?"

3

Montana June planned to meet Cara Johanson at the restaurant. It wasn't the first time June'd been to a restaurant since Logan died, but this time she intended to eat something. The first attempt, with Maura the week after the funeral, hadn't gone well. Both women ordered a salad and iced tea, then just stared at each other over their plates. Their eyes filled, their swollen throats wouldn't swallow the tea, and almost silently they agreed. Mom had thrown some bills on the table, and they left.

But now going out seemed possible, good to be among people. Cara was an old friend from college. In the early days of their marriages, the two couples—Cara and Peter, June and Logan—had partied often, and they'd socialized a couple times after that. When Logan died, June was surprised that the Johansons hadn't come to his funeral. Last night, on a whim, June called Cara to make a date for lunch. It'd be good to catch up, talk about happier times when neither had to worry about more than studying for finals and scrounging beer money.

As she parked at the Mexican restaurant in Victor, June saw Cara standing on the covered boardwalk that led to the door, leaning against the peeled log railing. She looked good: thinner, some new make-up maybe.

Slamming her car door, June called to her friend, "Wow, girl, you look fantastic. It's good to see you."

Cara ran and grabbed June in a hug. "Hey, you!"

The two linked arms and walked through the old-timey swinging doors. The good smells of salsa and spices made June's mouth water. The place was busy. June noticed Cara scan the crowd in the restaurant, as if she were looking for someone. Cara's look of expectation turned to disappointment.

The women were led to a table and sat down. Even before the waiter came, Cara brought up the subject that had bothered June. "I'm sorry I missed the funeral. You must know you were in my heart that day. I was completely devastated when I heard about Logan and didn't want to bring you down with my tears. How are you…really?"

June had almost learned to ignore how awkward people were in the face of bereavement. Finding the right words must be hard, but it often sounded like they thought their own grief was somehow worse.

"I'm getting there. It's a day-by-day process, but I guess I'll get through." She swallowed the lump in her throat. "You look marvelous! How are you?"

"Holy shit, I got so much to tell you. Been crazy busy with great things."

The waiter came with menus and took drink orders.

June, relieved that seeing her old friend made her think of their college years—better than remembering the foursome—said, "I want to hear, but first, know what this reminds me of, Cara?" She dipped a chip in the salsa. "Remember that time at Casa Grande after finals, we drank margaritas by the pitcher?"

Cara snorted. "And it wasn't until our *third* pitcher it dawned on us that they weren't putting much damn tequila in the mix. Shit, we were mad."

"Yep, when we should've been happy not to get stupid drunk."

The waiter came with their iced teas and took food orders. They sipped, laughing about the old days. For June, it was good to be out with a friend, feel almost light-hearted again. But soon, the laughter sounded tinny to June, and she glanced away. Not wanting to let go of the good feelings, she gulped a swig of water, hoping to relax her throat.

"So, how's Peter? What's going on?" June'd always liked Peter. He was a fun, gentle guy, more studious than most of their friends.

"Oh, Peter. That bastard. I've been wanting to tell you, I'm seeing someone else and you'll never guess who it is. But first I—"

"What? You're seeing someone else? What in the world happened?"

Cara flipped her hair and her eyes sparkled. "Well, Peter got so sedentary. And I wanted to keep on doing things, so I joined a gym and started working out. Peter didn't seem to notice how much weight I'd lost, didn't see the new definition in my muscles, and when I'd come home from the gym kinda late he'd act all, you know, pissed off." Cara kept on talking, not paying attention to June's silence.

June took another drink and swallowed hard, retreating into her head. She saw Cara's mouth moving, knew she ought to listen to what

Cara was saying. But tears threatened. *Please, not now. Let me hear her out. Perhaps I'm missing something.*

"My trainer, Ludwig—don't you love that name?—was great; we'd have a protein drink after workouts. One thing led to another, and now…," Cara took a breath. "I'm leaving that son-of-a-bitch husband and moving in with Ludwig. He's meeting us here, in fact. Should've been here already. I can't wait for you to meet him. He's gorgeous, all muscles!"

At first June just stared at her in disbelief. The noise of clinking glasses and people's lunchtime chatter seemed to grow, then fade. Cara, flipping her chic bangs out of her eyes, continued.

"Yeah, fucking Peter. I hate him now, can't even stand to see him. I wish he was dead. Dead and gone, so I wouldn't have to divorce him. Then I'd get on with my life. Like you're doing."

At that point, Cara must've noticed June's expression of horror, but kept going.

"Sorry, June. But you cannot imagine what a stupid ass he's being."

June's control broke. "You know what, Cara? I don't care how stupid he's being. Sounds to me like you're being pretty damned stupid yourself." She threw her napkin down; her voice was a low, angry growl. "You have a good man who works hard and doesn't sleep around. You're mad at him because he doesn't appreciate the new you. Yeah, I get that. And yeah, I get that he wasn't complimentary enough or whatever else it was that offended you. And you have this new guy who caught your eye." Her volume rose now, punching each word louder. "But to wish Peter dead? Especially to me? Oh, forget it. I'm out of here."

June pushed her chair back so hard it fell to the floor. Everyone in the restaurant was looking. She rushed past the tables and out the door.

"Shit. Shitshitshit!" June stormed down the boardwalk to the parking lot. "What the fuck is she doing, saying that? Go on with my life?" Her fury began to cede to embarrassment. She'd never lost control of herself in public like that before.

"Ah, shit!" June unlocked the door, jumped in, and put her head on the wheel. After a minute, she looked at the restaurant windows. People were staring. Too embarrassing.

She screeched out of the parking lot, turned toward home and hit the gas, trying to outrun the pain. Her eyes saw the road but her brain was seeing Cara's smarmy face, scrunched in indignation, mouthing those words. "I wish he was dead and gone, and then I could go on. Like you're doing."

Go on? Really?

Had Cara always been so insensitive? Self-centered and vain, maybe. But cruel? She screamed. The tires almost skirted off the road at the big S-curve. That scared her enough to slow down. *Okay, Juney. Calm yourself. Breathe. Forget her.* But there was no calming; her driving again became erratic.

Fuck it. Just drive. She sped up again. Rushing forward, she didn't care that she'd lost it back at the restaurant. *Fuck Cara. Fuck everything.*

The speedometer needle kept rising. No other cars came toward her. She flew. All it'd take would be a twist of the wheel and she'd be in the river, and Logan would be there.

Then she thought of Ranger, waiting at home. He wouldn't understand if she didn't return. June took a couple conscious deep breaths trying to slow her heart. She dashed the tears away from her cheeks with her forearm and eased up a little on the gas pedal. Perhaps she'd drive to the river, relax, forget Cara. She'd never have to see her again.

A road leading to a fishing access neared. June turned too fast. Gravel spun out from the wheels, but bumps and pot holes on the unpaved road made her slow way down. It'd been a long time since she and Logan had been to this fishing spot. Be good to sit by the river like old times.

Ahead, June saw the brown sign marking the narrow dirt road to the fishing access. Driving closer, she saw another, smaller sign tacked diagonally over the main one.

FISHING ACCESS CLOSED. NO ENTRY.

Just perfect.

She stewed for a moment, then shook it off. *So what? I'll go anyway. One little car, one woman sitting there won't hurt anything.* Following the dirt road around a corner, June saw that just ahead a barred gate blocked the road. A signpost read DEAD END.

She stopped the Jeep, keeping the engine running, and stared at the sign for a few seconds before she erupted. "Dead end? Are you fucking kidding me? Dead end? Who's dead now?" The months of grieving; the thing with Cara; the suicidal moment in the car; the anger, pain, frustration, bottled-up fear—all flooded over her in crashing waves. Her emotions boiled up into a mindless rage.

Breathing hard, June backed up the Jeep, threw the gear into drive, and hit the gas. The post holding the dead-end sign cracked but remained standing. Once more she backed up, slammed the gearshift, and sped forward, hitting the sign again. Again. Again. Again. At last, the signpost broke.

"Take that, dead end." Her rage spent, she put her head on the wheel and sobbed.

When June calmed sometime later, she was shocked to her core to realize she'd committed vandalism. She got out of the Jeep, walked to the front bumper. The sign was, well, dead, and the PTO winch on the front of her Jeep would never work again. The bumper itself was dented. Getting back in the Jeep, she turned the key and was relieved when the engine responded. Backing out, she heard no grating sounds. Maybe everything was okay.

Hedging around a bend, June spotted a vehicle blocking the road. A Fish, Wildlife and Parks truck. Great. Law enforcement, just when she'd vandalized public property. *Could this day get any worse?*

The officer got out of his truck. "Ma'am? Help you? Folks aren't allowed in right now. That sign back there's pretty clear, fishing access's closed."

June got out of the Jeep.

"Upgrading the safety signs at the weir," the warden continued. He looked at June, who was now staring at him. "Ma'am? You okay?"

That shock of white hair above his left ear. It was the jerk of a runner who'd knocked her down in the park yesterday. Guess the day could get worse, after all. Maybe he wouldn't recognize her.

"Officer, I'm okay, just had a really bad day." She sighed. "I better report an accident. I kinda ran into that dead-end sign." Trying to keep her head tilted so he wouldn't see her face, June motioned back with her arm.

Without warning, June's throat closed. She couldn't breathe. She was strangling.

"Ran into it? Guess I better grab a look." The warden started to walk toward the sign. "Jeez, guess so. What'd you hit it with, a semi?"

June made a gasping, squeaking noise as she tried to get oxygen in. The warden spun around.

"Hey. Hey, lady, take it easy. Here, sit here for a sec." He led her to his truck and lowered the tailgate. June's breath came in short, wheezy gasps, and her vision was sparkling around the edges.

He grabbed a plastic water bottle from his truck and handed it to her. "Don't think about breathing in," he said. "Just let the air come out…breathe out slowly…good."

Listening to his gentle voice, June calmed enough to inhale. And exhale. And inhale. Her vision cleared. She faced the warden. He furrowed his brow. "Better now?" She nodded, and he smiled.

"Yes. Thanks for the water," she said, embarrassed by the panic attack and contrite about the sign. "I'm sorry. Like I said, this's been one hell of a day. I was coming here to—well, to gather my thoughts after some unpleasantness with a friend, and—I guess there's no way to excuse what happened to the dead-end sign. I guess I killed it, taking out my frustrations. I don't ever do things like that, Officer. I really am sorry."

"Well, let me see what I can do." The warden walked to the sign. June, eyes closed, heard him kick at the ground, moving heavy objects. She waited, wondering how much trouble she was in.

"Ma'am?"

June startled.

"Should be okay. I stood the sign back up. Post is sure broken, but probably due to be replaced anyway. Don't worry, won't write you up or anything, but I do have to make a report. Need some info from you." He pulled out his notebook and pencil. "Name and address?"

"Montana June McPherson. Number eight—"

"Wait, hold on." His brow wrinkled again, and he looked up from his notes. "Your name's familiar. And you look familiar, kinda. But your name's unusual, rings a bell. Oh, hell. You're Logan's wife, ah, widow." He took his cap off and slapped it on his leg. "I'm so sorry about Logan. Knew him in high school. Such a shame. I'm really very sorry."

"Thanks. You knew Logan?"

He held his hand out. "Peter Pacinski, folks call me Pace."

"Nice to meet you." June shook Pace's hand. "Pace Pacinski. Maybe I remember Logan mentioning you."

"Here's my card," he said, handing her one. "Call me if you need anything." He grinned. "Especially if you need to access a blocked road. Probably get you in without damage."

She ducked her head and gave a tiny smile. "Thank you, Officer."

"Please, it's Pace."

"Okay. So, uh, what's next?"

"Well, that depends. You well enough to drive home?"

"Oh, yes. I'm fine now." June hopped off the tailgate, handed Pace his water bottle, and with a half-hearted smile, turned to leave.

"Montana June? Don't want to interfere, but since you've had such a bad day, I'm a little concerned. It's part of my job to make sure folks are all right. So, is it okay to call you tonight to double-check? Not really official, more as a friend?"

"Well, Pace, I guess that's fine," June said, supposing she'd let it go to voicemail. She was glad that Pace seemed to think the reason she looked familiar was because she was Logan's widow. It appeared he didn't remember running her over in the park.

After the extremely stressful afternoon, it was good June had an evening planned with Maura.

4

Maura lived on the mountainside across the valley from Montana June's farmhouse. Logan's parents had moved there after leaving the commune which now moldered into the soil farther up the mountain. The little house had an "old hippie" feeling. In the nearest trees hung wind-chimes made from wine bottles, silverware, bits of crockery and mirrors. The yard was kept in check by the nanny goat that wandered in and out of the barn, followed by her new kid. The first time June had seen this interesting house, Logan told her it hadn't always been so unusual. When his folks left the commune, Dad wanted to return to a more normal way of living. Logan's youth was spent close to nature but not quite as colorfully. When Dad died, Maura reverted to her younger hippie ways, decorating the house to match what she called "her real self."

Her real self was walking out of the house, watching June's Jeep coming up the drive. Maura's auburn hair, now mottled gray, was tied in a thick braid down her back. She was dressed as usual, in a long denim skirt and long-sleeved chambray shirt with the tails tied around her ample waist. Her feet were bare.

"Oh, my darling girl, it's been too many days." Maura flung open the Jeep's door and spread her arms for June to fall into. June stepped down and did just that. Ranger lumbered out, then wagged his whole body in joy at seeing the older woman.

"Mom, thanks for inviting us. This's been one hell of a week, and I guess I really needed to be with you. Thank you."

"You come right on over here and sit down. We'll have a grand view of the alpenglow while we rest and catch up. Ranger! Don't get too familiar with Kid!"

Ranger, an old friend of the nanny goat, was nosing the baby with a little too much exuberance. Nanny took care of matters and head-butted Ranger back to a more respectful distance.

Maura and June walked arm in arm to the table at the foot of the garden. It was already set with an open bottle and wineglasses.

"I thought we'd enjoy the early evening out here for a while, before we eat. By the time dinner's over and we have coffee, you'll be safe to drive home. Of course, if you'd rather, you can sleep here." Maura poured a glass of wine for each of them and plopped herself into one of the mismatched wooden chairs while June took another. They looked across the broad valley as it began its evening glow. The sun, setting behind the mountain on which the house sat, made the sky above their heads pink and apricot, melding into a deep blue across the valley. Through all this color darted a golden contrail of a jet following its daily route east. The two women exhaled at the view, then turned and smiled at each other.

"Let's have a toast," Maura said as she raised her glass. "Here's to us, taking it day by day and moving on." As they clinked glasses, June's sleeve slipped down her arm, exposing the new gold bracelet. "Oh, I see you found the box, Montana June. I wondered when you would."

"Yes, I had to clean out Logan's closet, even though I didn't want to. I don't want to give away his clothes. I don't want to even move! Damn it, I've been crying all day it seems." June pulled a handkerchief out of her pocket and blew her nose. "So, yeah. I packed up the clothes in his closet and, as you can guess, the last thing I found was the box."

"Honey, that day Logan and I drove into Missoula was such a gift; our first time out alone in so long. He felt quite a bit stronger, and we hoped he'd be able to eat some lunch, so we chose that little place by the river with tables outside, near Caras Park."

June nodded, remembering the spot.

Maura continued. "I gave him the money then. I'd been putting five dollars aside whenever I could, ever since you two got married. The money was intended, as I think Logan told you in the letter, for a college fund for grandkids, but you know, darling girl, none of us gets to choose how the cards are dealt." Maura used her thumb and forefinger to stop tears in the corners of her eyes. She cleared her throat. "We discussed how he should spend the money, and since the jewelry store was down the block, we went there after he finished not eating much. He wanted it engraved. I drove back to get the bracelet when it was ready the next week. By that time, he'd written his letter to you. When I got to your house, you were out in the garden picking tomatoes. Logan and I looked at the bracelet, cried a little, then I wrapped it and put it in his closet. I think you came in just as I was climbing off the chair."

June sipped her wine, then inhaled the piney scents of the evening. Bird sounds, soft and distant, floated up the mountainside. June spoke.

"I love the bracelet. I'll wear it the rest of my life. But I have to ask, isn't there a way you'd rather spend your money? You live on so little. You could've used this money yourself, or given it to your favorite charity, Save the Whales or something. I'm humbled that you gave it to Logan to give to me."

"Montana June. Listen to me and hear this, if you never hear anything I say again. When Logan became ill and it was obvious there'd be no grandkids, I needed to do something, anything, to give my blessed son some joy. The day we spent in town having lunch together and choosing that bracelet made memories I'd never want to forget. He loved you so much and didn't want you to die along with him. Well, that bracelet says it all. You were and are his own Montana June. And, in time, when you're ready, you will begin again."

As they looked across the Bitterroot Valley, the spring sun set behind them. The mountains in the distance began to glow. The long, beautiful song of a meadowlark floated up the hillside. Ranger came over and leaned against June's leg, putting his head on her knee. The two women sipped their wine, trying to swallow emotion. When June could speak again, she reached across and took her mother-in-law's hand.

"Thank you."

"Of course, my darling girl. Now, let's go inside and eat that veggie casserole waiting for us. I want to hear about the rest of your week."

The inside of Maura's house was an eclectic explosion of senses as they walked through the front door to the living room. The aroma of baking casserole emanating from the kitchen complemented but didn't overwhelm the usual herby fragrance of the house. Shawls of many colors were draped over the couch, chairs, and bean bags; bookshelves filled to overflowing with books lined the back wall of the small living room; books were stacked next to Maura's favorite chair. Houseplants and copies of ancient fertility figures sat on every horizontal surface, and a very large tuxedo cat was curled up in the center of the couch. Maura walked over and rubbed the cat's black back, then his white belly when he stretched and rolled over.

"Thought you might come out and join us this evening, you lazy old thing. Yet here you are, sound asleep where I left you. Ah, well, such is the luxury of being the most important being in the house, hmm, Mr. Mouser? Your buddy Ranger came to visit." Maura had left the door open, and Ranger walked through as she said this. The dog and cat greeted each other like the old friends they were. Ranger and Mr. Mouser had been little ones together, romping and chasing, puppy and kitten. Neither seemed to forget.

June walked down the hall, where Maura's bedroom and bathroom were and came back as Maura was taking the casserole out of the oven.

"Honey, grab the salad from the fridge. There's a loaf of crusty bread in the basket. Would you like iced tea?" Maura placed the hot dish on a trivet on the counter.

The two women gathered their meal and sat at the small table near the window that looked out on the rising mountainside behind the house. As they ate, June told her mother-in-law about the aborted lunch with Cara.

"Oh, yeah, that Cara," said Maura, "she's a piece of work. There's buzz in the valley about her and her German dude, Ludwig, and the big trip they're planning. I've seen them around together. They do make a picture."

June snorted. "Well, I'm glad she's out of my life." She went on to tell Maura about the incident with the FWP guy and the dead-end sign.

Maura smiled with memory. "Pace? Sure. Logan knew him in high school. He was such a nice kid back then, but a real loner. He was on the track and field team and won lots of regional races. I think that's how he got his nickname of Pace. Of course, it's also easier to say than Pacinski. I'm glad he came back to the area. Sounds like he's got a good position, now, too. Now, how about some coffee with dessert?"

"Mom, would you mind if I skipped dessert and took Ranger on home? I'm about talked out and ready for bed. It was such a wonderful evening. And I'll always love you for helping Logan with this bracelet." June hugged the older woman hard, and the two sniffed back tears.

June and Maura walked through the living room and woke up Ranger who'd curled into a ball by Mr. Mouser.

"Come on, Ranger, time to go home. Mom, I love you. Thank you again."

"Darling girl, take care. See you soon."

June and Ranger got into the Jeep. June waved as she turned around and headed down the mountain. The valley floor was in darkness now, but the way home was familiar and easy. June opened her window, letting the cool evening breeze blow her hair and caress her face as she drove home to the old farmhouse waiting across the valley.

HER PHONE RANG just as June walked through her door. It was her sister's ringtone, and she was tempted to let it go to voicemail, but decided it was easier to take it now.

"Hey, Sis," June said, her voice sounding tired even to herself.

"Hiya, doll. How you doing?"

"Ah, jeez. Some minutes I'm pretty good and some minutes I total-ly collapse. It's been a rough day." June filled Helena in, leaving out the near-suicidal speeding trip. "So, how's things in Florida?"

Helena lived near Cape Canaveral, with her husband Toby. She'd opened a needlework store, a small business to keep herself busy since their son started middle school. Helena and Toby'd had a hard time getting pregnant, perhaps because of Helena's weight. Helena had al-ways been big, but after marrying Toby, she'd ballooned. Following her son's birth twelve years ago, she'd gotten bigger.

Their son, Arnie, who'd always been a little brat, seemed to be grow-ing more unpleasant. Once, Logan had brought him a model bighorn sheep from Montana, which Arnie, about six then, broke right away. He threw a full-out tantrum because Logan didn't have a replacement. Arnie hadn't gotten any better since.

June tried to focus on what her sister was saying.

"I've been kind of worried, doll. I know you're still on leave from the school. How're you doing for money these days?"

June leaned back on the step. "No worries there for the time being. Probably should think about going back to work eventually. Gotta ad-mit, I'm not sure I'm up to dealing with kindergartners right now. But money-wise, Logan's insurance from the mill came in, so I'm set for the time being. Sure glad Max's place is almost finished. I can move soon."

"You've been working on that, like, forever. You and Logan were cleaning out the main floor before he got sick, weren't you?"

"Yep. Good thing, too, 'cause holy Hannah, all those stacks of magazines and newspapers. We'd just finished the dump runs when… well, you know." June's voice cracked and faded.

"Oh, damn it. Here I called to cheer you up and I'm getting us both all teary. Wish I was there to give you a hug."

"Helena, you're giving me a hug, right through this phone."

"Love you, doll. You gonna be okay tonight?"

"Yes, Hel. I'll be okay. No other choice. No way through this but through it. Can't take shortcuts, no matter how much I want to. Say 'Hi' to Toby and Arnie."

"Okay. Byee!"

The next time June's phone rang, she did let it go to voicemail.

"Hey, June? It's Pace, checking on you, make sure you're okay. Hope you kept my card. Listen, call if you need anything. At home, too, is fine. Here's that number."

June listened, with no intention of calling him. It may be, as he said, part of his job to make sure folks are all right, but she didn't need anyone else looking out for her, no matter what people thought.

5

Christ! What the hell was that? June jumped from the bed as thunder cracked over her head as if it would come through the roof. Hard rain pelted the windows. The branches of the Chinese elm raked back and forth across the glass, driven by a lashing wind. No wonder she'd been having a bad dream. June gathered a blanket around her shoulders and padded to the window to look at the storm.

Violent thunderstorms rolled down the mountains and bounced across the valley every spring, often bringing heavy rainfall, but yesterday'd been so warm and sunny that a storm of this magnitude hadn't even been on June's radar. Another thunderclap and burst of wind made June step back from the window. Turning, she caught sight of the sampler above the bed. "Never go to bed angry. (Just go to bed horny.)" It reminded her of the nightmare of an argument with Logan, quite similar to a real one they'd had a few years ago. She dug out her journal to find the place where she'd recorded it.

(excerpt from Montana June's journal)
I remember that horrible fight, when we
found out Julie and Jerry were
going to have a baby. I craved a baby,
needed to be pregnant. Like nature was
pushing me and I couldn't ignore it. I was
going crazy with longing. I told him,
"I'm thirty three years old! My biological
clock is screaming!"
And he said, (oh God, I remember this so
clearly) "Well, hit the Snooze button,
darlin'. We have our plan."
After the argument, when I was still crying,
I said, "What about me? I need a baby."
He said, "And I need you, Montana June.
Here, let me sit with you. Hold you."
He held me on his lap. We thought we had
all the time in the world to start a family.

What about me? How am I supposed to
handle this? How can I live through
Christmas, the winter, my birthday, the
rest of my life, without Logan
and without his babies?

Now, thunder rolling outside, June felt a wet nose nuzzle the back of her knee. She wiped her eyes and put the journal away.

"Heya, Ranger. Storm wake you up, too? Let's get you outside."

They walked through the kitchen—June hitting the switch on the coffeepot as she passed—then out the mudroom to the back porch. Ranger looked up as if to say, "Really? I gotta go out in this?" but then lumbered down the old wooden steps, walked to the corner of the yard, and took care of business. June looked up toward the mountains but could see nothing except blasts of rain and almost continuous forks of lightning. Ranger loped back to the mudroom and shook his coat, sending raindrops all over the little room and June.

"Gee, thanks, guy. Just what I needed to complete my wake-up call, a cold shower." June walked back through the kitchen into her warm bathroom.

Thunder reverberating there brought a sweet memory to replace the previous bitter one. The first thunderstorm two years ago had hit on a Saturday, a bit later in the morning. Logan and she had just awakened from a nap after making love early in the morning. Logan got out of bed, stretched tall, put his fingers on the ceiling, and said, "Okay, headin' to the shower, babe. Want to come with me?"

"Hmmm…nope. I'm going to stay right here. Save some water for me, though, okay?"

"Can do, darlin'."

He went into the bathroom, turned on the shower and started singing. He sang almost every time he showered, changing the words to songs. She couldn't hear what he was singing, but it was to the tune of a famous children's song from television. The sound of the shower was counterpoint to the rain pouring outside. Thunder cracked, the window lit up with lightning, but inside was warm and cozy. The shower stopped and June heard Logan's song.

"Junebuggy, you're so sweet. You have pretty toes and feet."

"Ta dah!" Logan jumped through the door of the bedroom and displayed his towel-wrapped body. "Gotta tell you, the modern amenity I appreciate the very most is indoor plumbing. Yessiree."

That whole day had been a delight. Logan and June spent the time playing games and laughing. Even Ranger had gotten in the spirit, bouncing around the house with a goofy grin, chasing dust bunnies.

Memories, good and bad, were precious now. Each one was a treasure.

AFTER THE STORM, Montana June decided to rent a U-Haul truck for the move to Grandpa Max's. Better than trying to take the few boxes at a time that would fit into her old Jeep. She still didn't want to move, but it was the smart choice, but daunting for one woman to shift all those boxes and furniture alone. Her friends were all busy with parent-teacher conferences. Perhaps Maura could help.

Entering the U-Haul Rental Store in Missoula, June walked into the answer to her problems.

"Hey, June! Sorry 'bout that." Gary Peterson, one of Logan's buddies from the mill, grabbed June's shoulders to steady her after she bumped into him. "How you doing? Been a long time. You getting by okay?"

"Gary! It's good to see you. Yeah, I'm doing all right. It's hard, of course it is." Actually, seeing one of Logan's friends for the first time in months brought tears to June's eyes. She wiped them away and flashed a tiny smile.

"What're you doing? In Mizoo for the day?" Gary asked.

"Well, I'm checking on truck rentals. I'm moving into town, and sure can't fit all the boxes in my little Jeep. You might remember we sold Logan's truck to help pay bills when he got sick. So, I'm here, looking at prices."

"When you gonna be making the move?" Gary's forehead wrinkled and his lips pursed.

"I don't have a set date. I'm maybe a week away from being ready, though."

"How about if I wrangle up some guys from the mill to help? I bet we'd get you all moved in a few hours. Hell, I don't know how you'd do it alone. 'Course I don't want to be pushy. Maybe you got it all planned."

"Oh, Gary, I don't. I was worried about how I'd move all the heavy furniture and boxes by myself. That'd be such a blessing. Jeez, thanks! It could be whenever the guys are available. I'll rent a big truck, and—"

"Now, there's no need to rent anything. You know us guys, we gotta show off our rigs. I'll call around, see who's free, then get back to you and we'll get'er done. Okay, June? I can say without even asking 'em that the guys'll be happy to help."

"That's wonderful, Gary. I'll wait to hear from you, then. Thanks."

"We've been wondering how you're doing. This'll be good for us, too." Gary smiled and waved as he left.

Later, Gary Peterson called to say that most of the guys were available the next Saturday, now six days away, perfect as far as June was concerned. It gave her time to finish her packing.

As move day neared and June had to defrost her big freezer, she took most of the frozen food into town and put it in Max's freezer. A remaining turkey she put in the refrigerator at the farmhouse to thaw. She'd cook it in time to feed the bunch of guys who were devoting their day off to help her move. She bought a few cases of beer, too, since she knew they'd be thirsty at the end of the day.

Getting the farmhouse packed wasn't easy. Often June would find herself staring at something in her hand that brought back memories of good times when Logan was alive and healthy. So many items required a decision, took an emotional toll. The hardest things were Logan's garage, Logan's desk, Logan's underwear drawer. June realized she was moving on, away from life with him and she wasn't ready. At times she screamed in frustration. Why did life-altering decisions always come down to money?

By the end of each day, June was empty, exhausted. She'd sit outside on the porch with a glass of wine, watching Ranger wander through the yard where he'd been a puppy, wishing she could afford to stay here forever. Then, June would take off her new bracelet and read the inscription that held Logan's last words to her: "To My Montana June. Begin Again." Selling the farmhouse would allow her to do just that, begin again. But, damn it. She didn't want to.

(excerpt from Montana June's journal)
"My heart bleeds with wanting him."

MOVE DAY DAWNED bright and sunny, promising to be very warm by afternoon. At 8:00 A.M., the sound of pickups coming down the road announced the cavalry had arrived. She walked down the front porch steps and into the arms of Logan's good friends; nine of them, all ready to work.

"Hey, Gary, John. Oh, all you guys! You're wonderful to do this for me. Thank you so much. Bring your coffee mugs into the kitchen and refill them from the big pot. There's cinnamon rolls set out, too. Then, well, you'll see the boxes, ready to go."

"Hmmm, that a turkey I smell?" Gary said as he walked into the kitchen. "What'd you do, put that bird in the oven at midnight?" He lifted the spigot on the coffee urn to fill his mug.

"No, at four. I was so nervous about today I couldn't sleep anyway. It'll be ready when we're done. I'll pack the roaster, and we'll have turkey at the new house. Beer and potato salad's already there, in the fridge."

June greeted and hugged the guys, then spent the next hour pointing out what needed to be loaded.

Soon the house was emptied of the things that'd been June's life with Logan. The pickups were filled. The refrigerator was strapped against the cab on the biggest truck. The guys stood, kicking tires, waiting for the final word. June took a last trip through the house. She drank a glass of water at the kitchen sink, unplugged the coffee urn, put the turkey roaster into the large cardboard box she'd saved for the purpose. Standing at the kitchen window one last time, she allowed herself a minute alone to reflect on this move. She thought about coming to this house as a bride, about all the Christmases and birthdays, the times of making love, the laughter. June dropped her head as the memories took over. She didn't hear someone come up behind her.

"Junebug," a voice whispered in her ear. "That's what Logan always called you, id'n it?"

Startled, June jerked around. Standing right behind her, so close her breasts almost touched the dirty T-shirt on his sunken chest, was Jeb Murdoch, a guy from the mill. He was tall and skinny with greasy dark hair brushing his shoulders. June had met Jeb once, and she'd been surprised to see him here today.

"What? What're you doing?" June's voice raised in alarm.

"Oh, hey, li'l lady. I just come in to check on you. We're all packed, ready to go, wanted to see what's holding you up. You okay, Junebug?" Jeb's voice oozed—too intimate—as he reached up and put a moist hand on the back of June's neck, squeezing.

"Shit, Jeb, you scared the bejeezus out of me. Let me get past." June almost ran out of the kitchen, straight into Gary Peterson. "Gary, hey. Guess I'm ready to go. I'll come back on Tuesday to clean everything, but now I need to…" June was so flustered from Jeb that she let her last statement fade. She picked up the boxed turkey roaster.

"Here, June. Let me carry that. Jeb, I thought you were outside with the rest of the crew. How'd you get in here?"

"Oh, I just come in through the backdoor to check on June. No worries. What's holding everything up?" Jeb barged through the living room and out the front door, leaving June and Gary alone.

"June, you okay?"

"Sure, Gary," June said, head down. "I was distracted and Jeb surprised me. That's all." She looked up. "We're good to go, now. Thanks." As she followed Gary out of the house, June shuddered. *Gah. That was really creepy. Should I tell Gary what Jeb did? No. That'd give Jeb the satisfaction of knowing he's gotten to me. Leave well enough alone.*

Outside, Gary stowed the turkey in the back of June's Jeep. June let Ranger jump in, then pushed him over so she could get into the driver's seat. Pickup doors slammed as the guys got in and turned on their rigs, then everyone started the process of backing out and driving down the driveway, headed to town.

All in all, everything went like clockwork. By the time everyone had gotten to town and the trucks were unloaded, it was noon. What would've taken June weeks by herself was accomplished in a few hours with all that extra muscle, the good friends of her husband. As the work drew to a close, some of the men called their wives, who brought salads and chips. By one o'clock, June's new backyard was full of people eating, drinking beer and soda, laughing and talking.

June was glad the wives came. Right after Logan died, she'd hated being around them. She knew each one was thinking, *Thank God it's you and not me.* But now, after all these months, the wives' presence at the end of the day made it a party, and she was grateful.

Now everyone was gone. The last guys had taken the picnic trash, the kitchen was cleaned, and boxes waiting to be emptied were disbursed. The living room furniture was set; June's bed was ready with clean sheets. For the time being, June could rest. She and Ranger walked through each room, June noting how different it felt with her own stuff in the house instead of Grandpa Max and Sarah's. She stood for a moment, looking out the big front windows toward the park as the trees glowed in the evening sun. It'd been a hard but good day. Tomorrow she'd start emptying boxes and putting things away, but not now. She got a glass of water, sat in the green tufted chair near the fireplace, and allowed herself to relax. Ranger settled at her feet.

June began the first night in her new house.

6

Montana June awoke early the next morning, feeling disorient-
ed. Of course. She was in her new house in the 'Snake, the
Rattlesnake Valley, across the street from Greenough Park. Confusing
dreams had disappeared with the coming dawn, though a fragment
lingered of searching, searching for Logan. June rolled over, stretched,
and looked through the window above her head at the rounded top of
Mount Jumbo, where in her old house she was used to looking at sky.

Not since going to the farmhouse as a bride had she moved into a
new house. All the days she'd spent in this house as a young girl when
Sarah was alive, the many hours she and Logan had been here with
Grandpa Max, all the time getting the house ready for her move—
though it was as familiar as her own face in the mirror, it wasn't yet
"home." Today, perhaps, would begin to change that.

As June looked out at Mount Jumbo and watched the sky turn pink behind the old mountain, she tried to recapture her dream of Logan, but it just wouldn't come. Her thoughts turned to yesterday and all the help she'd had from Logan's friends. Without their help, she'd still be moving box after box by herself instead of being ready to empty them and start making this home.

The one thorn in the whole day had been that weird incident in the kitchen with Jeb Murdoch. Thinking back on it, June's breath quickened. It was scary at the time, unexpected and threatening. Gary coming in stopped whatever might've happened. All was well. Once everyone was at the new house, Jeb must've had another pressing engagement. He left as soon as his own truck was emptied. Thank goodness.

Ranger moaned as he rolled over on his cushion at the foot of June's bed. He popped a loud fart, clopped his teeth together, and June heard him start the process of rolling his old body to a more upright position.

"Ranger, you 'wake? Wanna go out and see your new yard in the morning?" June got up, put on her robe, and squatted next to her friend. She scrubbed his ears and neck in the way he loved. "There you go, big guy. Come on, let's go see the world."

Ranger scrabbled up and padded behind June to the sliding glass door that led to the fenced backyard. Once outside, he snuffed his way around a tour of the yard.

As June watched her old friend, she stretched again then looked up at the mountain. The sun almost peeked over the rounded crest, and the sky was fresh and blue. A new day, a new house. June took a deep breath. "Logan?" She heard the sound of the breeze. "Help me move on without grieving. I'm trying to do what you asked, but I can't do it alone. Be here with me." She put her left hand around the gold bracelet on her right wrist and turned it. Though the words were hidden, she imagined them on the inside, imagined Logan's voice saying, "My Montana June. I'll be with you as you begin again." June closed her eyes to capture the thought, then opened them as the sun broke over the mountain. Yes, this was possible. She would begin again. In fact, she'd already begun.

Inside the house, June started the coffee, then jumped into the spanking clean tile shower. It was certainly a different experience from the tub at the farmhouse—no dealing with the cold shower curtain or stepping over the tub wall. Each mundane part of life was different now. June dressed in her jeans and work shirt. Unpacking was the job of the day.

When June had sealed each box back at the farmhouse, she'd labeled it with the name of the room where it belonged, so now there wasn't any heavy lifting to do. The kitchen boxes were no problem, with dishes and glasses, pots and pans all going where Sarah's had been. The bedroom was also a breeze. The surprise was in what little space her clothes, without Logan's, took in the closet.

Downstairs, June found a stack of boxes she'd labeled "Basement." Logan's tools she added to Grandpa Max's, all arranged just so on his hand-built workbench. June wasn't sure what all the tools were for, but they'd been precious to both men. In time, she'd learn what they were. The last couple boxes on the floor were Christmas decorations. June lifted those, putting them on the clean shelves, then rubbed her back. Time for a break.

Upstairs, June realized it was lunch-time. She made a turkey sandwich, added some chips, and decided she deserved a beer from what the guys yesterday hadn't finished. She chose a local brew. The name made her smile: Mount Jumbo IPA from Highlander, which'd been Logan's favorite.

She carried her lunch to the backyard, thinking about the boxes of Christmas decorations. It would be hard opening them in December. When those boxes were packed a year and a half ago, Grandpa Max was alive. He spent the holiday with them at the farmhouse, and they all had a restful, joyful time. One of June's favorite memories was of a drive around the Metcalf Wildlife Preserve to watch the winter birds settle in for the night. As they followed the gravel road around the ponds, snow came like big goose feathers. Logan started singing a favorite song about being happily in love in winter.

When he got to the part where the Parson Brown snowman asks if the couple is married, Logan stopped driving to kiss June. Grandpa Max took over singing, and soon they were all laughing in pure joy.

Max, Logan, and June took down the Christmas tree on New Year's Day while a football game played on TV. Grandpa Max died a few weeks later in his sleep. It'd been very sad for Logan and June, but a mere precursor of what was to come. Logan's cancer diagnosis had been in March of that year.

This past Christmas, three months after Logan died, June went to Florida to be with her sister. When Helena sent the ticket, June acquiesced in silence. At first, there'd been talk of Maura joining her, since it'd be her mother-in-law's first Christmas alone, too, but then Maura decided it wasn't possible. She wanted to stay home with Mr. Mouser and would take Ranger so he wouldn't have to be boarded. Maura would act as chauffeur for the airport trips. In Florida, nothing had felt right. June was empty, broken, too close to the horror of losing Logan.. Though it should've been good being with her sister, June felt packed in someone else's skin with a bunch of ants. She didn't know how to act, what to say, who she was. She hid in her room a great deal, and when that wasn't possible, took a glass of wine out to the dock on the canal, which was where she spent much of that long week. Helena would join her and they'd talk, but there was nothing right about any of it. The one bright spot was when a pod of manatees came up to the dock. Helena turned on the garden hose and put it in the water, and the big gentle beasts came up and sucked on the hose, drinking fresh water. This, too, had made June cry.

Going home was a blessing, but even that was fraught with difficulties. Bad weather diverted the plane to Great Falls. What should've been a ten o'clock arrival at the airport in Missoula turned into a bus ride over Rogers Pass in a blizzard. The bus arrived at the Missoula airport at 4:00 A.M. Maura met her there and the two grieving women drove homeward together. Their first Christmas without Logan had been a heartache, but it was over. They'd survived.

June shelved her memories as she finished her sandwich. Ranger came up for his traditional last bite.

"Well, Ranger, like your new yard? How 'bout a walk before we get back to work?" Ranger wagged his tail and smiled in agreement. Whatever June had in mind was okay with him, and a walk was always in order.

7

Montana June and Ranger returned to the farmhouse on Tuesday morning. The drive south through Missoula, then on across the Bitterroot River and through the small towns of Lolo and Florence should have given her time to get ready for the day. Instead, passing the Metcalf Wildlife Preserve, hearing the many Canada geese with new goslings honking, made June's heart twinge with memories of other springs. June tried to stay focused on the chores ahead. Seeing the farmhouse huddled among the elms, she felt her impetus for house-cleaning slipping away. A gray day, memories of Logan, being tired from moving. *Damn, I should've brought more coffee.*

"Well, Ranger. Let's get out and at least give it a try. You can spend the time wandering in your old haunts while your poor mom slaves away inside. If you had thumbs, you'd be helping." June opened the door of the Jeep and they both jumped out. Ranger headed straight to the backyard. The gray day evidently didn't dampen his spirits.

Inside, the farmhouse felt abandoned and sad. In the two days it'd been empty and closed up, it'd developed an odd smell. Used coffee cups sat on window ledges, left by the guys who helped her move; the coffee urn was unplugged, but hadn't been washed; and the carton of creamer June had set out and forgotten was long past its use-by date.

"Okay, Juney. Put on your big-girl panties and get started. You can do this." June spoke aloud while she walked through collecting the coffee cups. In each room, June turned on lights to dispel the gloom. By the time she reached the mudroom and turned on the old radio left on the shelf above the coat-hooks and ramped up the volume, she felt ready to dive in.

She started with the living room sweeping, mopping, looking for errant cobwebs, then moved on to the bedroom and bathroom. The country music coming from the radio set her pace, and she sang while she scrubbed. Once in the kitchen, she hoisted herself on the counter and was wiping out the upper cabinets when she heard Ranger bark from the front yard. The front screen door slapped shut.

June heard boots walking across her clean floor as she scrambled down.

It was Jeb Murdoch.

"Heya, Junebug. Come to see did ya need help."

"Umm, no, Jeb. Thanks, but I'm doing fine here. How'd you even know I'd be here? Don't you live in Darby?"

"Well, yeah, Junebug. But you tol' me you'd be here cleaning the old place today, said you'd be here on Tuesday, and here it is Tuesday, so I said to myself, I says, 'Well, the li'l lady might need a strong hand to help clean out the muck,' so I drove on down. Made a special trip. Come all this way, and it's a thirsty drive, too. Say, you got any of that beer left from the other day?"

While Jeb had been talking, he slouched closer. June could smell he'd already been drinking and it wasn't even noon. It appeared he wore the same T-shirt as on Saturday, even dirtier than before. His cowboy boots were dusty, worn down at the heels.

"No. The beer was all in town. Listen, I don't remember telling you I'd be here today and don't want help. So, thanks, but—"

Jeb took two more steps toward her, grinning as he came.

"Ah, come on, li'l lady. You're okay with ol' Jeb. I just wanna help out a good-lookin' gal. Be honest, I ain't much on house-cleaning, anyways, but I s'pose you might be ready for a break. I got some beers out in the truck, I'll go get 'em. We'll sit ourselves down out on the porch and rest a spell. Bet it's been long time since you been with a man. Hmmm. Months now, right? Here I am, ready 'n' able."

Jeb reached his hand toward June's head. She sidled away to the sink.

"Jeb, no. I don't need help, and I definitely don't want what you seem to be offering. You need to leave." June's heart raced. Damn, it hadn't even dawned on her to lock the door. June heard Ranger barking outside. "Jeb, I've got to see what's bothering Ranger. You go out the front door. Please go, now." June moved to her left trying to get around him.

"Oh, no, Junebug. Nope. Not gonna do it that way. Drove all the way down here jus' to help you out, and that's what I'm gonna do." Jeb stepped to his right and put his hand on June's shoulder, bringing with it odors of tobacco and too-strong cologne.

"Don't call me Junebug! Now leave. Get out of here!" Ranger scratched at the mudroom door, barking non-stop.

Jeb grabbed June's ponytail as she tried to turn away from him. That smelly hand stopped her from moving even a fraction of an inch. He reached his other hand to the left side of her face, turning her toward him as he leaned in. All June saw was his ugly lips with a crumb of chewing tobacco in brown spittle in the corner of his mouth, coming closer. His breath stank of stale beer and bad teeth.

"Oh, Junebug's a name just for Logan? Why, you'd share with an old friend. Come on now, li'l lady. You know you need this. Go too long, you get out of the habit and dry up. Just wanna help out an old friend by taking care of his lady." Jeb's lips were dry and peeling. His face slammed into hers, his crackly lips scratching her mouth. His hard-on ground into her waist as he shoved her up against the sink.

June felt panic taking over—and then she remembered something Logan had told her long ago. If she worked her knee over a little…

"Oh, you like that, li'l lady? Hmm-hmm. Yeah, move that way. Damn, feels good." Jeb stepped back a little to make adjustments. That was all June needed. June's knee slammed up between his legs just as Ranger broke down the back door.

Jeb collapsed on the floor, and curled into a fetal position grabbing his crotch.

"Bitch! Shit, you broke me!" he yelled. But he screamed when Ranger grabbed his throat. Perhaps he had major pain in his groin, but the threat of death by Labrador seemed to motivate him. Jeb, hunched up, scuttled out the front, chased by Ranger in full attack mode.

"Ranger, come here! Good boy." June called her dog, watching through the window as Murdoch lurched into his rusty black pickup.

He started the engine and backed up even before the cab door was closed. His truck turned and barreled down the dirt road, spraying gravel and careening from side to side. At the highway, Jeb didn't slow before turning right and speeding away.

June leaned against the wall of the living room, then slid to the floor. She grabbed Ranger's head and kissed him.

"Holy Christ, Ranger. That was close! You good boy." June's breath came in gulps. She scrubbed her hand over her face, trying to wipe away the taste of Jeb's mouth and the horrible crackle of his lips. Sweat beaded on her forehead, then suddenly she felt chilled. June hugged her legs to her chest, put her head back against the wall, closed her eyes, and tried to breathe.

"Ranger, thankyouthankyouthankyou. You and the knee in the balls saved me. That could've been truly ugly." June's hand shook as she dug her fingers into Ranger's fur. Adrenaline prickled her body. She jumped up and locked the front door, then walked through to the back. Well, there wasn't going to be any locking the mudroom door. Her furry rescuer had demolished it.

June's cell phone in her jeans pocket rang. Maura's ring-tone.

"Oh, Mom, thank you for calling!"

"Montana June? You don't sound good. What's up, darling girl?"

"Umm, I...I need help. You have some time right now?"

"Whatever you need, I can do. Got all the time in the world. Tell me."

"Okay, well, I'm at the farmhouse, and I need some wood to fix the mudroom door. I can't lock it and don't want to leave the house unlocked, and something's happened and I'd like it a lot if you came. I just really need you." June realized she was talking too fast, but it was a luxury to be able to spill out her worry and have someone come be with her.

"Absolutely. Give me half an hour. There's plywood in the shed, and nails and such. I'll bring some lunch, too, okay? You can tell me what's happened when I get there."

Close to forty-five minutes later, June heard Maura's little car banging up the road. June had washed her face and rinsed her mouth and felt almost in control of herself by the time Maura arrived. The sight of the old yellow VW bug with a piece of plywood tied to the top lightened June's spirits.

"Sorry it took so long. I forgot the wood wouldn't fit inside, and had to figure out how to tie it up on top of Baby. Then, of course, I couldn't drive very fast for fear I'd take off like a ladybug. But here I am! Now, tell me what's happened to your back door." As she spoke, Maura stalked up the sidewalk and grabbed June in a big hug. June felt immensely better having the older woman there.

"Well, Ranger happened to it, and thank goodness for him," she said, as they walked through the house to the mudroom. June squeezed Maura's arm tight. "See? Just looking at it makes me sick to my stomach—what might've happened." Her voice wavered.

"Holy lovin' shit. Look at the mess of that door!" Maura patted June's hand; releasing her own arm, she rubbed the spot. "You need to sit down, and you need something to calm you. I'll go get lunch from Baby's front seat. You can tell me all about it while we eat." Maura's voice faded as she went back through the house and out the front door. She returned with a cooler and jar of iced tea. "Ranger must've been pretty motivated to do all that damage. What the hell happened here this morning, Montana June?"

They sat on the porch step. Maura emptied the cooler, setting sandwiches and apples between them while June told her story.

"June. Stop right there. I think we should report this attack. Sounds like this Jeb jerk is really dangerous. Are you okay? Do we need to go to the hospital?"

"No. Mom, I promise, nothing more happened to me than having his disgusting mouth on mine. He pulled my hair—that's all. Then I used that trick your son taught me of the knee in the chops. That's when Ranger broke through the door and got Jeb moving. Wish you could've seen Ranger's jaws on his throat! Honestly, outside of being scared, I'm okay. I don't want to go over it with the authorities. Please. But, your phone call came at exactly the right time. Thank you so much for coming now."

"I'm glad I was available. I felt terrible I couldn't come on Saturday when you were moving to town. I had that date set up with the volunteer group at the Lewis and Clark Travelers' Rest for ages and couldn't break it. Being here now and seeing you makes me feel I haven't *totally* abandoned you in your move. After we eat, we'll fix the door, finish cleaning the house and all will be well."

June bit into the avocado and sprout sandwich, and took a conscious breath. This'd been quite a day, but it might've been worse. Jeb was a jerk, as Maura said, but now it was over and June had survived; in fact, she'd triumphed. She was determined not to think anymore about the attack. Jeb was a nonentity in her life. He lived sixty-five miles away, and though he knew where she lived, he wouldn't continue to be a problem. Because Jeb was an oaf and a coward, he wouldn't show his face again.

June took a swig of the iced tea then leaned back against the door frame. She reached down and rubbed Ranger's head as he waited, longing for his last bite of sandwich.

8

Montana June woke before sunrise the next day. Her bedside clock told her it was just 4:30, but when she looked out the high window at Mount Jumbo, she saw the sky was lightening already. Through the open window came the first sleepy chirps of birds nesting in the lilacs. It was Summer Solstice, the longest day of the year, and the birds were wasting no time getting started. She stretched long and deep in her bed.

Moving to Missoula had been hard. It would've been easier to stay at the farmhouse and hide, but now that it was done it felt okay. A new house, a new town. New beginnings.

June rolled over and hugged her pillow. Who was she kidding? She wanted none of that. She wanted Logan, the farmhouse. Her old life back. She wasn't brave enough to face the future alone. Tears came, hot and fast. Her sobs woke Ranger; he came close and nuzzled her hand.

Not even he could help this morning, though. June dissolved in grief, coming undone at the seams.

(excerpt from Montana June's journal)
I woke this morning with the same "pit of my stomach" fear I used to feel about my own death. The catch-in-the-throat fear, eyes-open-wide kind of fear of dying. Only this morning, I feel it at the thought of living not days, but years without Logan. These are the saddest words in the world. Without Logan. I'm so frightened at the prospect of trying to learn how to live without him.

The next time June looked out the window, the mountain was backlit by the rising sun. June's pillow was sodden, but her inner self felt lighter and clean. She'd read that tears shed in grief rid the body of toxins, so she stripped the pillowcases and threw them in the washer. June left the pillows to dry on her bed, called to Ranger, and stepped outside into the dawn. The air rang with bird calls, a choral festival celebrating the rising of the sun. June raised her hands up, stretched high to the mountain where the first bolt of sun shot across the sky, then leaned down, placing her palms on the dewed lawn in front of her feet. As she began a morning yoga ritual of the Sun Salutation Maura taught her years ago, June realized she'd taken another step in her healing. Her collapse earlier was a reaction to the work and stress of the last few weeks. She missed Logan with every cell and knew life was forever changed, but she also knew *she* could not stop living. She had to keep going or she'd be letting Logan down, letting herself down, and sometimes, like today, she'd have to do it when she was empty and sad.

As June finished her Sun Salutation and stood, reaching again to the sky, she saw the sun was now over the mountain. It was full day and promised to be hot. Ranger stood, staring hard at the screen door.

"Okay, big guy. Let's go in and get breakfast."

After eating, June decided she'd celebrate the Solstice by doing yard work. After some time she found the mower, under boxes at the back of the garage. Getting it out required shifting tons of stuff. By the time she was ready to start the mower, she was already sweaty and aggravated. She checked the gasoline, hit the primer bulb five times, and pulled the starter cord. Again. Again. *Damn it! Why isn't this stupid thing starting?* She knew the mower well. Mowing the lawn had been one of her jobs at the farmhouse, and she was well acquainted with the quirks of the beast. People walking by the house could see her struggling; June felt foolish. Okay, that was an easy fix. She pushed the mower into the backyard so at least she could struggle in private. She re-checked the oil and gasoline, but still wasn't getting even a hiccup from the mower. *What the hell?* She went into the kitchen for a glass of water, then came back outside to sit down. She didn't want another emotional breakdown and could feel one building.

Why isn't it working? It was fine before the move. What did the guys do to it? Oh. Yes. They'd disconnected the cable on the spark plug to make it safer to transport. *Well, duh.* Though June felt silly for getting upset, she was proud of figuring out the problem. She hooked up the cable, gave a tug on the starter cord, and cheered when the mower roared into life. Hurray! One success.

While June mowed the small backyard, she pondered why this minor incident felt like such a victory. Then it dawned on her she felt good because she'd chosen to avoid a break-down. She'd worked through a stressful situation and come through it without crying. She was making progress in her healing.

Finishing the backyard, she opened the gate to the front. Pushing the mower, one-handed, through the narrow opening while holding the gate required some doing, but she refused to turn the mower off. When the machine was hot it was notorious for not restarting, and she didn't want another struggle. Through the gate, she continued, enjoying beheading the dandelions in full bloom in the side-yard. As she reached the street, she noticed a runner coming toward her. The runner did a double-take when he saw her. *Oh, rats. It's Pace.* He waved at her.

"June! What're you doing here? Thought you lived in the Bitterroot. Hey, guess you didn't get my message." Pace stopped running, seeming to want to visit.

"Hi, Pace. Sorry, I gotta get this done!" June yelled above the sound of the mower.

"Yeah. Okay. Don't want to interrupt. Uh, some other time, okay?" Pace looked mildly put out.

"Sure, see ya!" June waved, but kept mowing. Pace turned back to the street, and, looking once over his shoulder at her, continued on.

June felt mean for not talking to Pace, but she didn't want to deal with a new friend while also trying to start life in a new town and new house. *One thing at a time.*

Continuing to mow, June turned her thoughts to a decision she'd been putting off. It wasn't something she wanted to consider, but her boss at school was going to need an answer soon. Would she return to teaching?

When Logan had fallen so ill just after his diagnosis in March the year before, June worked through the end of the school year, taking sick days when she had to get Logan to doctors. At the end of the school year, she and her principal believed she'd be returning in the fall, but by mid-summer it became obvious Logan's cancer was winning. June arranged to take a year's leave of absence. The staff had bake sales and fundraisers for Logan and June, and her colleagues brought casseroles so she wouldn't have to cook when they got home from the hospital. When Logan died in September, June was given the option of returning to school after the first semester, but she didn't have the intestinal fortitude, to use Grandpa Max's appropriate phrase, to do it. It'd taken all her gut strength just to get through each day. She used the full year of leave.

But the school year was now over. Her boss was expecting her back in six short weeks.

Lost in the roar of the mower, she made herself remember what it was like to be a teacher. She'd enjoyed the kindergartners and loved writing stories she'd read to them every day, but teaching was not a life's calling for her as it was for some. Added to that was the inherent sadness June knew she'd face every day of class.

When June had watched her tiny charges, she imagined what her own children, Logan's sons and daughters, would be like, laughing and playing. And now…well, now that would never be. June didn't want to be around other people's children. Not yet. Maybe not ever.

(excerpt from Montana June's journal)
We had such a good marriage – the kind
one hopes for and dreams of.
Together we were stronger and better. We
knew we belonged with each other from
the minute we met; that first evening we
talked about our grandchildren.

Finally finished, June stashed the mower in the garage, then admired her trimmed backyard. Ranger came up and put his head against her legs.

"Hey, guy. That noise you hate is over. Let's go to the creek for a break." They walked through the house, locking doors on the way. This was a new thing for June. It wasn't only the attack at the farmhouse; security was necessary in this bigger city.

They crossed the street to the path into the wooded park. Ranger ran ahead and was already chest deep by the time June caught up. She sat on a log, took off her shoes, and dangled her hot feet in the water.

"Yikes, Ranger, that's cold!" She smiled as Ranger jumped, pretending to catch a fish, splashing clear water into his face.

As June's sweat dried and her feet tingled from the icy stream, she reviewed her decision. Teaching had been a means to an end for her. She enjoyed it, had been good at it, and loved her students, but it was a job, not a career. She always planned to teach until she became pregnant, then quit to take care of their family.

Now that was no longer in the cards. Decision made.

But who would she be, if not a teacher? It'd been part of her persona for so long; what to do instead? The good thing was, money from the farm gave her financial leeway, the luxury of time in which to decide.

June realized this was the first time since Logan died she felt anticipation—the first time the future held some hope. She was healing.
Moving on. Tears came without warning, again.

Ranger stopped playing in the water and came over to June's log.
He put his big yellow head in her lap and licked her hand. She scrubbed
behind his ear.

"Damn it, Ranger. How do I make decisions on my own?" Ranger
looked as if he understood every word. The sun went behind a cloud
and a rumble of thunder rolled in the distance. June imagined Logan's
hand on her shoulder, and she reached up with her right hand to clasp
his. She saw the gold bracelet and remembered the inscription. *Okay,
Logan. I can do this, with your help. I need to go on.*

June got off the log. Ranger waded out and shook himself dry. They
walked back across the street to their new house. June had a phone call
to make to her old boss at Victor School.

After the phone call June wrote the necessary letter of resignation, then spent the rest of the day weeding the overgrown flowerbeds around the house. Thunder was a constant rumbling backdrop
to June's work, but with no rain the clouds offered welcome shade. By
evening, though, the sky was clear. June changed out of her gardening
clothes, then strolled with Ranger around the front yard, enjoying the
tidy appearance after the day's work.

A red pickup pulled up to the curb, but June paid no attention.
Folks often parked there to access the path into Greenough. It wasn't
until she heard someone walking up the steps that she turned around.

"Hey, June." Pace was coming toward her. "Hoped you'd be here.
I should've called first. Had a wild hare to come by on my way home
from the grocery." He was carrying a long, thin brown bag.

"Pace! Goodness, this is a surprise." She made an instantaneous judgment call. "Uh…want to see my new house?"

"New house? So you moved into town. Wondered what you're doing here. This's my running route, and…oh, wow," Pace said as they walked through the door into the great room with the polished hardwood floor and stone fireplace. "Gorgeous. How'd you come by it? Been house-hunting awhile?"

"No, I inherited it, and couldn't afford to keep both." June walked Pace through the sliding glass door out to the backyard, pulling the screen door shut. "Do you want to sit out here?"

"Sure. Holy shit…." He looked up. "Great view of Mount Jumbo. Hey, brought you some wine." He handed her the bag.

"Oh, thanks," she said, pulling out a bottle of red wine. "Perfect. By the way, this guy is Ranger. He's my live-in security system. Have a seat. I'll be right back."

June looked through the screen door as she returned with the cork screw and glasses. Pace was standing, arms crossed, still looking at the mountain. He was medium height and spare, had a pleasant face, a pointy chin, and bright blue eyes. His hair was dark blond, with that streak of white over his left ear. His eyes were serious as he turned to her. When he spoke, it was with that curious, halting speech pattern June had noticed.

"Uh, June. That comment, Ranger as security.…My work is, well, kinda quasi-law enforcement. Hear most of what goes on in western Montana. Greenough Park's nice, but well, maybe not all that safe. Lock your doors, okay?"

"Yeah, I've already started doing that. I had kind of a scare a couple days ago at the farmhouse, and it made me more aware of things. Oh, it was nothing much," June hurried to say as she saw Pace's expression darken, "but I know enough to be careful. Thanks for the advice, though. Here's your glass. Sit down, okay?"

"You bet, June. Nice evening. Solstice, right? Almost eight o'clock, and the sun's still high. Love living here." He sipped his wine and looked at the mountain again. "Umm, something I need to ask you.... Remember, I run by here often?"

"Yeah. I remember. In fact, you ran into me not too long ago."

"Oh, shit…was that you? Damn. Not my best manners, that day. A time-trial, but I should've stopped, made sure you were okay." Pace looked pensive. "Oh…that's why you looked familiar at the fishing access."

"Yep. No harm done. All's well. Anyway, what were you going to tell me?"

"Well, there's a local running club…uh, Run Wild Missoula. In fact, got a marathon coming up in July. But there's another race, the Missoula Mile, right downtown, this coming Sunday. Wanted to tell you about it 'cause, well, it's a fundraiser for prostate cancer research. Got a bunch of sponsors…wanted to ask your permission to use Logan's name on my shirt. 'Running in Memory of Logan.'"

"Oh, Pace." June's voice cracked. She sipped her wine. "Of course. What a generous thing. Logan would be very honored." June stood and walked to the edge of the yard, looking up. The sun was lower in the sky now, making the mountain glow. She pulled a tissue from her jeans pocket and blew her nose. "I never get through a day without crying."

Pace stayed seated, petting Ranger who had his head in Pace's lap, evidently quite happy with this new fellow.

June sighed and tucked away her tissue. She came back and sat down.

"Well, since you apologized for knocking me down that day, I guess I better apologize, too. When you ran by earlier, I didn't want to talk to you. I simply didn't want the added complication of a new friend. A lot's been happening and another person in my life was more than I wanted to deal with. And here you are, being nice about this race for Logan. I'm a real crumb."

"No need to apologize. Gotta take care of yourself, glad you do."

"Let me pour you some more wine. You don't have too far to drive, do you? Another glass'll be okay?"

"Actually, no problem. Thanks. I live in the 'Snake, too, a little farther up the valley. This'll be it, though. Let you have your evening to yourself. Thanks, too, for letting me use Logan's name. Race starts on North Higgins, in front of Runner's Edge. Nine o'clock, if you want to come."

"I'll come if I can. I can't always tell ahead of time how my emotions will be, but if I'm not a mess, I'll be there."

"Race day, even such a short race, lots of folks look a mess. Besides, you'd do me a favor. Always perform better if someone's watching." Pace actually blushed.

"Okay, I'll be there. And I bet Logan will be, too."

Later that night, after Pace had left, June was glad she'd made this new friend. No matter what complications it might bring, friendship was important.

9

The day of the Missoula Mile was beautiful: the sky a robin's egg blue, the crowd at the race exuberant. Montana June's first time stepping out in her new town was what she needed. She enjoyed watching Pace run and was amazed at his speed. "Like a cowboy on a quarter horse!" she told him. Pace introduced her to a friend, Ellen Painter, who headed a group of slower runners and walkers. Ellen invited June to go walking sometime soon to get better acquainted, and June jumped at the chance. Her winter plumpness bothered her, and exercise would be a step in the right direction.

In fact, June decided to extend her evening walk with Ranger. At the end of Greenough Park, a small hill led to the main drive which went farther up the Rattlesnake Valley. She and Ranger started to climb. It felt good to stretch her legs and put effort into her stride, and it was several minutes before she realized her dog was not in front of her anymore. She stopped and turned around. Ranger was a good twenty yards behind her, struggling on the hill.

"Ranger, what's the matter?" June ran back and kneeled to put her arms around him. His chest was expanding and contracting at an alarming rate. "Oh, damn me. I didn't even think about how this'd affect you. Come on over here, big guy, let's rest in the shade awhile."

June guided him to a grove of ponderosa and sat on the curb while Ranger caught his breath. This was a worrisome new behavior. He'd been getting slower, but nothing like this. When he seemed to have recovered, June stood up.

"Come on, my good guy. We're going back home. You can get a drink from the creek on the way, and then we'll rest. I'm so sorry I over-worked you, Ranger. Come on, buddy."

The two friends turned back down the hill, and June walked the rest of the way home with her hand on Ranger's head. They took it at his pace and stopped at the creek, with Ranger again walking all the way into the water to drink so he wouldn't have to bend his head. Back at the house, Ranger plopped down on the hardwood floor and went right to sleep, his breath ragged and snoring. June's eyes filled with tears at the thought of her sweet Ranger, her canine protector, getting older and infirm. Another loss she couldn't handle.

(excerpt from Montana June's journal)
I guess I'll always remember how Logan looked, down in that leafy gully, standing over the clear mountain stream, watching Ranger play. We thought it would last forever.

Ranger's veterinarian in Stevensville was Doctor Ben. Montana June called the next morning to make an appointment, and then she called Maura. Whatever June would hear at the vet's, she might need a shoulder to lean on afterward.

Ranger had gotten so used to the drive back and forth to the farmhouse, he didn't get his usual nervous-dog smell until they turned into the long drive leading to the vet's place. Doc Ben's clinic for small animals was in an outbuilding at his own farm; he visited the farms and ranches around the valley to treat livestock. Though Ranger seemed to like Doc Ben just fine, there always was some discomfort or undignified activity here, and judging by his shakes and odor he'd rather be elsewhere. June commiserated—she'd had enough of doctors' offices, too, over the last couple years.

Once parked at the front door of the clinic, though, there was no getting around the fact that doctors are necessary. June had to help Ranger down from the passenger seat of the Jeep. She kept her hand tucked inside his collar in case he decided to make a break for it. June swallowed the lump in her throat and said, "Well, come on, Ranger. Let's get this over with. Maybe all you need is a spring tonic."

Inside, the vet tech looked harried. Doc Ben was out on an emergency, probably be gone an hour. June sat. Ranger's shakes increased. The office clock's tick-tocking made time drag. Each tick of the damned thing made June's blood pressure rise. At the window, a fly bammed against the glass. TICK tock. Bam. TICK tock. TICKbam tock.

"Come on, big guy. Gotta get outa here."

Outside, things were better. Ranger crawled under the Jeep, hiding in the cool familiar space. June slid down the fender, wiggling her butt to a comfortable spot and raising her face to the sun. She reached under the Jeep and petted her friend, thereby comforting them both.

Doc Ben finally returned. The doctor was an old Montana man, rangy and rough. When he was outdoors, he always wore a Stetson over his bush of gray hair. Indoors, the uncontrolled hair added to his overall appearance of someone who cared only for animals and the folks who loved them. Ranger smiled his doggy grin at the doc, but couldn't stop the shakes. The exam proved to be every bit as invasive and uncomfortable for Ranger as June had feared.

"Well, June," Doc Ben said after the indignities were over, "we've got some bad news here. Ranger has congestive heart failure and his hips are becoming problematic. He's, what, close to twelve?"

"Yeah, that's right. He was a puppy when Logan and I were engaged. He was the ring bearer at our wedding."

"Ah, honey. Damn it. You've had enough bad news the last couple years. We'll keep Ranger going for good long while, with luck. I've got some diuretics that'll help with the congestion, and some anti-inflammatories for the pain." He petted Ranger, using soft strokes. "Gentle walks are fine, and his dips in the creek are okay, too. We'll do all we can to make him comfortable, but it'll be up to Ranger himself how long we keep it up. He'll let us know. Good news is, he'll feel much better in a couple days with the drugs I send home. I promise. How 'bout you? What can I do to help you feel better?"

"Doc, you know there isn't anything. Just keep my best friend feeling as well as possible for as long as you can. That's all."

Doc Ben gave June a hug, grabbed Ranger a cookie from the jar, then walked them out to the Jeep and lifted Ranger into the passenger seat.

"He won't need the boost after the meds kick in, at least not for a while. We'll wait and see how it goes. Call me when you need me, anytime. You hear?"

"You bet, Doc. We'll see you. Later rather than sooner, I hope," June said, smiling, then kissed Ranger's head before turning the key.

THE DRIVE TO Maura's house wasn't far, but June stopped along the way at the Bitterroot River. They didn't get out of the Jeep, since Ranger was still panting from the exam, but June turned off the engine and put her head on the steering wheel. With her right hand she caressed Ranger's neck. With her left hand she wiped the tears that wouldn't stop flowing.

He'd been the cutest puppy June'd ever seen. She'd fallen in love with him almost as much as she had with Logan, and even though Ranger was Logan's dog first, it was soon obvious to everyone that Ranger loved June with his whole big heart. Now that heart was failing. It was more than June could bear. With the dog's head in her lap, she cried, then eventually drove on.

At the last turn into Maura's driveway, seeing Nanny and hearing the wind-chimes in the trees, June's heart unclenched for the first time since leaving the vet. Maura, in the flowerbed, must've heard the Jeep. She stood, brushed her hands on her cut-offs, and walked toward her daughter-in-law.

"Hey, darling girl, I'm glad you're here. How's our Ranger?" Maura leaned in through the window and rubbed Ranger's head.

"Mom, can you help me get him out? He's pretty stiff and sore today, and the trip to the vet took all his energy."

The two women lifted the large dog from the seat and put him on the ground. Mr. Mouser walked up and nosed his old friend, sneezing at the obvious smell of the vet clinic on his fur. Maura and June laughed.

"My sentiments exactly, Mouse. Come on. I've got some iced tea waiting for us in back," Maura said as she walked up the flagstone path.

The wooden table in the backyard was pushed up against an old apple tree. On the table was a hand-thrown clay pitcher, dewed from the cold liquid inside it, covered with a cloth weighted down at the corner with beads. Ranger groaned as he lay down under the table, putting his head on his front legs. Mr. Mouser purred against Ranger's back.

"Here, darling girl, take your glass—lay in the hammock in the shade. Tell me about the visit to Doc Ben."

June set the iced tea on the ground while she climbed into the tasseled hammock, then reached to retrieve it. She told her mother-in-law all that'd happened at the vet's.

Maura sighed. "Damn it all. Our four-legged friends don't live long enough, do they? We need them so much. They're our friends and family, and there's no way we can make their life-spans long enough to suit. What's next with the big guy, honey?"

"Well, we'll take it day by day. Doc says the drugs will help, and Ranger should have a good long time left, so we'll hope for the best. I don't want to—can't—make the decision to…well, you know." June couldn't say the words.

Maura's voice was soft, sad. "One thing I do know, the day comes when it's easier to not go on. Ranger will come to that day, as we each will. It's *always* harder on those left behind." Maura leaned against the tree and stretched her legs in the grass. June drifted back and forth in the hammock, collecting her emotions. After a time Maura said, "Now, let's pick ourselves up. Tell me something happy, then I'll tell you something happy, too."

June took a deep breath and said, "Okay. Something happy. Well, I saw Pace again, and he asked me to watch him in a race to raise money for prostate cancer research, which I did. And, I've met someone who might be good for my fitness level. Maybe I'll even join Run Wild Missoula. How's that for happy?" June smiled as she said this. The two of them had, over the years, commiserated on how easy it was to get more fluffy, as Maura called it, and how difficult it was to exercise.

"Marvelous! Perhaps I'll join you in your fitness plan, and we'll go on walks and hikes together. That would be perfect. 'Cause guess why—I have a special reason for wanting to stay fit." Maura's eyes sparkled and her mouth curved up at the corner.

"Don't tell me you have a new beau! Who is it?"

"A lovely gentleman who volunteers at Travelers' Rest. He's a bit older than me, but so active and smart. He's half-Salish, and makes his own copies of tools used by them when Lewis and Clark came through. He's fascinating. I'll want you to meet him sometime soon."

"I would love to, Mom. You deserve someone special in your life. I thought you had a glow about you…and do my eyes deceive me, or have you had something done to your hair, too?"

"Uh-huh!" Maura grinned. "The gray got to be too much. You know, old hippie or not, there's no reason to look older than I feel. I'm only sixty-two you know, still young enough. I'd gone to a salon to ask for help with facial hair. Drives me bug-fuck-nuts how as I age, my eyelashes and the hair on my head get thinner, at the same blessed time my nose hair and mustache grows abundantly. Isn't fair, damn it.

So the beautician gave me some products to help with those problems and then suggested a way to trim up this old braid of mine and cover the gray. Look, what do you think?" Maura used her fingers to unbraid and comb out her long hair. She fluffed her hair over her chest and beamed up at June. The sun caught the new red and gold highlights, which enhanced her natural auburn color.

"It's beautiful! Maybe you'll keep your hair loose more often, so the highlights show."

"Oh, I do. I braided it to get into the garden. So, now back to you. Tell me more about Pace. This is what, the second time you've seen him?"

"Well, actually it's a bit more. He even stopped by with a bottle of wine on the Solstice, and we had a good long visit. But Mom, it's only nine months since Logan died. I'm not looking for anyone."

"I know, darling girl. I know. Just don't close any doors that open on their own. Logan would want you to be happy—you know that as well as I do." Maura got up and stretched. "Oof. Wish coloring my hair made sitting on the ground easier. So, when're you going to invite me to see your new house?"

June slapped her cheek, her eyes wide open. "You were waiting for an invitation? Oh, Mom, I'm sorry. Of course you must come. How about dinner tomorrow? I'll make something light and give you a tour of the house, and…could you spend the night? That way we'd have all the time we want to visit. Besides, I need you to help me decide something."

"Hot damn, of course I'll spend the night! What're you trying to decide?"

"I just don't have the heart anymore to go back to teaching. Yes, I know," June said, seeing Maura's smile, "you knew that was coming, even before Logan got sick."

"Mother-in-law's intuition, darling girl. Are you gonna make it official?"

"Well, actually, I've already quit. But the question is, now what? Holy Hannah, Mom, what do I do now? I went from college to being married and teaching, and that was all I was looking for in life until children would come along." She sighed, then sat up. Maura joined her in the hammock and they pushed off together.

June continued. "But now, I don't have a clue what I want. Sometimes I get panicky thinking I jumped too soon and should cancel my resignation. Without the framework of school and teaching, who will I *be*? I need to do something besides putter in my new house and take care of Ranger. I don't know. I need some guidance. Come tomorrow and help me make a list of possibilities, okay?"

"You've got it, darling girl. Ooh, what fun! A sleep-over and planning session, all in one. I'll bring the wine."

"We'll put on some of Grandpa Max's old records, and oh, this'll be grand. Thanks, Mom, for making this very sad morning into a much better day. Now, I'd better get my old buddy back home and tuck him in. Tomorrow, maybe he'll feel well enough to show you his favorite spot in the creek."

On the way back, June stopped at the market and bought the ingredients for dinner and ordered good crusty bread from Le Petit Outre bakery; great for a girls' night at home.

10

The problem Montana June faced in having over-night guests was the single bedroom. She solved this the next day by building a delightful little oasis in the great room, with a camp cot, a futon, several dramatic pillows, and a lacy bedspread. She'd be comfortable here, and Maura would have privacy in the bedroom.

By late afternoon, the house was clean and the meal ready. Ranger seemed to feel better, which made June's heart sing.

Maura drove up in Baby just before four o'clock. With a brief toot on the VW's horn, she pulled in behind the Jeep. She hopped out with her overnight bag and a grocery sack.

June called to her, "Hey, perfect timing! Come on in and I'll give you a tour, and then we'll take Ranger for a stroll through the park."

Maura had known Max and Sarah, having met them when Logan and June married, and shared many memories of dinners and cocktail parties in this home.

"I love what you've done with the place. You've kept the elegance and grace but added your own touches. The green chair looks perfect there by the fireplace. Hey, is that my bed? Oh, goody!"

"No, Mom. You're in the bedroom. I couldn't put you on a cot."

"Oh, no you don't. I'm taking this. I'll be the Queen of Sheba with all the lace and satin pillows. Hell, no. You're not taking this away from me. My pack is going on it right now, darling girl."

"Okay. If you insist. But if you get uncomfortable during the night, I'll switch. Now, where's that wine? Let's have a glass in the backyard before for our walk."

Maura opened the bottle of Saint Pepin from the Ten Spoon Winery a couple miles away, made from grapes grown right in the 'Snake.

The evening was a perfect respite: time for chatting, sipping wine, walking with Ranger through the park. As the sky deepened in color, after the food'd been eaten and the dishes cleared, they returned to their chairs in the back to watch the long evening sun start the mountain's fire.

June sighed and said, "I love the view of Mount Jumbo from here. The mountain almost glows. I've heard it was named after an elephant, but that's all. Do you know the story?"

"Mm-hmm. Back when the railroad first came through, when Missoula was getting started, a circus came in on the rails, complete with animals. Jumbo was their elephant. Folks noted how much the mountain looked like Jumbo when he lay down. See it?"

The mountain did look somewhat like an elephant lying on its side. The head and trunk stretched to the north; the large rounded rump sloped down to the Clark Fork River.

Maura continued. "You can also see the ridges left by the many shorelines of Glacial Lake Missoula, up there on the mountain. What a thing that must've been; ice dams making the whole region fill with water, then—swoosh—it rushed to the ocean all at once. Many times over." She sipped her wine, then pointed. "Hey, look! I didn't realize you could see people walking up the trail. And oh, my. There's a paraglider—where'd he come from?"

"Folks carry their canopies in backpacks up the trail, all the way to the top of the mountain. The evening thermals lift them off the crest. Sometimes they fly a long time. It's beautiful to watch, isn't it? Not my cup of tea, I'd be way too scared."

"Hmmm…I'd do it," Maura said. "Did you know I used to sky-dive when I was younger? But, no. Perhaps I'm not so adventurous anymore. So, on to our topic. What, thinking big, do you want to do now?"

"That's the problem: I don't know. I had energy during the move, but that's gone. I enjoyed seeing Pace race, and I'm getting used to meeting people again. I do love my new house. But…where do I go from here? I've never had to make decisions alone before." Her voice dropped.

"I'm going to ask a 'mother-in-law' question. How's the finances? When'll you get the money from the sale of the farmhouse? What kind of time-span are you looking at before you need an income?"

"Logan's insurance money is taking good care of me for the time being. He bought an extra policy before he got sick. The sale of the farm will be finalized next month, and that's another good chunk of change. And we were always careful, anyway, so money isn't a problem. I have Logan to thank for that." She sniffed and blew her nose.

"Now, don't go getting teary. We start, we'll be blubbering all night. Keep focused, darling girl." Maura's kind voice softened her words.

June inhaled. "Okay." She blew her nose again and said, "I've considered going back to school, getting my master's degree. The university's so close it's an easy walk. Or is that delaying things? I can't think what I'd want to study. Not education. I don't want to work in a school again."

"Perhaps an MFA? You're a good writer and have other artistic skills. A master of fine arts might be the ticket. Meantime, you could volunteer. What else can we come up with? Let's have another glass of wine and we'll brainstorm."

By the end of the evening, when the mountain above them was dark and the candles had burned down, they had a list for June to consider. Some of the ideas were crazy, like becoming a stand-up paddle board instructor on the Clark Fork River, but some were realistic. At least June had things to think about.

On their way to bed, Maura again insisted on the cot. Ranger started the night next to her, but before long wandered back to his usual place at the foot of June's bed. Through the open windows, June listened to the calls of the night birds. As she rolled over, she spoke to Logan.

My angel. Thank you for your mother. Being with her brings you closer to me.

WAKING UP TO the smell of coffee brewing and bacon frying was a luxury June hadn't had since Logan died. She heard Maura talking to Ranger in the kitchen. She jumped out of bed and pulled on her robe to join them.

"Hey, sleepyhead!" Maura smiled as June entered the kitchen. "Pour yourself some coffee while I finish making breakfast."

June filled her mug and took a deep sip. "Hmmm…you make good coffee. Thank you for taking the initiative. I should've been up making these things for you, yet here you are, pampering me, as always."

"Nonsense, darling girl. Now. Any epiphanies while you slept about what's next?"

"No, darn it, though you tickled something when you mentioned writing. I should start journaling again, at least. You also suggested volunteering. Maybe I'll go down to the Run Wild Missoula office today and see if they need help. It'd be a great motivator for my new exercise plan, being around runners more. The marathon's coming up soon, they probably need people right now."

"Oh, goody. I'll come with you. And then, I'd better head home to Mr. Mouser. He's okay for an overnight on his own, but he'll be wanting some company soon. Now, breakfast is ready."

After eating, Maura and June took Ranger around the park. The early morning sun spangled the tops of the cottonwoods and lit the hill to the west of the narrow Rattlesnake Valley. The crisp air was invigorating.

"Would you look how glorious everything is today?" Maura said, as they walked at Ranger's slow pace.

"Days like this, when I start feeling good, Mom, I kind of forget, then it all comes crashing back. Hard. The grief never ends."

Maura stopped on the bridge over the creek and rested her arms on the railing. "Montana June, grief ends. It does. The missing doesn't, the loving doesn't, but the gut-wrenching, soul-destroying grief does finally come to an end."

June leaned into Maura's shoulder. "It's such hard work. I'm exhausted all the time."

"You just have to take my word on it, darling girl. These are still hard times. We aren't even a year into it. But, I think we're making good progress in our healing. You've moved, you're making new friends, and thinking about the future. I have a new beau and I'm busier than ever volunteering. I believe our Logan would be proud of us."

"Maybe you're right. I dream about him often, and I feel his presence all the time. I miss him so much." Her voice choked as the tears started.

"Honey. Don't cry. We're making progress, remember? Oh, look there." Maura pointed to a pair of mallard ducks with new babies, in the creek. "Oh, those dear little balls of fluff. Five ducklings. And isn't Papa proud!"

The drake, in his emerald and brown feathers, swam behind the flotilla of babies, his neck stretched high watching for threats. The hen at the front was busy grabbing food as she led the family to a haven under branches. Montana June swallowed her tears and watched them.

"It wasn't long ago Ranger would've already been in the water chasing them," June said. She rubbed his head and sighed. "This reminds me of a time when he was a pup. We were on our honeymoon, in fact, at the campground at Georgetown Lake, with a floating dock. Ranger saw some ducks several yards out in the lake, and ran right off the end of the dock, not realizing the water wouldn't hold him up. He couldn't swim yet, being so young, and he panicked. Logan had to pull him out of the water by his collar. Took him weeks to get used to the water after that." June reached down and scrubbed Ranger's ears. "Do you remember that trip, my old friend? You were such a cute puppy. Oh, dang it, Mom. I don't want my Ranger to be old and sick."

"Darling girl, I know." She hugged June. "But he's better with his new meds. He's walking well, it's a beautiful morning, and we are *not* going to borrow grief from what's coming. Enjoy what we have while we have it, that's my new motto."

"Okay. I hear you. Let's take the big guy back to the house before we walk to town."

AT THE RUN Wild Missoula offices, they were greeted by several people Montana June met at the Missoula Mile race. June bought her membership to RWM and put her name on the volunteer list for the marathon. This close to such a big event, the office was a hive of activity. As Maura and June turned to leave, June saw a familiar face.

"Hey, Pace!"

"June, great to see you. Hey, Mrs. McPherson. I remember you," he said, giving her a peck on the cheek.

Maura beamed. "Heavens, boy, you've turned into a looker! You were nothing but sinew and bone the last time I saw you…oh, my. Must've been more than fifteen years ago, when you and Logan graduated from high school. I'm glad you've made friends with my darling girl. June tells me you're with the FWP."

"Yep. High school's a long time ago, Mrs. Mac." His eyes sparkled as he seemed to struggle to keep a grin from surfacing. "My job now's to tackle the worst of the bad guys who poach wildlife…or run over dead-end signs." A snort escaped as he lost the battle. "Sorry," he said, dodging June's slug to his bicep, "guess that's top secret."

"No, Mom knows all about it, but still, you shouldn't spread rumors. Hey, I just put my name on the volunteer list for the marathon. You're running in it, aren't you? Excited?"

"Heck yeah…hope to qualify for the New York City Marathon. But training's gone well. Want to volunteer tomorrow morning setting up the bib packets with me? Office labor here, but you'd meet lots of folks."

"You're on. What time?"

"Not me," said Maura, "I'm working at Travelers' Rest. But I'll come cheer on race day. Even bring my cowbells."

"Great, Mrs. Mac!" Pace walked to the base of the staircase. "June, meet me here tomorrow at 9:00. Now, gotta go earn a paycheck."

"Okay." June gave him a quick hug. "See you tomorrow."

"Take care, you two." He turned, and ran up and out the door.

"Ooh, darling girl," said Maura, "he's matured nicely. A real hunk-a-hunka."

"He's a…what?"

"Good goddess, you *are* a child," Maura said, sparkling. "Well, I guess that was long before your time. Even I was a mere babe. But you never heard Elvis sing about burning love?" Maura, despite her broad hips, gave a good impression of Presley's sexy shimmy. "I do hope you keep seeing him."

"Mom, I told you," June said, laughing. "He's just a friend. I'm not looking for anything more. But, yes, I enjoy his company. Now, are you ready to walk back to the house?"

"Yep. I need to get on home to Mouser. This has been a mini-vacation, spending the night with you."

The walk back to June's house was a perfect culmination to that mini-vacation. The shaded streets were cool; the porches of the houses in this old section of town were decorated with pots of geraniums. They didn't even have to wait at the crossing, where often traffic was stopped for many minutes as the trains rumbled into the siding.

Later that day, June reflected on what Maura'd said on their walk through the park with Ranger. "We are not going to borrow grief from what's coming. Enjoy what we have while we have it." They were making progress in their lives and were healing. Both of them needed to concentrate on the beauty and joy of each day and not borrow sadness from what was to come.

11

The next day, Montana June enjoyed working with Pace at the Run Wild Missoula office. To start, she got a quick lesson in what went in each of the race bags: a paper bib imprinted with a racer's number and timing chip, four safety pins to attach the bib to shirt or shorts, and tons of race and community information. This marathon had several times been voted best in the nation by the readers of *Runners' World Magazine*. The pride and excitement was palpable in the work space. June quickly became part of the crew. The woman who'd taken June on a hike, Ellen Painter, was there volunteering, too. A green Back of the Pack bandana was tied around her neck, just below her brown-gray hair.

As work progressed, Ellen shared her own story of how she'd started in Run Wild. She'd been an overweight fifty-something woman who was motivated when a Missoula policeman had died. He'd been paralyzed ten years previously after being shot in the line of duty. His wife ran the Missoula Marathon to raise money for the Christopher Reeve Foundation, for research for the treatment and cure of spinal cord injury. Ellen was inspired to take on the challenge, too. "From the beginning, the folks here treated me as an athlete. And now, years later, I enjoy something that brings joy and fitness to my life."

"That's a wonderful story. Pace"— June glanced at him by her side—"is raising money for prostate cancer research, and you for the Reeve Foundation. Running must attract wonderful people."

"Oh, I'm no runner," said Ellen. "I walk all my races. But yes, we're mostly good folks. You ever do a race?"

"Nope. But I'd like to try."

"Hey, great! We aren't all studs like Pace." Ellen grinned at Pace, who blushed and snorted. She laughed, then continued. "You know, there's a 5K race, just over three miles, the day before the marathon. Why don't you sign up?"

"Maybe I will."

Ellen said, "Oof. I'm bushed." She looked, unsuccessfully, for another box of bags. "Hey, believe it or not, I think we're done!"

LATER, MONTANA JUNE and Pace Pacinski walked up and out of the downstairs RWM office into the early July sunshine together. June felt a sense of growth. She'd signed up for the Missoula 5K.

As they left the parking lot behind the building, Pace cleared his throat. "Uh, hey, June…you have plans for the Fourth of July? Gotta work that day, but my evening's free, and some running buddies close to my place are having a barbecue. It's a week before the marathon, so no one'll be overdoing the food or drinks, but…well, should be fun. Want to come?"

"You know what, Pace? I think I'd like that. Where and what time?" June smiled, knowing she'd need something to take her mind away from the previous Independence Day.

As Pace climbed into his truck, he gave June directions to the party. He reached through the open door to grasp June's shoulder.

"Thanks for today. Glad you'd hang out with me. See you on the Fourth. I'll bring some beers, but the food'll all be provided....Later!" As Pace drove away to his shift at FWP, June waved and began the walk home.

On the way, June thought about the last Fourth of July. Exactly a year ago Logan had been going through chemo, which was intended to attack the cancer. He'd have a treatment, then go home and throw up all day. The folks in the chemo ward tried to make things cheery with patriotic decorations, and most of the folks sitting in recliners hooked up to the bags of chemicals dripping into their veins were as happy as they could make themselves be. But June had to fake it. The cancer was winning; chemo wasn't helping. The vigorous man June had fallen in love with wasn't there anymore. After that last long session of treatments, Logan swore he'd never go through it again. Though of course he didn't get better, being away from the chemo allowed him to not feel so very ill—a blessing for them both. On Independence Day, Logan had not quite three months to live.

June walked down the shaded street toward the railroad crossing, remembering. Her grief now included sadness at moving away, moving on. She touched her gold bracelet and wiped her eyes. Just then clanging bells signaled the train barricade would soon be closing over the street. June startled and began to run, crossing the tracks as the barricade slammed behind her. She watched five big engines, indicating a very long train, rumble over the crossing.

INDEPENDENCE DAY, LATE afternoon sun shone very hot, so June lowered the windows of the Jeep and tied her hair into a braid under her hat. The party was farther up the valley, close to the trailhead that led to the Rattlesnake Wilderness Area. June followed Pace's directions to the large meadow with a beautiful big house next to the creek. There were already about fifty people lounging around the tables, many she recognized from RWM. As she parked the Jeep, Pace hurried toward her.

"Hey, June, you're here! Glad you came…well—" Pace seemed suddenly shy. He reached out and grasped June's hand, pulling her close for a kiss on the cheek. "—Just glad you're here."

"Me, too, Pace," she said. "But, this is the first large party I've been to for a long time. Don't hate me if I can't handle it and leave early. I'm not expecting that to happen." She stepped away from him, feeling at odds about the kiss.

Ellen was putting a bowl on the salad table near the grills heating up for the burgers. June called to her, happy to focus her attention away from Pace's greeting. "Heya, Ellen. How are you?"

Ellen waved and came toward them. "Hey, June! It's great you signed up for the 5K on Saturday. Pace, you ready for the marathon?"

"You betcha, Ellen. You doing the full or the half?" Pace grabbed a bunch of chips from a nearby bowl and handed some to June as they talked.

"Oh, the half. I gave up doing full marathons some years back. I love the distance of a half marathon. Feels like I've accomplished something, but I can still walk later in the day."

The three friends continued their banter as they walked toward the shade of trees. Ellen veered off to talk to another friend, and Pace led June to a log near the creek.

"Like a beer, June? Got some stashed in a cooler…right here." As always, his voice was quiet, halting.

"Sure. Oh, you have the good stuff. Yum." She popped open a Bayern Dancing Trout and took a deep swig. "Dang, Missoula has some great breweries. How'd work go today?"

"Ah, hell…had to play bad cop on the river. Folks jumping off the bridges, not looking…too many floaters, too much drinking. At least nobody got hurt on my watch. Glad for the end of the shift."

"I bet. I heard about someone hospitalized by a jumper last year. A holiday, hot weather, lotsa beer, I 'spose it can lead to problems." June leaned back and looked down the valley southward toward town. Ponderosa offered shade near the stream but didn't obscure the view. The field they were sitting in nestled between Mount Jumbo and Missoula's North Hills, now turning from green to golden-brown. "Hey, you said you live near here, right? Where's your house?"

"Well, between here and your place, past the winery, near the school. We get tired of these folks, we could go there, but we'd lose the view of the city fireworks. Too close to Mount Jumbo's flank. Ranger okay with fireworks?"

"He hates them, but he's in the basement, so maybe he won't be bothered. He's failing, now, too. I just had him to the vet. He has congestive heart failure. I don't think I can handle it if he dies."

"Damn, June! That…sucks." Pace cleared his throat and took a swig of beer. He threw a stick into the stream and watched it float down, then looked toward the tables. "Hey, want to eat before the band starts?"

"Music, too? Sure, let's go. I'm hungry and it'll take my mind off Ranger."

They loaded up with burgers, potato salad and chips. Back on their log with full plates, Pace offered June a fresh beer to help wash the food down.

June bit into the juicy burger, chewed and swallowed. "So, tell me about yourself. Maura said you grew up in the Bitterroot, attended school with Logan. What else?"

Pace's burger was already half-gone. He grabbed a chip, took a drink of his beer, and turned on the log to face June. "Well, we were in the same class most years growing up. Logan had that strong, good-guy image...even then. Lost touch after high school. I went to Washington State for college. The folks divorced....lived with Dad in Vancouver. Worked hard, played hard...you know the story. Fell in love."

"Oh, yeah? Tell me." June sipped her beer.

"Thought she was the love of my life. Dad tried but couldn't talk sense into this young stud who knew it all." Pace's quiet voice was full of irony. "Guess Dad saw past her beauty to the...shit; turned out to be pretty ugly stuff underneath. All I saw was a gorgeous female, seemed to want me. After I graduated, we eloped. Ignored family...lived in a little cabin on the coast. Got a job working for the state park nearby. She stayed home getting crazier and crazier. Less 'n a year later, the trouble was obvious. Tried to get her to a therapist, salvage our marriage, anything. Came home from work one day and...she'd cleaned out the whole cabin, taken our nest egg, all the furniture, everything. All gone. Found out later, she'd been hanging with a creep at the local bar. They had a truck, loaded everything up...sold it all."

June stopped eating and took his hand. "Holy Hannah, Pace. What an awful thing."

"Yeah." Pace scuffed the dirt at his feet. "Butt-ugly for a while. Cindy, that's her name; Cindy had a mental disorder. Called me a year or so later from a mental hospital where she'd been court-ordered to go for rehab. Drying out, said she'd been diagnosed with bipolar disorder, and was sorry…yeah, right. Soon as she's out of the hospital, she's back with the creep. They pulled some even worse stuff. She's in a women's prison in the Southwest now."

"So, are you still married?" June's voice was quiet to match Pace's tone.

"No. We divorced, long time ago. Never hear from her anymore." He took a deep breath and laughed. "Never think of her, either, except times like this. So, that's it…moved back to Montana, got a real job with Fish, Wildlife, and Parks, and started running again. And now, I'm sitting next to someone whose beauty is real inside and outside, not a faked-up view of herself." Pace smiled, his eyes crinkling at the corners.

"Why, thank you! It's been a long time since I've gotten a compliment like that. At my age, too." June felt her face flushing, adding to her embarrassment.

"Oh, come on. You're…what, twenty-nine? Thirty? Logan was probably my age, thirty-six."

"I'm thirty-five and proud of it. I've always been glad to get older. Oh—" she choked a bit, took a sip of beer, then wiped her nose "—until this year, anyway. My last birthday was one I'd rather forget. It's been a horrible year."

The two finished eating silently, listening to the band tuning up in the background. The evening light faded. Pace gathered up their empties and paper plates, put them in the trash, then offered June a hand.

"Want to go down to the creek before the music starts?"

"Yes. That'd be good."

AS THEY WATCHED the fireworks later, June felt a glow of happiness. She watched the colorful explosions rise and fall over her new town, and once again touched her gold bracelet.

Logan, my angel, do you see me? Is it okay for me to be here now? Give me a sign from you, sweetheart.

At that moment, the finale of the fireworks took over the southern horizon. Blue, red, gold, and green flowers as big as the sky came one after the other. Time after time, the rockets rose to explode into millions of sparks, breaking apart to make more flowers, more colors. June's heart thrilled with each explosion. Pace took her hand, wove his fingers with hers.

He said, "I think Logan would've loved that."

She squeezed his hand, then disentangled her fingers. "Yes. I know."

12

Much to her surprise, at 8:30 the morning before the Missoula Marathon, Montana June was standing in front of the Wilma Theater on Higgins Avenue, just north of the bridge, in a large crowd of people. Her race bib was pinned on her shirt. Her new shoes had been broken in, and she'd worked up to walking three miles at a pretty good pace. She knew that for someone who'd started training less than two weeks ago, she was as well prepared as possible, but her heart was going crazy with first-timer nerves. Why had she thought she could do this?

Other people jogged on the sidewalks to warm up, but June had walked from home, so her muscles were ready. Folks were checking their watches, drinking from water bottles, adjusting their laces. And laughing. Everyone was talking and laughing. Music blaring from loudspeakers was often interrupted as the announcer whipped up the crowd.

"Hey, June, you came. Marvelous!"

June turned around and saw Ellen Painter, ready for the race, wearing the marathon T-shirt and her green bandana.

"Oh, hey! I'm glad to see someone I know. I'm terrified." June laughed.

"Stick with me, you'll do fine. I know you got this, since you did great on our hill climb." Ellen patted June's shoulder. "Need water?"

"Nope, I'm good. We're pretty close to time, aren't we?"

"Yep. Clock says one more minute. What a great day, not too hot yet. Damn, I love this!" Ellen jumped up and lassoed the air. "Yee-haw!"

As the seconds counted down on the time-clock, June tried to slow her breathing.

BANG!

The crowd moved forward. Ellen kept to the right, so June stayed with her, allowing runners to pass on the left. As they crossed the bridge heading south, June looked around at the clear, fast flowing river, the mountains encircling the valley, the deep blue sky. She was doing a thing she wouldn't have imagined even a month ago. Here she was, in a race. She'd never done anything so spontaneous.

As the crowd of racers turned west through a neighborhood June hadn't seen before, she realized most of Missoula came out to support this race weekend. Folks lined the streets, cheering on the runners and walkers; for awhile, June smiled and waved. Soon, though, she needed all her energy to put one foot in front of the other. By the time the route took them back to the river toward the university, June was exhausted.

"Hey, Ellen…I'm sinking." She was dripping with sweat.

Ellen poured water on her bandana and handed it to June. "Here, wipe your face."

"Jeez, you're not sweating at all." June wiped her neck, face and arms. "Thanks, that sure helps."

"Okay, let's slow down a little. Empty your lungs, let them fill naturally. Take shorter steps, don't pick up your feet as much. Scuff them, that way you'll save energy. Bend your arms into a right angle…there, that's it. Better?" Ellen watched June make the changes.

"Oh, amazing difference." June panted. "Yep, I feel better. But you go on ahead, I'll get there. Promise."

"Nope. No rush. I'm enjoying the day, saving my energy for tomorrow. Okay, here. We turn and go under this bridge. Less than a mile to go."

Within ten minutes, the finish line came into view. June's face still ran with sweat, but there was the end, and she saw volunteers putting medals around the necks of the finishers.

"Hey, June, good work." Pace cheered her on from the other side of the finish line. "You can do it, come on!" June put a spring into her step. And then, she crossed the line.

"Your first race! Congratulations." Pace put the medal around her neck and gave her a quick hug. Ellen joined in, patting June on the back.

"I can't believe I did it! I was ready to quit when we got to the riverbank. I didn't think I'd finish. Thank you both for encouraging me."

June handed the bandana back to Ellen. "I should wash this first, I guess, but thanks."

"Nonsense. I'm glad you could use it. Now, Pace, how about the three of us do the Expo together?"

For a while, June walked through Caras Park with them, looking at the Expo tables, where businesses sold racing duds and advertised other races. By 11:00, though, it was time to head home to Ranger. Trudging back, she realized she'd been over-confident to walk to the race. She was tired; her feet hurt. She didn't even mind when she had to wait at the railroad crossing for an east-bound train to clear the street. She sat on the curb watching the graffiti-splashed cars inching by.

At home, June let Ranger out in the backyard, then collapsed in the shade of the big maple. The thrill of the morning disappeared. She realized, though she was proud of herself for completing her first race, she longed to share that experience with Logan. She leaned back on the grass. Ranger came and lay beside her, and they rested together, watching the sun dapple through the leaves above.

THE NEXT DAY, Maura and June stationed themselves near the Bitterroot River east of the Maclay Bridge. It was early, but they knew Pace would be coming soon. He wouldn't be in the first rush of elite runners who came from all over the country for this marathon, but he'd said he intended to be crossing the river at about 8:00, which would allow him to finish the race, as Pace said, at "a sub-three time" or in less than three hours, faster than necessary to qualify for the New York City Marathon. Maura and June arrived separately but parked together and walked to the race route. As promised, Maura brought her noise-maker cowbells to cheer on the racers.

Only about fifteen minutes passed before June saw Pace.

"Oh, look, there he is! He's wearing his 'Logan' shirt." She waved wildly. "Pace! You look great."

Pace ran right up and grabbed her.

June squealed just before he kissed her smack on the mouth.

"Thanks for being here, June, Mrs. Mac. Sorry about the sweat. Gotta run, bye!" Pace waved as he left.

"Well," said Maura, "that was brief but exciting. How about that kiss, darling girl!"

"Salty but fun! Now what? You want to go watch him cross the finish line?"

"Nope, I'll stay right here and keep on cheering. I bet folks'll be coming for hours. You go ahead, watch your guy. Now, more cowbells!" Maura shook them wildly.

June hurried to her car and drove to downtown Missoula. Streets were blocked because of the marathon, but she found a back way to the Higgins Bridge in plenty of time. A huge colorful arch made of hundreds of balloons marked the finish line in front of the Wilma Theater. Spectators lined the bridge, cheering for the tired, happy runners and walkers nearing the end of their race.

Before long, one was Pace.

"You're doing great!" June looked at the time-clock below the balloons. "Still sub-three!"

He grinned in triumph as he passed. June wove through the throng to the finish line, and watched a volunteer place a finishers' medal around Pace's neck. He looked sweaty but happy, accepting a water bottle from an aide.

"Pace, you did it!"

He walked gingerly in circles, gulping his water. "June, thanks for coming here." Pace stopped near the barricade and reached over it to hug her. "Hey, meet me down by the river, okay? By the other side of the fish sculptures…gotta sit in the water a few minutes."

By the time June snaked through the crowd to the river, Pace sat hip deep in the river, soaked. It was just after nine in the morning, but he didn't seem to mind the chill of the water.

"Isn't that cold?" June sat at the water's edge.

"Hell, yeah. But cold water's good for the muscles…keeps 'em from aching more later. Learned that from an elite runner, always try to do it after a long run. Truly helps, believe me. What a great run. Love this marathon. Can't wait to see how New York does it….Guess the views'll be different, anyway."

"I'm so proud of you for qualifying, Cowboy. Congratulations."

"Big Apple, here I come!"

13

Montana June dropped Pace at his house to clean up and rest after the marathon, then drove home to prepare a celebratory dinner for him. First, though, she walked through the park with Ranger so he could wade in the creek. It wasn't even noon and already hot. By mid-afternoon, it'd be a scorcher.

June sat on the stream bank and dabbled her feet in the cold water. A patch of watercress grew close by. As June reached for it, she reflected on how much had changed since Pace had run into her six weeks ago, down this path. That day she'd been picking lamb's quarters and dreading a solitary dinner of the greens and a burger patty at home at the farmhouse. Now she was harvesting cress to add to the salad she would serve Pace this evening. Her thoughts drifted over a recurring worry—that she seeing too much of him. But he was sweet, calm and very shy; and she enjoyed his company.

June shook the wet greens. Ranger ambled up out of the creek, and the two turned toward home, Ranger's hips slowing him and June's sore muscles from yesterday's race making the pace feel good. June had bought a bottle of excellent red wine and two great steaks to celebrate Pace's sub-three marathon. Along with a loaf of crusty bread, a peppery watercress salad, and a cool lemon sorbet, it'd be a fine dinner. Her concentration on dinner prep was interrupted as she stepped around a black pickup. This jerk hadn't even parked, just jammed into the shrubs across the path. June squeezed between the front bumper and a snowberry bush, then crossed the street to her yard.

June unlocked the front door of her house and went to the kitchen to wash the watercress, then wrapped it in a tea towel and stepped through the sliding glass door to swing the cress dry outside. Ranger pushed in front of her, barring her way, hackles raised, a low growl coming from deep in his throat.

"What is it, Ranger? What's the matter?"

He exploded with loud barks and bounded off the patio, tearing around the back of the garage. He yelped once, then—silence.

"Ranger?" June ran after him, around the corner of the garage, straight into the chest of Jeb Murdoch. Pulling back in surprise, June saw Jeb's eyes were blood-shot. He had several days' growth of beard. The front of his shirt was stained with beer and chewing tobacco.

"Holy Christ! What're you doing here? What did you do to my dog?"

"I recalled that yellow devil from the last time I come to see you, so I's prepared this time. Picked this up across the street." Jeb sneered as he hefted a branch, his hands dirty, nails black and broken. Ranger lay collapsed, blood on his head, his chest rising in jerks.

"Ranger!" She fell to her knees and touched his head.

"Oh, no, li'l lady. Don't you be waking that devil, or I *will* kill him. You and me got unfinished business. I come to help you awhile back, shit-long way down from Darby to your place at Metcalf, and this here hell-hound near tore my throat out after you attacked me. All I's after was a bit o' cuddle, and you attacked me!" Jeb's words slurred.

"I've got to get Ranger to the vet. Let me go call, right now!" June's blood ran ice-cold. Kneeling next to Ranger, she looked up, but Jeb blocked the sun. He loomed over her, threatening.

"Nope. Not gonna be doing it that way. You come on over here, now." Jeb reached down and grabbed June's shirt, yanking her up by the sleeve. His breath was foul, his armpits rank as he tightened his grip around her. "I been waiting here on this couch you got set up in the shade, all nice 'n comfy. Brought some beers, we'll have ourselves a fine ol' time." Jeb dragged June around the corner of the garage, kicking Ranger in the ribs as he passed.

"Leave my dog alone, Jeb. Get the hell out." June's throat tightened; she was nearing panic. "If you go now I won't report you, but—"

"Oh, you do got a funny idea of what's happening here today, don't you, li'l lady, Junebug girl? No, that just ain't it. You gotta pay for what you did to ol' Jeb last time." Jeb shoved her down to the chaise lounge, holding onto her shirt. The cloth ripped, exposing June's bra. She screamed. He slapped her face hard; her head whipped back.

"Quiet, bitch. Now you ruined it. We gotta go inside." Jeb hauled on the remnants of June's shirt, ripping it further as he hefted her off the chaise, then pushed her through the doorway. "Get in. One more sound, you'll regret it."

June stumbled, falling face-first on the hardwood floor. She tried to scramble away from him, but Jeb grabbed her shorts and pulled, one torn fingernail scratching her butt as her pants came down. She screamed again. Maybe the neighbor was in her garden and would hear. Maybe Pace would come early. Maybe Ranger…oh, God, was Ranger dead? The thought sent June into true panic and she bucked her way to her knees.

"Let me go—I need to see Ranger. Stop!" June got one leg under her, but her shorts were around her knees. She tripped as Jeb's right arm reached around her throat.

"Shut the fuck up, bitch. Tol' you you'd regret it." He slammed the sliding glass door behind him with his left hand, pressing tight on June's throat. She couldn't breathe—gripped his forearm—tried to pull his arm away. Jeb pushed her forward, her legs hobbled by her shorts. At the door of the bedroom, he slugged a glancing blow at her left cheek then threw her on the bed. "Not one more sound, bitch. The life of that cur out there depends on how you handle yourself right here and now. You take those sweet li'l shorts rest a' way off and spread those pretty legs for ol' Jeb. Do it."

June felt sluggish; each second was an eon. Her fingers reached under the band of her shorts and pulled them off. As she leaned forward, her torn shirt fell off, leaving only her bra. Her face was hot, stinging from the blow. She tried to get oxygen into her lungs. *Breathe. Think.*

"Jeb. Listen. It doesn't have to be this way. Ummm…there's beer in the fridge. Why don't we have a couple, okay?"

"Sure, Junebug. Sure. Jeb'll have a beer or two. Just use my belt here, tie your hands to the bedstead." Jeb grabbed her wrists with one hand and whipped off his leather belt with the other, then secured June's wrists over the post of the headboard. "You keep that pretty li'l pose you got there, and I'll be back with some cold ones." He stomped to the kitchen, hitting the doorframe as he lurched through it. Things on the refrigerator door rattled as Jeb jerked the door open; he was rummaging, grabbing bottles, then he slammed the fridge closed. June tried to calm herself while she struggled to lift the tightened belt up and over the bedstead, succeeding only in loosening it a little by the time he stumbled back.

Jeb had one beer almost empty in the time it took him to return. Two more were clutched in his grimy hand.

"Brought you a beer, Junebug, jus' like a gentleman. Here, I'll hold it for you, since you're kinda tied up." Jeb's voice gurgled as he laughed. He upended the bottle in front of June's mouth. Cold beer sluiced down her face to her chest, soaking her bra.

"Oh, that there's a pretty picture. Wet T-shirt contests got nothing on a wet bra, eh, Junebug? Let's jus' get that little bit of bother taken care of, too." He used the finger with the broken fingernail to pull down her bra, leaving a deep red scratch on her breast. "Ooh, too bad. Jeb'll kiss it, make it better."

Jeb leaned forward to reach June's breast but lost his balance and fell onto the bed. "Damn, this bed's not steady. Din't you set it up right when you moved in? Pro'ly ol' Gary Fucking Peterson doesn't know how to set up a bed. I shoulda stayed and fixed you up that day, but you had all those damned people here, and…ah hell."

Jeb stood—clapped a hand to his mouth—stumbled toward the bathroom, falling—splatter sounds as he vomited on the floor. *Now!* She lifted her arms up and scraped the loosened greasy belt over the bedstead. By the time she got to her feet at the bottom of the bed, Jeb was standing, wiping his forearm across his mouth.

"Jeb, listen. Leave. Go now and I won't report you. You aren't in any shape today. Go home."

Jeb's stomach heaved again. His eyes widened as he looked at her bruising face, her wrists bound by the belt, the bed, the mess on the floor. He seemed to deflate in front of her. June worked her hands free from the belt and thrust it at him.

"Go. Take this thing and go!"

He turned and tried to run, stumbling to the front door. June heard him struggling to unlock it, then the crash as it slammed opened; the next sound was his truck engine whining and a roar when he sped down the street.

June's first thought was for Ranger. She grabbed her bathrobe from the hook in her closet, threw it on, and ran out the back door and around the garage. Ranger lay still, but was breathing. His chest raised, paused, and lowered.

June ran back into her house, grabbed her phone and called 911, then Pace.

MUCH LATER, AFTER hours with the police and more with doctors, Pace and June sat on the back patio, Ranger at their feet. June had called Doctor Ben, but his service said he was away from the area. They recommended an emergency vet, the only thing open on a Sunday. It'd been expensive, but without doubt, worth it. Ranger had stitches on his head and was sore. The vet said his ribs weren't broken, but probably bruised where he'd been kicked. He'd recover.

So would June. Pace had insisted on taking her to NowCare while Ranger was being treated. June's cheek and lip were swollen from where Jeb had slugged her, and an impressive black eye was blooming from the slap. She knew she was incredibly lucky it wasn't worse. The difference between a trip to NowCare and an ice pack versus the emergency room and a rape kit was the simple fact that her attacker had been too drunk to complete what he intended to do.

Pace brought June a glass of water and adjusted the light blanket over her shoulders.

"It's funny—it's hot out but I'm so cold I can't stop shivering," June said. She gave him a small, one-sided smile.

"Effects of shock. Really glad you called me after 911. Good to get here at the same time as the police, but…I should've been here earlier. Could've stayed here instead of going to my house."

"Don't be silly. You had to be home after your marathon. No one could've foreseen this. Poor Ranger." June reached to pat him as he moaned and rolled over. "You tried to protect me again, and it almost got you killed. Pace, thank you for coming and taking care of us. And cleaning up the mess in the bedroom. That was way above and beyond."

"Hey, girl. No worries. Glad it's hardwood, not carpet. Hot water and Lysol, no problem." Pace cleared his throat, preparing to ask the next question. "So, uh…you knew this guy? Jeb, right?"

"Yes…well no, not really. He was a coworker of Logan's, and somehow got included when Logan's buddies helped me move; that's how he knew where I lived. He kind of made some moves on me, but I never thought he'd pursue it, not at all. I wonder what the police will do. I'm sure they'll have his address. Will they arrest him? Will I have to testify against him?"

"Well, don't know. Hope the good guys'll win this one." His pocket buzzed. "Hey. That's my cell. Asked one of the cops to call with an update. I'll take this in the house."

June leaned back in the chaise and stretched her legs, putting her head back. Pace's voice mumbled in the great room but the words weren't clear. This'd been an incredibly long day. What to do about dinner? The watercress and towel were still in a flowerbed where she'd dropped them.

Pace was gone a while. When he returned to the screen door, he used his elbow to open it. Each hand held a glass of red wine.

"Here, you better take a drink." Pace gave a tight-lipped smile as he handed her the glass, watching until she brought it to her mouth and sipped. "We got good news. That was the officer who took Jeb's name and the description of his pickup. You said Jeb lived in Darby, right?"

"Yes, at least he used to, last I knew."

"Well…they told Ravalli County law enforcement about Jeb. Our guys just heard back. That black pickup went off the road into the Bitterroot River north of Hamilton. Witnesses said he'd been speeding, driving erratically and…he lost control. Son of a bitch's dead, June. Drunk driving accident."

June gasped, hand to her mouth. "Oh, my lord. Did he hurt anyone else? What should I do?"

"No one else involved. Nothing to do. Your troubles with Jeb Murdoch are over. He died a drunken coward's death." He raised his glass up, took a big swig and motioned for June to do the same. She sipped; her sore mouth allowed a small, sad smile.

"Now," Pace said as he leaned forward, forearms on his knees, "you stay right where you are and rest. But how 'bout some food? Starving, here…bet you are, too."

"Oh, those steaks! I'm afraid my face is too sore to chew that much."

"Yep, with you there. Maybe something from that Mexican restaurant downtown? I need protein and carbs, and…well, we both could use comfort food. I'll call in an order and go pick it up. What do you say? Then, after we eat, I'll make sure you're tucked in, locked up tight then get out of your hair. Bet you're exhausted."

"Me? You're the one who ran a marathon today. But, yes. That sounds fine. Ranger and I will sit tight, and we'll allow you to pamper us. I'll return the favor someday. Thank you, Pace, for being here for me. I'm very grateful."

June reached over and touched his arm. He stood, leaned toward her, tucked a lock of hair behind her ear.

"No worries, girl. Happy to do it."

14

Montana June moaned as she rolled over in bed the next morning. Her body was sore, her face aching. She'd swallowed some extra-strength pain relievers last night, but the effect was long gone. Her eyes opened to take in the bedpost where she'd been tied. She clamped her eyes shut again and shivered. *Focus on good things, Juney.* Through the window came the sounds of the birds in the hedge, the whistle of a train. At the end of her bed, Ranger's breath caught as he changed position.

Last night Pace had walked around the house and garage before he left, checking each lock, making sure everything was secure. Even though Jeb was dead, June knew the attack would remain in her psyche a long time. A wave of longing for the way things used to be, with Logan at the farm and a life of security, flowed over her. Tears, again.

The next time June awakened, a gentle rain was falling. Ranger stirred, groaning as he moved.

"Hey, guy. 'Morning." June wiggled to the foot of the bed, reached out and patted his neck, staying away from the stitches. "Pretty ow-y still, huh? Let's get you outside." She disentangled herself from the sheet and stood up; her left hand touched her inflamed cheek. "Ouch. We both have some sore spots, don't we, Ranger?"

At the sliding glass door, June took out the broomstick security bar Pace made for the track. Opening the door, she inhaled the fresh smell of rain. Ranger padded out to the yard, taking time going about his business.

Back in the kitchen, June made a decision. This wasn't a day to be alone. She started the coffee, then picked up her phone.

"Mom? Sorry to call so early. Umm…a lot's happened since I saw you yesterday on the marathon route, and I'm wondering if Ranger and I could come spend a couple days with you."

Maura's voice was warm, but concerned. "Of course, darling girl! Of course you can come. But you don't sound good. Are you all right?"

"Well, we are now, but it's a long story, and I can't tell it over the phone. If it's truly okay, we'll be to your place before noon. Thanks. Please don't make a fuss, and don't worry. We're fine."

June's next call was to Pace. He sounded relieved she was going to her mother-in-law's and would be taken care of there, since he couldn't miss work. The call was warm, and June half-smiled as they ended it.

She took another aspirin and got out some ice for her face before she poured her first cup of coffee. She leaned on the kitchen counter, staring out the window as she took careful sips. Seeing the place Jeb's pickup had been yesterday made June's chest constrict. She tried to fill her lungs, but the breath caught.

June's next sip of coffee was tepid; she must've been leaning there in a fog for some time. She stretched, then began the process of gathering what she and Ranger would need for a couple days away.

THE SOFT RAIN had lifted, but the sky was overcast as June drove the Jeep up the mountain road to Maura's house. Turning into the driveway, June felt overwhelming relief as she saw her mother-in-law come out the door, rushing down the path at the sound of June's arrival.

"Holy shit, my darling girl! What in the world happened to your face? And look at poor Ranger. You get in the house right now. I'll carry your bags. Don't say a word until I get you on the couch." Maura's bustle and concern were a balm to June. Some of the tightness in her chest released.

"Oh, Mom. Again the tears. I think I've been crying for years," she said as Maura tucked June onto the couch with a handmade afghan. "I'm not sure I even believe what happened yesterday."

June's story about the attack, and the trips to the vet and NowCare, took the better part of an hour. Maura jumped from sitting on the edge of the couch to pacing back and forth. Mr. Mouser remained curled on June's tummy, his thrumming purr comforting her.

Maura's voice was colored with concern and anger. "Christ. You poor kid. I've paid attention to news of Jeb, since that incident last month; as you know, the valley has a pretty good backwoods telegraph for gossip. He's a bad one from long ago. No loss that he *has* killed himself. Good riddance, I say. Let me call Doc Ben, though. Perhaps he's back, and can see Ranger. He'd make a house-call, I bet."

"Thank you. I cannot tell you how grateful I am to be able to come here."

"Nonsense, darling girl. Of course you should be here. You go to the guest room and take a nap. I'll call the doc. Oh, by the way, my beau is coming over this evening—no, don't worry," she said, seeing June's grimace. "You'll love him and I promise you won't feel uncomfortable. In fact, I bet it'll be just what you need. Now, you get unpacked and tucked in. I'll bring you some soup in a couple minutes. Good thing it's a cool day because soup is what you need."

June was able to breathe fully for the first time as she allowed herself to be taken care of. She listened as Maura made the phone call to the vet, then gave a one-sided smile when Maura brought a tray into the guest room.

"Here's an ice pack, too. And some aspirin and a glass of cool tea. I've taken Ranger outside to pee, and he's curled up on the couch. Doc Ben is coming in a couple hours, after he finishes at the clinic. All's taken care of, and there's not one little thing you have to do except eat, and then sleep. I'll come get you when Doc arrives." She bustled out.

June sipped at the cup of soup and then cuddled in the summer quilt on the bed. She liked this room, what long ago had been Logan's. Now, Maura's sewing machine was in the corner, a bookcase against the wall. The open window let in the cool, rain-soaked air filled with birdsong. June finished the soup and went to sleep.

SOMETIME LATER, MUCH later judging by the way the light came through the window, June heard Doc Ben's voice in the living room. She got up and brushed her hair at the mirror before joining her friends.

Doctor Ben straightened from tending to Ranger and said, "Hey, Montana June. Oh, my. Look at your poor face. Between the two of you, I'm not sure who had it worse."

"Hi, Doc. Thank you for coming. I guess by the time Jeb got to my place he was so drunk he wasn't thinking. If he had been, he probably would've killed Ranger right off the bat."

"Well, I called the Emergency Vet you visited, and after talking to them, I think this bang on Ranger's head won't be too problematic for him, long term. It could've been a lot worse, from what Maura said."

"Yeah." June gulped. "Jeb must've grazed Ranger's head—enough to knock him out, but not enough to…oh, thank God, not enough to kill him. That kick, though, that was plain mean. Can you tell, are his ribs broken?"

"No, not broken, just sore, so I won't tape them. Keeping him quiet and as still as possible is the best medicine. By the way, word is, Murdoch'd been in a real downhill slide for a few months. You hear he lost his job at the mill this spring because of his drinking? And he got a DUI a couple weeks ago. This's no great surprise to anyone in Ravalli County. Folks up the valley've been keeping an eye out for him, to stay out of his way."

Maura pushed out of her rocking chair. "Pfft. As I said to June earlier, good riddance, though I do wish he'd killed his sorry-assed self before he damaged two of my favorite friends. Doc, can I offer you a beer?"

"No, but thanks, Maura. I've got to get on home. We'll see you soon. Ranger, keep it quiet, okay, old boy? Don't give your mom grief trying to be too active. And I hope you aren't going to have to come to her rescue again." He stopped petting the dog, then put his cowboy hat on and held the door for the women. "June. Maura. You both take care. See you soon." He had to step around the goats in the front yard. "Well, I see Nanny and Kid are doing well; dang near the same size. All right. I'm on my way." Doc Ben waved as he walked, bow-legged, down to his truck.

Maura and June stood side by side on the stoop and waved, too. Ranger wagged his tail, quite obviously happy to see the doctor leave, though it'd been better than at the clinic.

Maura turned to June and said, "Well, honey, did you sleep? You were down quite a while."

"I slept so soundly. Thanks." She stretched her arms up, humming. "Dinner smells delicious. When's your guy coming?"

"Anytime now, I bet. Would you like a bath before dinner? Or sit outside and rest? It's up to you. There's some good ginger bath salts I made. It'll help detox your body from all the tensions and poisons of the last few days. They're in that crystal jar on the sink."

"A bath, maybe. Ranger, good guy, want to come lie in the bathroom with me? Oh. No, I guess that means you'll stay out here with Mr. Mouser," June said as Ranger and Mouse curled back up together on the couch. "You two stay quiet, okay?"

As June soaked in the tub full of ginger-scented Epsom salts, tears came again. Her face hurt. Her heart hurt. She was crying for Logan. Had he been alive, none of this would've happened. *Logan, where are you? I need you, darling.* She imagined lying in his arms, blessedly supported by him. Through the open window, the evening sounds and smells of the mountain floated in on the cool breeze. She breathed in and let the bath work its magic.

Drying off, after the water had cooled and her tears subsided, June felt an odd scratchy pain as the towel rubbed her breast. She glanced down and saw the gouge Jeb made with his broken fingernail was red and puffy. June wrapped the towel around herself and opened the bathroom door.

"Mom? Do you have any antibiotic cream?"

"Sure do. It's in the bathroom cabinet. Why do you need it?" Maura stepped into the small room.

"Look." June lowered the towel away from the scratch. "I suppose the one on my butt's infected, too. I hate to imagine what was under his fingernails to cause it to fester like this." June turned to show her backside.

"Oh my, those are both ugly. This cream is old, but we'll get some new stuff at the drugstore tomorrow. Here, I'll dose this back one for you. Unh. That looks very sore."

"I didn't even think about these when we were at NowCare, and forgot them until I was drying off. Oh, well. My battle scars, I guess." June tried to laugh, but it came out as more of a sob. Maura finished dabbing the cream, and hugged her.

"Honey, I don't want to borrow trouble, but if you need to see a counselor over this, we'll make that happen. Do not, do *not* let this thing haunt you. That evil shit-head is dead and can't hurt you again." Maura stroked June's hair. Then, cocking her head, she said, "Hey, I bet that's Richard coming up the drive. You okay to finish getting dressed?"

"Sure, Mom, thanks for the help. I'm good." June gave her sore half-smile and let Maura close the door. She dressed in the flowing caftan she'd brought for evenings. It was cool and pretty and wouldn't put pressure on the scratches.

Maura and her beau were sitting outside in the front yard, waiting for June to join them. They had a bottle of wine opened, three glasses ready, and a pitcher of water with lemon slices, along with a plate of cheese and grapes. As June walked toward them, the older man stood and came forward. His hair, bright white and well-combed, was the same color as the crisply pressed long-sleeved shirt. The folded-back cuffs revealed strong brown wrists.

Maura said, "Richard, I'd like you to meet my dear friend and daughter-in-law, Montana June McPherson. Darling girl, this is Richard Donner." Maura's voice had the deep chuckle of a stream going over boulders.

Richard grasped June's hand, looked in her eyes, and then placed his palm against June's swollen cheek.

"June, I am happy to make your acquaintance. Maura has told me much about you and I hope to learn more on my own." His hand cupped her face. "You appear to have been through the wars, recently. May I?" At June's nod, his index and middle fingers moved up, and with a soft touch traced the rim around June's eye. June felt a strange sensation coming from Richard's hand. She couldn't stop looking at his eyes—they were deep as mountain lakes, calm, clear, soothing.

Richard broke contact and stepped back. June's own hand went to the place on her cheek his hand had just left, exploring the new sensation.

"How odd! My cheek doesn't seem to hurt now. And my eye feels better too." June walked to the table and sat down. "I've never experienced anything like that before. You must be magic."

"No. Certainly not. But when I was little I learned from my mother's people, Salish, an empathy for things in pain, and sometimes I am able to...well, do just that." Richard poured wine for them and turned his chair to look out across the valley, drawing attention away from himself. Ranger came and sat at the man's feet. Richard's hands drifted over the dog's sore ribs, caressing damaged tissues.

Maura said, "I told you he was marvelous, didn't I? Full of marvels is Richard. I don't know where he's been all the years I've been alone on this mountain, but I'm sure glad to have found him now. Richard, tell Montana June about the work you do with aboriginal tools at Travelers' Rest. I know she'd like to hear."

As they chatted, watching the light change on the mountains, Ranger and Mouse, Nanny and Kid wandered around the yard. Evening settled in. Maura brought out an easy-to-chew supper with fresh steamed veg from her garden, saying she insisted on serving her two favorite people. June realized that by coming to Maura, she'd done exactly the best thing to help herself step away from the trauma of the attack, the stress of the last week. June smiled fully, her cheek and eye no longer painful.

15

The next morning, the sun was still below the horizon when Montana June took Ranger out to greet the day. A few fluffy clouds over the mountains were deep coral and pink. Shafts of gold came from the hidden sun, shooting up toward the last of the stars.

June sat on the front stoop with her coffee and touched her injured face. It wasn't swollen; there was no residual pain. When Ranger completed his meanderings, she rubbed her hands over his ribs, massaging ever deeper. He didn't cringe or step away. June's breath escaped in a soft "hmph."

What was this skill Richard Donner had, this odd, mystical healing ability, that he could touch a hurt and make it disappear? She resigned herself to wait until Maura woke up to learn more. Until then, the dawn's light-show was thought-provoking enough.

June's coffee cup was long empty and the sun rising above the mountains when her mother-in-law came through the door. Maura, without speaking, began the Sun Salutation. June joined her. The deep stretches and bends worked air into June's lungs. She imagined sparkles of light-energy flowing through her veins.

When they finished, June wiped her forehead and said, "Golly. Thanks for reminding me. I know you do those every day. I do them for several days, and then forget."

"Good morning, darling girl. I've done those exercises every day for so long, I do them without thinking. It's as natural to me as peeing, and as necessary." Maura's face crinkled with laughter. "Mmm, now time for coffee!"

When both women had collected their coffee and were again outside in the morning sun, June asked her question.

"Mom, what does Richard do with his hands? I massaged Ranger's ribs, and it seems as if there's no pain there at all. And look, my face isn't swollen anymore, and the bruise on my eye is almost gone. What happened?"

Maura stretched back, putting her face in the shade. "Well, I'm not sure. I know he takes no credit for his ability since it's been with him since birth. He's told me when he touches someone who's hurting, he senses the source of the pain, the seed of it. Then he imagines the seed shrinking and disappearing. It's a type of drawing in, like being an empath, if you know what I mean. In my case, as soon as he held me in his arms, my own grief at losing Logan, though it didn't disappear, subsided and changed so I saw death as part of life. Richard healed me, too. But don't say that to him; he doesn't call it healing. He says anyone can do it. He doesn't understand that to us it seems magical."

"He's an amazing man. I loved learning about the Native tools and toys he makes. I wanted to listen to him forever, and it was frustrating when I started falling asleep. I was a wuss going to bed so early."

"Montana June—honey—let me tell you it didn't hurt our feelings one tiny bit you left the party early." Maura's tone held a smile. "We took full advantage of being alone…and well, let's say the hammock works fine as a bed. The rocking…mmhmm…added to that man's considerable natural abilities like you wouldn't believe!" She chuckled and tucked her long auburn hair, with new highlights, behind her ears.

"Mom!" June's face grew warm with embarrassment as she reached over and pushed Maura's arm. "But I'm so happy for you. It's marvelous you've found a good man." June's voice turned wistful.

Maura grasped June's hand. "You also, darling girl, will find someone again, when the time is right. I'm sure of it. And perhaps you've begun the process. I'm glad, and grateful, that Pace was able to help you on Sunday, when you needed him so much. Is he someone you might be interested in?"

"No. I don't know. My heart isn't ready. I stop and listen for Logan's steps, sometimes; still think 'Oh, I can't wait to tell him that!' and then it all comes crashing back. Give me time. Perhaps someday."

"Of course, Montana June. Someday it'll happen. Now, we have chores to do, if you feel up to helping me. We need to milk Nanny, since Kid's done nursing. Weed the garden. Later, we'll go to Stevi, get a newspaper, and buy some antiseptic for those nasty scratches. Think about what you might like for dinner tonight, okay? We'll restock the larder."

IN THE SMALL town of Stevensville, the newspaper they picked up had an article about Jeb Murdoch's car wreck. The only new information it held was that his blood alcohol at his death was three times the legal limit for driving.

June read the article aloud as Maura drove the old VW bug back home. When she finished, she said, "It's odd I somehow became involved in Jeb's self-destruction. If it hadn't been for me needing help moving, I wonder if he would've spiraled down so fast. Seems like when I rebuffed his advances at the farmhouse that first day, that's right around when he got fired. Later, he came back and tried again. If I hadn't rejected him, maybe he'd still be alive."

Maura pounded on the steering wheel. "Oh, my god. I do *not* believe it. He might be alive and you might be what, his new girlfriend? His drinking partner? Listen, Montana June. You did not cause this. You were his victim, not the instigator. You didn't make him come on to you. You didn't ask for the attack at the farmhouse. You didn't cause him to drink so much he lost his job. You didn't ask him to come to your house to rape you. And you certainly didn't make him drink so damn much he drove into the river and killed his worthless, shit-hole, sorry-assed self. We'll never know, hell, I don't even *want* to know, what demons Jeb Murdoch struggled with, but from everything I've heard over the years, he's been a slob hanging on to decency by his dirty, poisonous fingernails. And quite obviously he lost his grip. If you so much as hint again that you're somehow responsible for what happened to that son-of-a-bitch, I swear, I will whop you upside the head. 'Might still be alive,' as I live and breathe."

When June stopped laughing at Maura's diatribe, she said, "Okay, okay. I get the message. Thanks, Mom, you're right; of course I wasn't responsible. What I meant is life takes a strange path. The paths converge, separate, sometimes cross again, or maybe don't. It's just interesting."

"Well, good. Don't you forget it, either." Maura snorted with laughter, but her eyes were flashing. She parked and put on the brake. "Now, help me get the bags into the house."

June grabbed the bags from the tiny area behind the seat of the vintage bug while Maura opened up Baby's front trunk and got the ones from there. Maura had bought Baby new, and it was as dear to her as one of her animals. She'd done all the minor work on Baby herself—each oil change, every tune-up. Though Baby wasn't pristine, it'd aged gracefully, as Maura herself had done.

Ranger and Mr. Mouser came from the backyard at the sound of their arrival and were rubbing up against the two women's legs, tails wagging.

June bent to them. "Hey, you two. Okay, okay. Let me put my bags down before I trip. You're not such a big help, you know. Here, I'll scrub your heads." Ranger licked June's face as if she'd been away a month. "Goodness, thanks for the exuberant welcome." Right then, June's cell phone rang. Caller ID said it was Pace.

"Hey, Pace. How are you?" June sat on the grass to talk. Maura came back out, gathered up June's bags, and mouthed to June to invite Pace up for dinner that night.

Pace sounded happy as he accepted the invitation. June reminded him how to get to Maura's house, since he hadn't been there since he and Logan were in high school. A bit later June disconnected and went inside.

"Pace said thanks, and he'd love to come for dinner. How can I help and what do we need to do?"

As the two women put away the groceries, they discussed plans for dinner. Maura called Richard and invited him as well. They decided this would be a grand event, celebrating Pace's spot in the New York City Marathon, Richard and Maura's new relationship, and June coming through Sunday with no lasting damage. They were, in fact, celebrating life.

Maura's eyes sparkled as she said, "Ooh, such fun—a party! I'll get out my fairy lights, and we'll string them in the back garden. We'll have candles and wine, perhaps a fire in the fire pit. You can wear that smashing caftan again, and I'll loan you some earrings. I'm going to wear my new long skirt and slinky blouse. What else, now—oh, would you go out and pick an armload of flowers from the side garden for me?" Maura handed June some clippers, and turned to climb into the attic for the fairy lights. Her muffled voice floated down. "Good thing I keep these close to the ladder-door. Lots of dust up here!"

BY LATE AFTERNOON, all the preparations were made. The back-yard was transformed into a hidden arbor of beauty. Lights had been strung and the table set with a lace cloth and colorful linen napkins. Vases overflowed with flowers; candles dangled from branches of the apple tree, each in its own vibrant glass jar hanging by wire, away from any leaves. The steaks were marinating, salad tossed, wine was breath-ing, and fresh bread was ready for slicing when the time came. The heat of the day began to dissipate. They realized there was less than an hour to clean and ready themselves before the men arrived.

"Good goddess," Maura said. "I'll dive into and out of the shower, then it's all yours. It's lucky we're both natural beauties, since we haven't much time to dress." Her laugh was deep and soft.

After June showered, she discovered some gorgeous long earrings on top of her caftan. The deep blues and greens surrounded by gold wire perfectly matched the colors of the cloth. The earrings were long; their elegance made her feel dressed to the nines.

"Mom, these are gorgeous! Where ever did you get them?" June raised her voice a little so Maura could hear her in her own room.

"Logan's father made those for me years ago when we were living in the commune. They were such a splurge back then. None of us were supposed to spend any money on ourselves, you know. It was all about the community. In fact, now I think about it, perhaps those earrings precipitated our leaving the commune. We'd decided by then we weren't quite as good a fit for communal living as we'd thought. We wanted our privacy, and to spend what little money we made on things we wanted, not on the group. We left the commune and started saving money for Baby and this house. Logan was a toddler. It was time."

June came and leaned against her mother-in-law's bedroom door, listening. Maura didn't speak often about the commune. June found it fascinating.

"Logan's dad made these? They're beautiful. I had no idea he was so talented."

"Yes, indeed. That's how he made money, by making and selling jewelry. Didn't you know that? Funny how many things we think we've shared. Now, help me with this necklace. He made this, too." Maura turned to face the mirror, her hands behind her neck holding the ends of a hand-made gold chain. June managed the clasp, then put her hands on her mother-in-law's shoulders, while they both looked in the mirror. Maura's blouse was variegated burgundy, its plunging neckline now enhanced by a beautiful chain on which dangled a single tear-drop stone in deep red. Maura reached to caress it.

"This was the necklace he gave me on our wedding day. Garnets are my birthstone, you know, and though he couldn't afford it, he traded a great deal to get this. It's so valuable I rarely wear it. I should."

"You're beautiful tonight, Mom. The color of the blouse and stone brings out the highlights in your hair."

"Not bad for an old broad." She chuckled again. "And you, also. You look marvelous. This's perhaps the best we've been since before…"

"And before we start thinking about that *before* and getting teary, there's a car coming. Let's see who's arrived." June gave her long blond locks a final fluff as she turned from the mirror.

Richard and Pace arrived almost at the same time. Introductions were made, the women accepted high compliments from the men, and the party moved to the backyard. Ranger and Mouse offered the early evening entertainment: the cat chasing butterflies and the dog moving from person to person to receive his pets and head scrubbing.

Pace was Ranger's current choice. "Huh…is it my imagination, or does the big guy seem better? And June, gotta say your bruises are almost gone. You better, too?" He settled himself on the ground, leaning against the apple tree.

"Yes, we're recovering. It's amazing what Richard did for us." With excitement, she explained how he'd helped. "I've never experienced anything like it. Richard, you should sell your services as a healer. You'd be a millionaire in no time." She sat in the hammock, bringing her legs up carefully so she wouldn't tumble out.

Richard's voice was low, a deep soft rumble. "June, it is nothing special, rather something anyone can do if they focus. A matter of listening, of going deep." The older man seemed uncomfortable being the topic of the conversation, and he ran his hand through his white hair, making it stick up.

Maura said, "See, what'd I tell you? He believes because he's always had the gift, it's something we must have, too. But let's not embarrass him. Pace, tell us about your race on Sunday."

"Well…great day for the race." Pace stretched his legs in front of him. "Cool at the beginning, 'cause it starts at six A.M.. Coming out of Frenchtown, making that long straight run toward Blue Mountain… luckiest guy in the world. Sun rising, the river, the birds. The exhilaration of running on a day like that is almost unexplainable. Thanks for waiting for me there, you two, cheering. That was great. My best race ever. Hope it'll be as good in November in New York." Excitement lit Pace's face, highlighting the white streak of hair. "But, June, tell us about the 5K. Person's first race ever is important. How'd it go?"

"Oh. I'd rather forget that. I certainly wasn't fit enough."

"Well, keep your training going. Another race's in late August, a little longer…four-miler, called the River City Roots Run. Lots of folks walk it. How 'bout it?"

Maura looked up from the wine glass she was refilling. "Darling girl, let's do it together. It'll be motivation for me to get off my ass. There's almost six weeks to get ourselves in shape. Surely we can pull it off."

"Okay. You've talked me into it." She stretched back in the hammock. "I should start the grill for the steaks." June's voice was languid. The other three laughed.

Richard rose from the willow-branch chair. "Well, my dear, you appear entirely too comfortable at the moment to be getting soiled with charcoal. You two have done all the work for tonight. Grilling is the least the men can do." He lifted the lid on the cooker to begin preparations.

Dinner was quiet but festive. The food was delicious, topics of conversation varied, with many stories and much laughter. By the time it was over and the dishes cleaned, darkness had fallen. The stars over-head were bright. June poured the last of the wine into Maura's glass, and coffee for both Richard and Pace. The three of them settled down around the fire pit and June went back into the house to return the coffeepot, then stepped into the front yard. She walked away from the house and trees to see more of the night sky.

As always, after a time of enjoying herself, after getting back to life, June felt guilty moving further from Logan. She wanted to reconnect with him in her heart.

Logan, my angel. I wish you'd been here tonight. Your mother is so beautiful and she seems happy. I hope you're watching us, and know we love you. Darling, you will always be in my heart. As she thought this, June noticed a glow in the north sky. Green spirals of light, greens as deep as the ocean and as pale as a duck's egg and every tone in between, whorled and grew in waves toward the south. Soon half the sky was taken up with this tremendous light display.

June ran to the back and said, "Come quick, the Northern Lights are coming out!"

Everyone hurried to the front, then down the slope where they had the best view. The entire sky filled with swirls of emerald. Maura lay down—saying zoning-out at a light show required being comfort-able—and soon the four friends were lying together in the cool grass, holding hands, entranced. A zephyr teased the wind-chimes, adding celestial music to the auroral display.

After nearly an hour, the light show faded as it had begun.

Richard, grunting, stood. "My friends, we have been blessed. I can-not imagine a better way to end this evening, unless, Maura, you will allow me a kiss." He leaned in, holding her head with both hands.

"Hmmm, thank you, sweetheart. Now, I will leave. Pace, it has been good meeting you. June, my dear."

"Yes…thank you, Maura and June," Pace said as they walked toward the vehicles. "Gotta leave, too—later than I planned. Long drive to the Rattlesnake. But what a finale! Maura, you end each party like this?"

"Of course, dear boy! Oh, thank you for coming." Maura kissed Pace as he opened his truck door. "Come back anytime, even if June isn't here. You're a welcome addition."

June hugged Pace, and turned to hug Richard as well. Her heart was full of the beauty, her throat full of tears; no one seemed to notice she didn't speak as the rest said their goodbyes.

The women watched the trucks' tail lights go down the hill then wink out of sight.

"What a marvelous night. I came out here while you were all at the fire, to speak to Logan, and it seemed he answered by sending the Northern Lights. Do you think he sees us?"

"Darling girl. Of course he sees. Don't you know he was painting his love for you across the sky? He was telling you once more, 'Montana June, begin again.' "

June touched her gold bracelet. Begin again.

16

The next morning, Montana June and Maura honored their commitment to the upcoming race with a walk. They started with Ranger, down the lane and back, but it was soon obvious to June he wasn't up to a longer hike. They returned and put him in the house, where he curled next to Mr. Mouser on the couch.

"Okay, Ranger. We'll be back soon. You guard the house," Maura said, closing the door. "Poor guy. He's not doing well, is he?"

June and Maura walked to the end of the drive then turned uphill, increasing the pace. The air was cool, and the pine trees' scent flowed into their lungs with each deep breath. Barbed-wire fences bordered the dirt road on either side; tall summer grasses and milkweed were interspersed with wild roses. A mare leaned her big head over the fence, blowing warm breath on June's hand when she stopped to pet the velvet nose.

June took some time to respond.

"No, he isn't doing well. He struggles for breath sometimes, and doesn't have the energy I'm used to seeing. Would Richard help? I see progress with the drugs Doc Ben prescribed, but maybe there's something else, something deeper."

"Hmm…honey. This is a thing I've wanted to talk to you about, but needed the right time to mention. After you went to bed the other night, we spoke about you, and about Ranger. Richard's concerned you now view him as some sort of magical healer, and I admit, it must be hard not to, when the inflammation left your face like that. It's not magic, but he seems to have a deeper understanding—can see inside other beings in a way you and I can't. He told me when he touched Ranger and soothed the soreness in those ribs, he felt a true illness in our old friend's heart. It saddens Richard deeply, but he wants you to be prepared. Ranger will let you know when he can't do it anymore, and that time is coming, darling girl."

The two women continued, turning a corner. A small stream meandered down the field, passing under the road. June stopped on the tiny bridge and looked into the flowing water.

Maura spoke again as they watched water-skippers dance on the clear pool. "Water's still flowing. That's a good sign. It's getting hotter, so soon the spring run-off will be gone, and we'll start to see things dry up. I hope this won't be a bad forest fire year."

June wiped her eyes and swallowed the lump in her throat. She knew Maura was giving her time to control herself before responding. "That's pretty much what Doc Ben said. I was just hoping." She blew her nose. "Did Richard say anything about when he touched me?"

"Yes. No doubt this won't come as a surprise to you, but he said he felt inside you a deep hole, an emptiness. Tendrils of healing are starting to cover the hole, but it's a long process. We both know you're better now than a month ago, much stronger than on your birthday in March. This incident with Jeb, goddamn him, no doubt eroded your progress some, but you're truly *making* progress. You've a new friend in Pace, you've got plans and fitness goals. That's all good. Take it step by step, darling girl. Don't expect magic, not even from Richard." Maura put her hand on June's shoulder. They continued on.

Maura's mention of June's birthday brought back a bad memory. It'd been an ugly time for her, the first birthday without Logan. She'd come, desperate, to Maura's house. After a fresh flood of tears subsided, Maura had made tea while June tried to put words to her depression. "Mom, I should've died when Logan did. Some days I don't even want to get out of bed. If it weren't for Ranger, I wouldn't. I come to you for strength and you're always propping me up." June's voice took a whiney edge. "Aren't *you* ever sad?"

Maura straightened, stalked to the window, stared out. Long moments later, when she turned back to June, her expression was flat, her posture stiff.

"Montana June, I'll forgive you for that, because I believe in my heart, perhaps even at your age, you've some growing up to do."

June drew in her breath. Prickles crawled up her spine and her gut turned cold. Maura had never spoken to her like this.

Maura continued. "Yes, you do come here, and I never want you to stop. I do prop you up, because I love you. But don't forget, Montana June, that Logan was *my only child*. He was the light of my world, as he was the light of yours. And before we lost him, I lost my most precious love, Logan's father. I do know what it means to lose a husband." She spun back to the window with a sob.

June's heart beat loudly in her ears, nine, ten times before she could find words. "Oh, God, Mom! I'm sorry. I didn't mean to be cruel." June went to her mother-in-law and hugged her from behind.

For long minutes, Maura's shoulders continued to quake. Then she inhaled, took a tissue from her pocket, and wiped her eyes. "No, darling girl. Of course you didn't. And that's why I needed to talk through this with you." Maura turned around and hugged June hard, then sat again at the table. "We each grieve in our own way, June. Being a brassy broad doesn't mean I'm bullet-proof. Believe me, I've done more than my share of crying. You asked me if I'm ever sad. Yes, but when I am, I find relief in action, and many times it isn't *heal*, it's *deal*. I have to *choose* to be optimistic." Maura's voice again became hard. "Take my word for it, child. Sometimes it ain't easy."

Remembering that time, almost five months ago, Montana June grasped Maura's hand as they walked. "Mom, thank you. Sometimes I do feel good, then I feel guilty for feeling good. I guess that's all a natural part of healing. In a few short weeks, it'll be the first anniversary of Logan's death. I cannot fathom how it's a whole year. He's so present to me. It helped to move out of the farmhouse, I guess. But he's still here." June struck her chest with her fist.

"And he always will be." A few steps later, Maura added, brushing sweat from her forehead, "Let's head down to Four Corners, then we'll go back home."

They arrived back at the house about an hour after they'd left. Maura had obligations at Travelers' Rest, so she showered and dressed for her volunteer work. It was time for June and Ranger to leave.

BY THE TIME she arrived back at her new street in Missoula, June was disgruntled. Her lawn would need mowing, and with the temperature well over ninety degrees, the prospect was disheartening. As she neared her house, though, June realized the lawn was not at all shaggy. In fact, someone had cut it; June noticed mower stripes.

"What the heck, Ranger?" June said, as she got out of the Jeep, then helped her dog out as well. She grabbed her overnight bag from the back and walked up to the front door. When she pulled the screen door open, a note fell.

"Hi, June. Hope you don't mind. Drove by - saw your grass needed a hair trim. Brought my mower down early this morning before work. Call you later. Pace."

"Well, I'll be. What a pleasant surprise." June unlocked the door and they entered. The house was cool, the blessing of a brick house. She filled Ranger's food and water dishes, drank a glass of water herself, then walked to the sliding glass door, intending to inspect the flowerbeds in back. As she headed to the door, though, a flashback hit. She saw herself lying facedown on the floor just there, struggling to stand, half-naked and terrified.

She spoke out loud again. "I cannot let that incident rule me, won't let those bad memories affect every day to come." Montana June closed her eyes, filled her lungs, and concentrated on memories of walking over this floor with Logan, going out to the patio to enjoy an evening with Max and Sarah. When she opened her eyes, the flashback was gone. With deliberation she turned, opened the sliding glass door, and stepped through. She picked up the towel the watercress had been wrapped in, shook it free of the last dried bits; snapped it harder, imagining her negative memories flying away before folding the towel edge to edge, then again, and setting it on the table. The shade of the maple tree looked inviting. She walked over and sat down, leaned back on the shorn grass, stretching her arms over her head. Ranger, having explored the corners of the yard, snuffed his nose deep into duff at the place he'd been attacked, snorted, then peed where Jeb had stood. He came back to June and lay down next to her, panting with a big doggy smile. She scratched around the sore spot on his head.

"Well, big guy, you said it better than I could've. 'Piss on him.' He cannot damage us again." June petted her friend as she watched the light dance through the deep green leaves above. The dappled sun was warm, the leaves offering just enough shade in the heat of the day. June yawned and stretched again, and soon she was asleep. She didn't hear her cell phone ringing in the house, tucked inside her purse.

MONTANA JUNE AWAKENED from her impromptu nap under the maple tree with grass clippings stuck to her bare legs and itchy spots from no-see-ums in the lawn. She looked at her watch and realized she'd been out for over an hour. Ranger raised sleepy eyes.

"Yep, we gotta move. Golly, we get home and kapow. Asleep again. I wonder why I'm sleeping so much. Come on. I need to unpack."

Later that evening, after dinner, June took a glass of wine outside, then heard her cell ringing. She got to it as it went to voice-mail, and she heard her sister's voice. "Doll, don't you ever answer this damn thing? Call me."

June called back. "Hel? Sorry. My phone was in my purse. Did you call earlier? I've been bad about checking."

"Yes, I called. Really, you'd think no one would be concerned about you, the way you don't keep in contact. It's been weeks since you've called. Jeez."

"I'm sorry, Sis. You're right. A lot's been going on, some of it good and some bad. I just got back from spending a couple nights with Maura. I'm sorry I haven't called."

"Okay, doll, start in. I have time and want to hear it all." Helena's voice softened as her irritation faded.

June settled herself on the chaise lounge, took a sip of wine, and told the long story of all that'd happened in the last weeks. They talked a long time about Jeb's attack, and then moved on.

"Heavens, doll. You have had one busy month. I forgive you for not calling me. Not to change the subject, but I've got something kind of sensitive I wanted to talk to you about, and that's another reason why I called. So, well. Here goes. Juney, I know the anniversary of Logan's death is coming up. Do you have plans? I don't think it'd be good for you to be alone."

Montana June was quiet for a moment, and used the time to breathe away the tightness in her throat. She glanced at the mountain above her, now glowing in the evening sun. A paraglider was flying close to the side of Jumbo, coming over the yard. He angled his canopy and turned with the thermals, rising again into the sun.

"June, you there?"

"I'm here. Trying to decide how to answer. Not sure what I'm going to do. There's good days and bad days. I'm sleeping a great deal. I don't cry as much as I used to, but I never know when the tears will start—can't seem to predict them at all. I don't want to deal with the anniversary of his death because I do not want it to be *a whole year* without him. I'd rather have taken care of him, changed the catheter bag, moved the walker, helped him in and out of the recliner, for the rest of my life."

"June-doll. You know he didn't want to live that way. He was so miserable. I wouldn't want to live like that. I'm sorry to bring this up, but haven't you been thinking of it yourself?"

"Oh, yes. Maura and I talked about it. It's just…"

"Well, here's an idea. I haven't seen what you've done with Max's house and it's been a long time since I've been back home. It was awful I couldn't come for Logan's memorial service, what with Arno being so sick—"

"*Arno?*"

"Oh, God, yes. He insists on being called Arno now. Evidently it's more grown up than *Arnie*. But what I was saying is, how 'bout I come for a visit? Toby says it'd be okay, and Arno will've started school. The store can get by on its own for a while, since I've hired my great assistant. I'd love to see my little sister. What do you say?"

"Well, uh. Yeah, okay. But you remember this house has one bedroom, right? When Maura stayed over for a girls' night, she slept on a cot. That's it for guests, I'm afraid."

"Oh, I'll sleep with you, doll. It'll be fine, like when you were a little girl, and we'd sleep together. Okay? It'll be great! I can't wait. Oh, goody. I'm going to hang up right now and make my reservations. I'll let you know when to pick me up at the airport. Talk to you soon, Juney. Byee!"

June set her phone down, poured herself another glass of wine, and downed half of it before she looked up at the mountain again. Okay. This should be fine. Her sister was right: it'd be good to reconnect.

Without a doubt, the anniversary would be difficult. *But.* She was pretty sure she didn't want to share it. Maybe the nearby hotel had reasonable rates. Maybe Arnie, uh, Arno, would get sick again and Helena wouldn't be able to come. Maybe Toby would decide the three of them ought to go on safari instead. Maybe.

Oh, hell.

(excerpt from Montana June's journal)
All these months later. How am I going to live without him?
No. It doesn't get any easier. No matter what they say.

THE NEXT MORNING at 6:30, Montana June was outside on the front walk picking up her newspaper. As June stood back up, she saw Pace running down the street.

"Hey, June." Pace's voice was light. He stopped at the stairs and put up a foot to stretch his ham-strings.

"Pace! Bless you for mowing my lawn yesterday. What a treat it was to come home and find my work done for me. You shouldn't have, but believe me, I really appreciate it. Have time for some coffee?" June, still in her nightie, belted her summer robe around her waist.

"Well, no…not really. Could use some water, though. But gotta clean up and get to work. Working in the Bitterroot again, checking fishing accesses." His eyes sparkled. "Gotta guard the dead-end signs."

"Oh, all right, give it a break," she said, laughing. "Come on in." June gestured Pace through the door in front of her, and then went to the kitchen for a glass. As she filled it and Pace emptied it, they talked about Maura and June's decision to sign up for the race. June asked for directions for training walks, and Pace gave her several ideas.

"Sure would like to go with you today," Pace said as he returned the glass. His finger slid down it and touched June's; he leaned a bit closer, his eyes showing concern. "June, you okay here? Worried you'd be scared coming home."

"Well, there were some bad moments, but I'm determined to let Jeb stay dead. We're okay, Ranger and me. Thanks for asking." She put the glass on the counter and stepped back. The silence lengthened. "So, what time do you need to be at work?"

"Oh, damn. Yep. Better go…well, thanks for the water." Pace went to the front door and opened it. "So, be seeing you."

"Sure, Cowboy. Thanks again. Don't work too hard today." She gave him a quick hug.

Pace turned, jogged down the walk, and started running up the street. June watched until he disappeared around the curve in the road, then returned inside to dress for her own exercise.

ALONE ON THE road heading north, following Pace's directions, June thought about his visit. She didn't think she was imagining his growing affection. While she felt somewhat guilty, she appreciated the attention of a male her own age. When they'd all been at Maura's house the night of the dinner party, and Pace first saw June in her flowing clothes and dangly earrings, his eyes had glowed. It was wonderful to feel attractive again, and June guessed Pace was someone she might become involved with, someday.

But not yet. June wasn't ready in her heart. How could she look at another man when she was still in love with Logan?

Nearing the top of the hill, June's stride shortened, her arms bent and she was breathing hard. Her forehead grew damp. The movement felt good, allowing her brain to focus.

Logan had died in September. The anniversary of his death was five weeks away. June caressed her gold bracelet and spoke the words, "Begin again." She walked on awhile, then added, "Much too hard, Logan, much too hard."

She tried to imagine what she'd tell a friend if she were giving advice to someone in her shoes. *Take it step by step. Like preparing for a race. Step by step in the right direction.* But sometimes those steps were damned hard.

17

Early on the Sunday morning of the River City Roots Run, Maura drove up the drive to Montana June's house in Baby, giving her customary toot on the horn. Her VW bug looked as cheery as the morning sun.

"Hey, you! Ready for the race?" June called, as Maura walked toward her.

"Goddess help me, I guess. Whose idea was this, anyway? I'm three-quarters nervous, darling girl. I dropped Richard off at the finish line, to cheer us across, given we make it that far. Listen, I know you wanted to walk to the start, since it's only a mile away, but let's go in Baby. That way, when we've completed the race, we can saunter with Richard a few blocks to the car instead of slog all the way back here. Humor your elders, please?"

"Okay, Mom. Let me get Ranger in from the backyard, and then I'm ready to go. We might even find a parking place closer than we are here."

Down near the tracks where the race would start, a crowd gathered, a feeling of festival in the air. Maura parked in the bank lot nearby.

"I'm glad we're doing this, Mom, though I totally get what you mean about being three-quarters nervous. But we've put our bodies through more miles than this in the last month, and with any luck we'll do okay. We've lost weight, we look tighter, and I don't know about you, but I feel more fit. And it's not like we're running a marathon. We're walking four miles. That's all."

"Hmmpf. That's all? Don't take away my thunder, girl. I'm dang proud of this!" Maura slapped her daughter-in-law on the arm.

"Yep. Believe me, I'm proud, too." She watched people migrating to the start. "Hey, folks're clustering; must be close to time. Let's get over there."

June and Maura joined the back of the group. There was a wide range of people—all sizes, ages, and apparent fitness levels. The volume rose and the crowd pushed closer. June caught a glimpse of someone familiar, up toward the front.

"Hey, Mom. There's Cara, next to that tall, buff guy."

"Oh, yes, that's her all right. And, darling girl, that big guy is her beau, Ludwig." Maura laughed. "Wow, Cara looks out of sorts, kinda bitchy." BANG! She jumped. "Yikes, we're off!"

The racers made their way toward the train tracks and Mount Jumbo. Maura and Montana June started slowly, knowing it would give them more energy later in the race.

The route led past Greenough Park, then straight up the steep hill on Rattlesnake Drive. That was work. Though they'd trained for a month and went slow, both women were gasping for breath when they reached the top.

"Ugh. Breathe. Shit." Maura mumbled to herself, but June teased her anyway.

"Breathe—yes, please. But maybe not the other, okay? At least not until we get to a porta-potty." She dodged the slap, grinning when Maura stuck out her tongue.

As the route continued north and June's pace leveled out, she had time to enjoy the vista beyond the colorful stream of chattering, laughing people to the mountains in the distance—the tall peaks of the Rattlesnake Wilderness Area—deep blue-green and strong. To her right was Mount Jumbo, its sloping sides turning a golden brown in the late summer.

She spoke again to Maura, her words and breath choppy from effort. "There's an elk herd that winters there on Jumbo....The city closes access to the upper trails in the winter to protect the herd....Pace says you can see them easily when there's snow....Deer, of course, no big deal, had them in the valley and...lots of urban deer in Missoula, but be great to see elk!"

They turned the corner onto Missoula Avenue. Racers were spread out far in front. June turned to check—yes, there were plenty of racers behind them as well; they weren't the last. The route turned back toward town, coming close to June's house. There was no temptation to quit and slink home. They were tired, but this was fun. June used the quiet, repetitive movement, and the surging oxygen in her blood to think about what this new exercise was doing for her. She was getting stronger, fitter. And with each day's exercise, June felt more able to face her future on her own. She was becoming someone she'd never been, like a chrysalis breaking open.

A half hour later they were on the river walk, coming down the same last few yards toward the finish line June had covered in her first race on marathon weekend. June glanced at Maura's face: red, moist, but determined. Probably her own face matched.

"Hey, there's Richard. Don't slow down." June was encouraging herself as much as Maura. "Smile pretty!"

The two women held hands and passed the finish line with a final burst of speed. They accepted their water bottles, then walked the few yards to where Richard awaited them.

He threw an arm around each woman. "Strong work, you two! You make me proud, my racer girls." He gave Maura a bigger hug.

"Ack! Don't get too friendly, I'm all sweaty." Maura beamed at her tall, handsome man as he kissed her red face.

"You have never been more beautiful, woman. I saved a place for us to rest."

As they walked toward a bench, June spotted Cara again. Once more, Cara's face looked like thunder. She limped in circles, holding a running shoe in one hand and massaging her thigh with the other. Ludwig seemed to be nowhere around.

Maura voiced discomfort. "Actually, instead of sitting," she said, wiping her sweaty face, "I really need to pee. Do you two mind if we just leave? We might find a porta-potty on the way to the car, but I'm ready to go back home and clean up."

As the three walked toward the lot where Baby was parked, they passed the beer tent, complete with tables.

"Hey, Mom. Look there. Cara is waiting out in the sun, obviously hurting from the race." June pointed into the tent where a large blond man was cozying up to a young, pretty, voluptuous redhead. "But isn't that Ludwig?"

"Ho ho—it most certainly is. Oh, poor Cara. He seems too interested in those big boobs to be planning a three-week cruise with Cara. Ah, well. I shouldn't find that funny, but I do. Now, I would much rather use the bathroom at your house than a porta-potty. Could we please hurry it up?"

18

"'Lo, Helena," Montana June groaned, answering her sister's call long before she wanted to get up.

Helena's chirpy voice came back, "Good morning to you, too, doll! Oh, damn. Were you asleep? You'd think I'd remember the time difference. What, it's nearly six o'clock there? Sorry. I'll call back."

"Nah. I'm up now. You talk. I'll get my coffee." June shuffled into the kitchen, yawning.

"Okay, grab a pencil, too, 'cause I have flight information."

June held the phone away and groaned again. She found a pen and paper. " 'kay, shoot. I'm ready."

After writing down Helena's arrival info, one week away, June poured coffee and listened to Helena's chatter. Unsurprisingly Arno wasn't happy his mother was abandoning him to the care of his father.

June tuned out most of this. She took Ranger outside, taking her coffee and wandering with him while listening to her sister.

When Helena gave her usual "Byee!" June realized she'd better start making preparations for this visit. She badly wanted to tell Helena not to come.

If June could choose, she'd spend the anniversary alone with Ranger, visiting places they used to go when Logan was healthy. Maybe have dinner with Maura. She didn't want a house-guest. *Damn.* It'd been stupid to not stop Helena's plans at the outset. Ah, well. Better make the best of it. Maybe sharing a bed with her again wouldn't be so bad. Helena was right: probably shouldn't be alone on the anniversary of Logan's death.

JUNE WAS AT the Missoula Airport waiting for her sister on a gorgeous early September day.

She was surprised to feel excited. Helena hadn't been able to come when Logan died. Arnie-Arno had gotten a bad cold, and Toby complained work wouldn't let him take care of their son. The two were masters of manipulation, and Helena had no defense against their neediness. June's crushing grief and inability to function made Helena's absence a non-topic. And then, June's trip to Florida last Christmas was best forgotten.

But Helena was coming now, down the stairs on the other side of glass doors. June watched as her sister took it step by step, leading with her left foot, gripping the banister. She had a carry-on and a huge purple purse slung over her shoulder. Reaching the bottom stair, Helena put the carry-on down, adjusted her purse, patted her brown helmet-shaped hair, and looked around. Seeing June through the glass, Helena gave a broad smile, then pulled her bag through the revolving door.

"Finally. What an ordeal. Oh, doll, you look fantastic! Heavens, it's good to see you!" Helena's purse swung around, whacking June on the back as they hugged.

"Hey, Sis! I'm glad you're here. You look—well, you look great, too." June swallowed as she looked at Helena. "Here, let me take those bags for you. The luggage carousel is right through here."

"Potty first. You know how those long flights are." Helena went into the ladies' room while June waited outside. Helena was different. The last time they were together, Helena had a waist. June wondered if her sister's added girth was due to happiness or the opposite. *Damn! I should've set up the cot, even if I sleep there. Will we both fit on the bed?* June's thoughts were interrupted.

"Whew, barely in time! I swear, those seats get smaller all the time. Flying used to be glamorous. Not anymore." Helena, returning, chirruped like a wet hen. "Now, let's see if they've succeeded in losing my bag."

As they waited at the luggage carrousel, June asked about her sister's yarn and quilting store. "So how's 'Come to Helena Teacup'?"

"Just fantastic! We've got a group of ladies who meet to do handwork together, we call ourselves Belles of Hel. Isn't that cute? And I made you a present. It's in my carry-on. I'll dig it out."

Helena opened her bright pink carry-on and rummaged to find a gift bag with floral tissue paper escaping from the top. "Oooh, I'm excited. Open it right now, okay, Juney?"

June smiled at her sister's exuberance. Presents from Helena had always been a mixed pleasure, since their tastes were very different. The gifts ranged from mildly overdecorated to way over the top. Now, she grasped the bag and pulled out the tissue paper.

"It's adorable." June held up a dishtowel embroidered with a depiction of a cute little Halloween-style devil with a delightful grin, sitting in a teacup, knitting a brightly colored flame. The teacup was almost tipping off its saucer as it slid down a slippery slope. Underneath, in elegant script, was written, "Come to Helena Teacup!"

She laughed at June's expression. "These sell like hotcakes at my store. Now, don't just leave it in the drawer, like all those hankies I made you."

Under the towel was a box of tea. When June looked up questioningly, Helena explained. "When my Belles get together, we actually do drink tea in nice cups. And at the store I sell different teas, but this is my own blend, sort of a take on the hell theme. It's ginger, and believe me, it's hot. Yummy, too."

June hugged her and said, "Hel. You sweetie." A harsh sound interrupted them. "Oh, there's the buzzer for the luggage."

Walking outside after collecting her suitcase, Helena looked around the valley.

"Oh, my. I've missed Missoula, especially in the fall. The air smells like apple cider—so crisp and clean." Her eyes fell on the vehicle they were headed to. "Don't tell me you're still driving Dad's old Jeep. Goodness, isn't it time you upgraded?"

"I keep it because it reminds me of Dad, and it's a classic. Runs like a top. It's worth more than you'd think. Someday maybe I'll buy a smoother ride. Not yet."

June opened the back. "Here, I'll lift that up for you." She lugged Helena's suitcase in. "Holy Hannah, what's in there, gold bricks? I'll put your carry-on back here, too. Now, hop in. Five minutes, we'll be home."

MUCH LATER, AFTER dinner, the sisters sat outside having vodka tonics, from a large bottle Helena had brought in her suitcase, presenting it to June as a second hostess gift. June oohed over pictures of Arno's swimming and Scout activities. Though she wouldn't say it, she was glad her nephew was in sports, as his weight reflected that of his parents.

Helena's first drink went down fast. When she came back with her refill she said, "So doll. Not to bring up sad topics, but the anniversary is the day after tomorrow. I could organize something. Or shall we wing it?"

"I already know what I want to do." June told her sister about her plans. "I can't believe it's been a year." June dug a tissue out of her jeans pocket and blew her nose.

"Mmm, poor doll." Helena took a big swig.

June looked at her sister. Was it was tiredness from the flight that made Helena seem unfamiliar? Of course, it might be her own sadness and raw emotions that made this situation awkward. But that "poor doll" sounded condescending instead of sympathetic. *Surely I'm misreading this.*

But minutes passed and Helena offered no other comments—she made inroads on her drink.

June searched for something to say to bridge the silence. "Maura and I have always been close, as you know, but we've become really good friends this past year. Her new beau is an amazing guy, and they're such fun to be around. I hope you'll enjoy them as much as I do."

"Oh, I suppose I will. Hey, guess I'll toddle off to bed. Listen, I always sleep on the right side of the bed, hope you don't mind. See you in the morning."

A whiff of vodka followed Helena as she went to the bedroom. The second drink she'd poured herself must've been very strong. June stretched back in the chaise and thought about her sister.

After their parents died, Helena had put her own life on hold to make sure Montana June got through high school. June thought about all she owed her sister. And now Helena had many responsibilities in Florida as mother, wife, and business owner. Helena deserved a vacation. It must be quite a relief to escape, and after the stress of travel, relaxing drinks were well earned. June was glad, at that moment, her sister had come.

A couple hours later, though, June was not quite so glad. The times they'd shared a bed were many years and many pounds ago. June found herself clinging to the wrong edge of the bed, since she also slept on the right side. Helena's boozy snores were enough to rattle the windows, and each time Helena turned over, an arm or leg would flop and hit June. She gave up, leaving the bed to her sister. She'd set up the cot tomorrow. The couch, though not a pull-out, was the quickest option for this night.

19

Montana June's goal for this day was for the two to become re-acquainted. They had breakfast at the diner in Bonner, then toured their old haunts in Missoula, taking Ranger out for a walk at Fort Missoula. It was a good day, but marred by a strange incident. During the walk, June asked for a swig from Helena's water bottle. The embarrassed way Helena refused, claiming a sore throat, seemed… odd. After stopping at the fort's museum so June could rehydrate, two tired women and one very exhausted dog loaded into the Jeep. As they drove home, Helena talked about places she remembered from when she was young. Her voice got more wavery and emotional with each story. June's cell rang once, and it went to voice mail.

At home, Helena headed straight to the bedroom to take a nap. The missed phone call had been from Pace. June called him back and invited him over to meet Helena.

MONTANA JUNE AND Helena were sitting on the patio in the cool late afternoon. A plate of crackers with cheese and fruit was ready, along with a bottle of wine. Helena had a vodka tonic going and offered to pour one for June.

"Thanks, Sis, but I'll wait until Pace comes. I'm glad you got a long nap. I'm like that, too; travel takes it all out of me." In fact, June'd been worried Helena wouldn't wake up in time. She'd slept for hours.

"So, doll. This guy. Are you two an item? Seems strange he'd be coming over tonight of all nights. Tell me more about him." Helena cocked her head, giving the look that used to send warning signals through June's veins when she'd come home late from a date. "I want to make sure all is above-board here."

"Jeez, I'm not a teen-ager anymore, Hel. He's just a good friend. Don't get excited. Besides, Maura knows and likes him a lot. And he saved my bacon, too. I told you he came over right after the attack, took me and Ranger to our respective doctors. Thank goodness for that." June's voice was tense. Now she tried to relax. "All's well. You don't need to act like a big sister."

"Hard not to." Helena drank deeply, spilling a bit on her front.

At that exact moment, Ranger woofed, announcing an arrival. June said, "Hey, I think he's here."

All three walked to the front door, Ranger's tail going crazy. Pace was there with a big grin and a bouquet of flowers.

"Oh, Pace—you didn't have to do that," June said as she welcomed him in.

"Thanks, but…uh, these aren't for you. Figured anyone who traveled all the way from Florida deserved some of Montana's best. Stopped at the Farmers' Market on the way here. Helena, welcome to Missoula."

Pace handed Helena the bunch of vibrant sunflowers. He leaned down to pet Ranger who doubled his wagging and gave a big doggy lick. Pace wiped his hand on his shirt, then kissed June on the cheek.

"Well, aren't you sweet," Helena said. "How nice. June, do you have a vase big enough? Oh, look, an aphid. Maybe we should put these outside."

A few minutes later, the sunflowers were in a gallon jar on the picnic table. June poured wine for herself and Pace.

Pace dove onto the crackers and cheese. "Yum. Brie." He mumbled through a mouthful. "My favorite...so hungry. Had a long run earlier, kinda forgot to refuel." He took a deep swig of his wine and leaned back against his chair. "Love this view of the mountain. My place's too close to see the glow."

Pace asked Helena about her family. Her demeanor brightened as she filled him in on her favorite subject, the raising of a teenage boy.

June's attention wandered, thinking back to a year ago. This night last year, Logan was in the hospital. It was obvious his struggle and pain were almost over. As he faded into a coma, June believed her world was ending with the life of this man in the bed. Her world hadn't ended, but it had assuredly changed.

Since then, June had experienced horrible anguish. Not even the loss of her parents came close. Many days during the winter the only reason June got out of bed was to take care of Ranger. She survived the dark, deep cold until spring because of her friendship with Maura and the love of her dog. They allowed her to keep breathing; she didn't want to live, but she could take one more breath.

Now here she was, with a new friend and her sister. Montana June let these memories wash over her as she gave a silent toast. *Logan, my angel. I will never forget and I'll never be the same.* She looked at the glowing mountain and sighed.

"Gonna go to the little girl's room, be right back." Helena picked up her glass and pulled open the screen door. Once inside, she took her glass to the side-board, then turned into the bedroom.

"Thanks for having me over to meet your sister. Sorry I decimated your cheese tray." Pace reached over to hold June's hand.

"No worries." She smiled, and squeezed back. "I've got sandwich makings for dinner. I'll get up and make something in a few minutes. You two seemed to have hit it off. Hopefully she didn't talk too much."

"Nope. Not at all.…Sounds like she carries a heavy load in Florida, with her family and store."

"Mmhmm." June leaned back again and sipped her wine. "Logan and I went down to visit a few years ago." June lowered her voice. "Her son is a real pain. She's so proud of him, but he doesn't treat her well."

"Yeah, he looked pretty cranky in the photos. What's planned for her visit?"

June inhaled. "Tomorrow's the anniversary of Logan's death. I wanted to spend it alone, but I've rearranged things." Her voice faded. "I wish—"

"Hey, you two!" Helena pulled the screen door open and stepped onto the patio. A full drink sloshed as she closed the door behind her. "Oops! Sorry." She dropped into her chair. "Well now, isn't this pleasant? Pace, tell me about yourself. I wanna hear allllll 'bout you. What're your intentions with my little sister?"

"Helena!" June tilted her head and narrowed her eyes. "Mind your manners."

"You bet, doll. Jus' asking. I'm interested, is all." Helena stretched her lips into something like a smile.

"Oh, it's okay, no secrets about my past," Pace said, ignoring the question about intentions. "But...can I order a pizza? Pretty hungry here. Sorry to be such a guy...ate all your snacks."

"No problem, Cowboy. I'll go make those sandwiches. It'll just take a minute."

Montana June left the patio as Pace started telling Helena his history. Walking past the sideboard, June replaced the lid on the vodka bottle.

June made sandwiches and put chips, salsa, and cans of soda on a tray, taking maybe ten minutes. As she carried the food to the patio, she heard Helena's voice raising.

"Really?" Helena was saying, "this's what you expect of my sister? You know she's very, very fragile right now. I cannot think why you're hanging around."

"Helena? What in the world's the matter?" June said as she put the tray on the picnic table. Helena's face was bright red. Pace's eyes were enormous. His mouth opened and shut, seemingly unable to form words.

"This guy. Don' know why you let him hang around. What the hell, doll. Logan's jus' a year dead and you're pickin' up men already?" Helena's voice slurred, and she leaned forward, pointing at Pace.

"June, no idea what happened. We're talking about your race, our dinner at Maura's. And then...she just—snapped." Pace's face was white and his voice sounded panicked. "Helena, uh...so sorry."

June stared at her sister, astounded.

"Oh, sorry, is it. Sure. You betcha. Sorry'll fix everything my poor sister's gone through. Why'n't you jus' leave. Quit hangin' around like a horny kid. I see the way you look at her, don't you think I don't." Helena's voice got louder, and she took another big swig from her drink.

"Okay, guess I better leave," Pace said, getting up from his chair.

"Pace, don't. Please stay." June touched his arm, then rounded on Helena. "I think you're the one who should leave. Quite obviously you need to go to bed. What the hell are you thinking, yelling at my guest like that?"

"Your guest, huh. I come all the way from Florida and he's the guest. This's the way you treat me. Sure. I'll go to bed." Helena actually harrumphed, then grabbed her glass and tried to stand, but her free hand slipped off the armrest of the chair. "Oops. Yeah," she said, finally up and moving, "I'm outta here!"

June pulled the screen door closed. She watched as Helena slammed the bedroom door, then turned to Pace.

"Good heavens, I wasn't gone long. What in the world happened?"

"Holy shit, June…no idea. Seemed pretty obvious she'd started drinking a little early, but we were fine…talking about this summer… then it was like she clicked off. Kept getting louder and louder, then you came back and, well, you saw."

June put her hand on her forehead; her eyes squeezed shut. "Damn. It's my fault. I should've made sandwiches earlier. I had no idea she'd had so much to drink. But, when we were at the Fort today, something seemed a bit off. She wouldn't let me share her water bottle." She opened her eyes. "Maybe it wasn't water in it? Oh, hell. I'm sorry about this." She sat down and tried to smile. "Well, let's have a sandwich."

"Great. I'm starving." He took one from the tray, and bit into it. Then, still chewing, said, "Yum. This's delicious. You okay?"

"Yeah. You know, Helena's changed. She was so stable when it was just her and me. Something major is different. Since I don't see her often, I only know what she tells me about her life. Maybe it's a relief to be away. But it sure doesn't excuse her behavior." She leaned forward and looked at him. "Are *you* all right? She was way out of line."

"No problem…just didn't make any sense. It's okay." His big bites made short work of the sandwich. He reached for another. "Pass me a soda?"

Dusk was falling. Montana June lit the candle. They ate in silence for several minutes, letting the calm evening settle their nerves. Ranger sat at their feet, waiting for last bites.

"Grandpa Max used to call this time of day 'the gloaming.' I love that term. It's one of my favorite times, when things quiet down and the world draws in on itself. Thanks for staying."

Pace leaned back in his chair and looked at the sky. "No worries. Helena's suffering from stress and travel. Hey, look! First star of evening. You make a wish? Always did when I was a kid."

"Yep. Don't tell me what you wish for, because then it won't come true."

As the two friends watched the stars come out, the sky darkened into night. Tomorrow would be another day. For June it would mean the end of firsts—the end of the first year without Logan. June raised her glass toward the mountain in a silent toast, grateful she'd survived.

20

Sometime during the night, Montana June rolled over yet again, coming out of her unsuccessful doze on the camp cot.

She decided to stop trying to sleep and instead return in her heart to exactly one year ago this dark, dark hour of the night. She'd never told anyone of the moment Logan died, not even Maura. Logan's coma had deepened, but there was no way to know how long it would continue as his life drained away. Maura was exhausted to the point of shattering, so June had sent her home. June was exhausted, too, but her *home* was lying here, on this bed.

For a long time, she sat, holding Logan's hand, these long fingers that had caressed her, worked hard for her. The nighttime hospital sounds and smells faded away. Everything important in the world came to pin-point focus.

Time stopped. June left the hard chair and crawled into the hospital bed, enfolding Logan in her arms. She sang their wedding song and told him stories of Ranger as a puppy. Her breasts, pressed against his ribcage, felt his slow breathing slow further; her heart heard the cardiac monitor hesitate—hesitate—stop. Montana June held Logan as his body cooled. The two things she prayed for hadn't happened: Logan hadn't lived; she hadn't died.

THE STARS WERE fading in the morning sky when Montana June left her cot and walked outside with Ranger. She began her Sun Salutation, reaching to the dawn then bending to put her hands flat on the dew-damp grass, her movements slow and deliberate. She completed two full Salutations. This day she'd need all the internal strength and grace she could gather.

Finished, June stood still, balanced, solid, pulling in and emptying life-giving air. The sky lightened, pinking the few clouds that floated over Mount Jumbo's round hip. The day promised good weather, and for this blessing, June was grateful. She walked back in the house and poured herself a cup of coffee.

June tried to retain the calm and clarity from her yoga, but was losing the battle. Helena's behavior last night had to be addressed. June's thoughts whirled. *What the hell happened? Do I want a pissing match with my sister? On this, of all days? Damn it! How will I handle this?* June decided that today she needed to take care of herself. She'd see what Helena would say, but this was no day for confrontation.

The toilet in the bedroom en suite flushed, and June had time to soften her expression before Helena came into the kitchen.

June's voice was calm as she said, "Good morning, Helena. How do you feel?"

Helena poured herself a cup of coffee. "Oh, fine. I slept soundly, as usual. That's quite a good bed you have, doll. How long did Pace stay? Guess I went to bed before he left."

"Really, Helena? You don't remember what happened last night?" June frowned at Helena's back as her sister doctored the coffee with sugar and cream.

"Well sure, I remember the cheese and crackers, talking and having a nice time. That's it, really. Why, did I miss something?" Helena sat down across from June at the breakfast table.

"Umm. Hmm." She cleared her throat. "Well, we can talk about it later. Let's say you really enjoyed your drinks and decided to hit the hay early. Pace and I had sandwiches and watched the stars come out. Then he left. He told me he's going to a conference for a week, so you won't see him again. Which might be a good thing."

"He seems like a nice guy. Too bad he'll be gone, I'd like more of a chance to get to know him."

June looked at Helena and frowned. "Yeah? You liked him? Huh."

"What? You're acting weird this morning, doll. Of course I liked him." Helena smiled. "So, we're driving south today, right? To see Maura?"

June appreciated the change of subject. "Yes, Sis, we'll meet Maura at the river picnic area at Metcalf, near the farmhouse. We'll take some sandwiches and stuff. Then stop at the cemetery on the way home. I don't want to plan any more than that. Take the day as it comes. Sound okay?"

"You bet, doll. Let me make the sandwiches and stuff for us. You worry about you and Ranger."

Montana June couldn't understand what'd happened. Helena seemed to have no memory of her behavior last night and this boggled June's mind. Either Helena'd had an alcoholic black-out or she was lying, pretending to not remember, and June didn't know which was worse. Whether or not she'd confront Helena with her rudeness to Pace was a question for later. This day was meant for other things, and June needed to make sure she herself had the emotional energy to make it through. She wasn't going to worry, for this one day, about what other people thought or did or felt. June would table the whole situation. She got out the cereal and bowls, bananas and berries, and they ate breakfast in companionable silence.

FOUR HOURS LATER, June parked at the Lee Metcalf Wildlife Preserve. Ranger needed to be helped out of the back area. Since there were no rear windows out of which he could put his head, he'd slept the whole way on the rubberized mat June kept on the metal back floor of the old Jeep, and his muscles were stiff. June hoisted her friend to the gravel.

"Poor old Ranger," Helena said as she grabbed her purple purse. "He's really failing, isn't he?"

"Oh, he does okay. He and I look out for each other just fine. Hey, I'll lock the Jeep. You don't have to lug your purse." June ruffled Ranger's ears. He shook his head and went to anoint a fencepost.

"I don't mind carrying it, 'cause it has my water bottle and lip gloss. Girl has to stay pretty, you know!" Helena put on a large sun hat decorated with crocheted flowers, then pulled her blouse down over her belly. "Guess I'm ready to go. Is Maura's car here?"

"Yep. That's Baby right there, the VW bug. Maura will be at the river already, no doubt. It isn't far. We're lucky the day is so pretty." June shouldered the lunch cooler backpack.

They crossed the slough on the footbridge, then followed the trail that lead to the river. The cottonwoods were bright yellow, glowing against the deep blue sky. There was a hint of woodsmoke in the air. A flight of Canada geese in tight formation headed south. Their honks sounded exuberant, calling Ranger's attention skyward.

"You remember, don't you, big guy?" June said as she petted his head. She said to Helena, "Logan used to do what he called hunting, but was really sitting in a duck-blind on fall days like this. They never brought back birds. Logan just wanted to be outdoors with his dog. He told me once he wouldn't shoot geese because they mate for life. He didn't want to leave one grieving. Oh, damn." June reached into her pocket and pulled out an embroidered handkerchief. "I brought one of the hankies you made me. I knew a tissue wouldn't last long." She blew her nose and wiped her eyes, as Ranger guided her down the trail.

Helena walked in silence for a while, then said, "Logan hunted, though, didn't he? I remember him telling hunting stories when you two came south."

"Oh, sure. He hunted deer and elk. Pronghorn, too, when he got enough time off to go to eastern Montana. We needed the game to fill the freezer. But he never killed geese or swans. He told me a story of a working buddy who went swan hunting, killed one, and then had to deal with its mate, who flew back and was walking around the dead bird, calling and beating its wings and, well, *crying*. After he heard that, he refused to do it himself."

The trail curved through small meadows, past a swampy area, before reaching the river. June saw Maura, her long auburn braid hanging down her back, standing at the riverbank facing the water.

"There she is." June called out, "Mom, hi!"

Maura turned and waved. Ranger saw her and started a slow lope. His head was pushed into her legs, Maura rubbing his shoulders, by the time June and Helena arrived.

Maura's voice was calm and low. "Hi, you two. Helena, come here. It's good to see you again." She pulled Helena into a hug, then fussed over how pretty she looked in her bright top. June slipped off the cooler backpack and set it on the picnic table. "Darling girl. You too. I need a hug from you so badly," Maura said as she released one sister and held the other. "I've been watching the river flow, thinking about how difficult and strange this year has been. And yet, we've both had things happen for which we are grateful. Life flows on. A year. Who'd ever have believed it, Montana June?"

"I know. I miss him so much." June buried her face in Maura's shoulder.

"As do I, honey. As do I." Maura stroked the back of June's head. "Now. Let's eat. I think we all need some fuel in our tanks."

Helena said, "Okay, but first I need to empty my tank." She took her purse and headed to the nearby porta-potty.

As Helena closed the door on the little plastic hut, June whispered, "You see she had her purse with her? We had an incident last night when Pace came over. She exploded at him, completely out of control and now doesn't seem to remember. I think she's secretly drinking. Help me keep an eye out, let me know what you think." Her voice faded as the door to the porta-potty swung open and Helena walked toward them again, her eyes bright and her cheeks rosy.

Maura nodded, not looking at June, and opened her own cooler. "Look. I brought dessert. I made Logan's favorite lemon bars and brought ice cream wrapped with some dry ice. It'll stay frozen for awhile. We'll have sandwiches first."

Lunch in the open air, the sound of geese overhead and the cool breeze riffling the yellow leaves, was perfect. The sad reason for being there, not forgotten, made it all more poignant.

After they ate the sandwiches and softened ice cream, Maura rewrapped the lemon bars. "We'll save these for later. Now, I'd like to sit right at the water's edge. Want to join me?"

June didn't hesitate. "Yes. Definitely. Some time to remember all the times Logan and I came here. Ranger? Want to go into the water, my friend?" June woke the dog, sleeping in the sun.

"I'll come, maybe, but I need to go to the little girls' room again. Dang this small bladder," Helena said, once again picking up her purse and heading to the porta-potty.

June and Maura exchanged glances as they climbed down the steep embankment. There was a rock beach perhaps ten feet wide before the water. The women found flat rocks to offer relative comfort for their backsides. Ranger walked chest-deep into the river and took a good long drink, then came back to June before shaking.

"Oh, thanks a lot! You couldn't shake off next to the river, you have to come stand by me? You goof-ball." June put her arm around Ranger's shoulders hugging him to her, not minding the wet. Together they watched the water flow, carrying golden cottonwood leaves. A fish jumped downstream. The honking of geese, the chirrup of grasshoppers, and the gentle chuckle of the river were background music.

Maura sat with her arms wrapped around her knees and leaned back to let the sun hit her face. There was no other place to be. Nothing else to do. For June and Maura, this place Logan had loved offered a healing balm, wrapping them in soothing comfort. The primeval sounds of nature played a hymn of healing.

Perhaps a half hour later, Maura stood and stretched her arms to the sky, then bent, putting her hands on the rocks. She rolled her spine straight bit by bit, and said, "Ooh. That feels good. At my age, rock sitting's hard, if that's not too redundant." Maura gave her deep, musical laugh. "Darling girl, you ready to go? We'll lose our light soon."

"Yes, Mom. This was a blessed time. I felt him here. Did you?"

"Oh, yes. And here." Maura placed her hand on her heart. "Now, one last stop in our day."

The two women turned and clambered up the slope where Helena sat at the table. She pulled her hand out of her purse and wiped her mouth.

Helena's words were slow. "Good. You're back. I figured if I climbed down that slope I'd never get back up again, so I didn't even try." She hiccuped. "Oops! Excuse me. I've repacked all our stuff."

In the Jeep, Helena slept. The drive to the cemetery took about thirty minutes. It was a private cemetery on land owned by friends, and Maura had received special permission from the county for Logan's interment. The small graveyard was very old, with graves dating back to the first settlers in the area; the most recent burial was in the 1950s until Logan was placed there. It lay in a meadow which sloped up the mountainside, looking out to the Sapphire Range across the valley. With the vibrant colors of grass, trees, mountains, and sky, it was achingly beautiful.

Montana June parked the Jeep and waited until Maura brought Baby up next to her, then everyone got out at the same time. June helped Ranger from the back. No one said a word as they walked to the newest grave. June knelt down and with her handkerchief wiped the dust and leaves away from the simple headstone bearing Logan's name and dates.

"I've wondered, Juney," Helena said, "why Logan was buried rather than cremated, as our parents were."

June took time to fill her lungs and relax her throat, before answering. "Logan had plenty of time to think about it before he died, Sis. He decided he wanted to be buried, to remain here on this hillside so he could become part of Montana. He was not—oh God, this is so difficult—he wasn't embalmed."

June reached for Maura's hand. "Mom and I washed his body together. He was different by then: no muscle left, and his skin was like ivory. We washed him and dressed him in his favorite jeans and flannel shirt. His boots. He's lying in a plain pine box made by a carpenter friend of ours. That's what he wanted, and we did everything possible to honor his wishes. I believe it's a pretty good place to spend eternity." June turned to face the far mountains. The evening glow was beginning as the sun set behind the mountain on which the graveyard lay.

Maura walked back to Baby and opened the front trunk, taking out a bouquet of flowers and a cardboard box. Her eyes and smile were sad as she rejoined them. "The flowers are from my garden, from perennials Logan planted for me when he was a boy. As I tend those plants, I think of him and how much he loved this land. And how much he loved us." Maura put the flowers on Logan's grave next to Ranger, lying with his head on his paws. "Yes, Ranger, he loved you, too. This I know: if Logan could've arranged life to suit his bidding, he'd be here with us, rejoicing in every day. But neither he nor we get to decide the roll of the dice. Here, I made Logan's favorite cookies. I brought them, though perhaps we'll choose to eat ours later."

Maura took one lemon bar out of the box and placed it on the ground at the base of Logan's headstone. She gave one to Ranger, and then offered the box to June and Helena. Each shook her head. Maura closed the box, closed her eyes, and said, "Logan, we miss you. We love you always. My blessed boy, you gave such joy to me and to this woman here. Thank you for your life. And now, to quote my precious son, I'll say this, 'Montana June, begin again.' " They shared the silence in sweet communion and looked across the valley as the sun faded from the mountains. At last, their eyes went to the evening sky.

Maura took a deep breath. She began singing in a deep alto voice, her tone pure and beautiful. She sang something familiar to Montana June. The words were calming, but it was the smooth dark voice like melted chocolate that moved June's soul. Maura sang:

Abide with me, fast falls the eventide.
The darkness deepens, now with me abide.
When other helpers fail, all comforts flee
Help of the helpless, O, abide with me.

When Maura finished singing, all three had tears coursing down their faces. June held her mother-in-law hard and long.

Maura said, "And now, dear girls, please come to my house for coffee before you begin your long drive back to the Rattlesnake. Montana June, give me a five-minute head start so I can get the pot going, okay?

I'll see you soon." She hugged each woman, then jumped in her bug and drove down the mountain toward her home.

Helena meandered, looking at headstones, back to the Jeep. Ranger leaned against June's leg. She put her hand on his big head, inhaled, then turned to the mountains again. The first star of evening sparked into view. Montana June touched her bracelet and sighed, then turned to go.

AT MAURA'S HOUSE, coffee and lemon bars were served in the small living room, with Mr. Mouser in his tuxedo acting as master of ceremonies. He walked from woman to woman, winding his rotund body between their legs, purring hard, looking up as if to make sure his attentions were having their intended calming effect. Helena curled on the couch, put her head on the corner pillow, and was soon asleep. June motioned to Maura that they take their coffee outside.

"See, Mom?" June said when they were far away from the sleeping woman. "She fell asleep, or passed out, on the way to the cemetery, too. I guess she keeps a flask in her purse. You wouldn't believe how sudden and violent her explosion at Pace was, accusing him of taking advantage of me. And she appears to have no memory of it at all. It pisses me off that she's doing this. I mean, she came up here to support me. What kind of support is that?"

"Oh, let her be, June. She'll be all the better for the rest, now, and we'll wake her up when it's time for you to drive home."

"Mom, she was drunk! And truly mean to Pace. I'll have to have it out with her eventually. I put it out of my mind today, but really, I'm so angry, I don't know what to say."

"Darling girl, you're hurting now and have a right to be self-protective. But the world doesn't stop because *we* are grieving. We all deal with stress in different ways. I myself've had the odd glass or two too many at times." She grinned. "I suppose you have, as well. I imagine she's letting her hair down, being away from the responsibilities of being a wife, and mother to a difficult boy. Maybe there're more problems. You might ask her what's happening at home."

June thought for a minute, then sighed. "You're right. I guess I'm being self-centered. I'll ask her if there's something wrong. Thanks."

They sat, finished their coffee, letting the quiet night soothe them. June continued as if no time had passed. "And thank you, too, for today. That hymn you sang was beautiful."

"You're very welcome. Though I haven't attended services in years, the old hymns offer solace. Sometimes, I change the words. Now, another cup of coffee?"

"No, we'd better get on the road. It'll take an hour to get home. I *am* glad we had this day, but it's good to get it over with, isn't it? To be past the one-year mark. Though we won't miss Logan any less, we'll never again have to think 'This is the first' whatever."

"Yes, darling girl. Let's go in and wake the sleepers. I do believe Ranger is passed out as well."

21

Rattlesnake Creek ran cool and clear the next morning. The cottonwood trees at this lower elevation were only tinged with color, but some shrubs already shone bright red or deep orange. The scent of woodsmoke held an under-note, the subliminal announcement of autumn. Helena planned to spend part of the afternoon visiting old friends in Missoula, but for now, the two sisters sat on the log, dangling their feet in the stream while Ranger lay at the water's edge.

"Ranger," Montana June said, "aren't you going to jump in the water today? Poor friend. Our late night really took it out of you, didn't it?" She rubbed his back with her wet toes. "And how do you feel today, Sis? You've been pretty quiet this morning."

"I'm fine. Well, I've got a small headache," she said, "but…I'm halfway through my visit with you, and it seems I just arrived." She kicked her feet hard in the water, then stopped and raised her hands. "I don't want to go home, doll. Isn't that a horrible thing for a mother to say?"

"Hell no, Sis. Who would want to go back home to housework, the store, laundry, and hauling Arno hither and yon? Stay as long as you want."

"Wish I could. Toby'd kill me if I spent the money to change the ticket."

"Helena, can I ask a personal question? I know it isn't my place." June's voice was almost lost in the sound of the creek.

"Well, if it isn't your place to ask, it's no one's. We're family. That counts a lot in my book. Ask away. If I don't want to answer, believe me, I won't."

"Okay. Here goes. Couple things I want to talk about, but first, would you tell me how things are at home? You've told me about Arno's activities and some about Toby, but I haven't asked you how things really *are*, if you get my drift." June turned on the log toward her.

Helena wiped her face with wet hands. Her shoulders slumped. "Well, to be honest, things aren't all that damn peachy." She sighed, deflated. "Arno is horrible. Toby refuses to discipline him and won't let me do it, either. Toby's father was abusive, so Toby's way too lenient, but I'm not asking him to be mean, just rein the boy in a little. Nothing we do for Arno is ever good enough. I'm truly worried about him, doll. To be brutal, there're times I don't like him very much. I love him, but I worry about what kind of man he'll grow up to be."

June touched Helena's arm. "Damn. I was afraid there must be something like that. I'm sorry, Sis."

"Yeah. Thanks. And, I think Toby's seeing someone else. Shit. There aren't any glaring signs, I mean no lipstick on his collar or anything, but he stays late at work often, and there's not much going on in our bedroom. I can't believe I told you that. Probably it's because I've gotten so big."

"Okay, stop right there, Helena. If he loves you, your size wouldn't matter. He's not thin, himself. You're a beautiful woman, even if you are a plus size. He's lucky to have you."

"That's sweet of you to say." She tipped her face back, eyes closed. "There's something else, doll. It's my first time away from them, ever, and it felt good to be away, but I screwed up—wanted to feel young again. I tried something that's too embarrassing. I guess I don't want to talk about it." Helena got ponderously up from the log, and walked through the shallow stream to the bank where she'd left her shoes and a towel. "Thanks for guarding these, Ranger. Good boy."

June hopped off and waded to the bank as well. She sat down next to Helena and accepted the towel, wiping her own feet dry before slipping on her flip-flops.

"Sis? Umm, I might know what your secret is. Were you afraid to tell me you have a nip from a flask now and then?"

Helena turned, open-mouthed.

"Honey." June's voice was gentle. "You're not all that surreptitious about it. I first suspected when Pace was over the other night. Did you know you exploded at him, accused him of taking advantage of me?"

Helena blanched and her eyes widened. "Oh, shit. I thought I'd dreamed that. I'm sorry, doll. Does he hate me? He must think I'm a terrible drunk." She put her face in her hands. "Oh, my God, I'm so embarrassed."

"On the contrary, he said it's probably the stress of travel and exhaustion. But I'm worried about you, Sis. Have you been doing this a long time?"

"Heavens, no. Not at all. Toby'd throw me out of the house if I drank all the time. I mean, we have the odd cocktail, but…I just wanted to have a real vacation and relax. I should've realized I couldn't handle it. I'm such a fool." She grabbed a handful of pine duff and threw it into the stream.

"Helena, you aren't a fool. You have a lot to deal with, and you are on vacation. How about if we start fresh? You know, yesterday's been hanging over my head and now it's over. I'd also like a vacation. Let's go away for a couple days, you and me. We'll go up to the lake, have drinks, go out to restaurants, do whatever we want. Just promise me, if you want a drink, say so. Don't hide it in your purse anymore, okay?"

"Oh, doll. You got it. You're such a sweetheart. I'd enjoy going to the lake. I do need to see those people this afternoon, but after that, Flathead, here we come!"

They bumped shoulders, sun dappling their faces. June said, "To quote my sister, 'We're family. That counts a lot in my book.' "

MONTANA JUNE DROVE with a light heart toward Maura's house. The trip to Flathead Lake had gone well—they'd had a grand time dining, shopping, driving around the lake, picnicking and playing. The gorgeous weather sparkled everything with a relaxing sheen of *vacation*.

They'd stayed until the wee hours of the day Helena had to return home. As they said goodbye at the airport, June realized Helena looked rested and happy. The idea of the trip had been a stroke of genius. June reveled in a new-found strength; by helping Helena come to conclusions about life in Florida, June was growing out of the depths of her own grief. She was learning that healing comes in many forms, at different paces, in unexpected ways.

Now she was excited to be picking up Ranger at Maura's; she'd taken care of him while the sisters went north. As June turned into the drive, she saw her good dog lying in the sun near the front stoop. She stopped the Jeep and opened her door.

"Hey, Ranger!" June ran forward as Ranger got up and walked toward her. "Oh, I missed you." She kneeled to kiss his head, reveling in the familiar smell of his warm coat.

Maura came through the front door, saying "Darling girl! Welcome home. How was the lake? Did Helena get off okay?" She gave June a hug.

"The lake was marvelous, and yes, she's gone. We had long conversations, and I think she's ready to go back. She decided it's vital to stand up for herself. It won't be easy to change, but she's determined they all must treat each other better. Thanks again for your wise advice, to ask her about what was wrong. We talked through everything, which might not've happened otherwise." As June spoke, they all walked back into the house, where Mr. Mouser wound around her legs in greeting. She reached to pet him, too. "So, how'd Ranger do while I was gone?"

"I think he did…okay. He slept most of the time, and of course couldn't go on walks. His breathing's become very labored, but I'm sure you know that. Richard came over several times and massaged him, and that seemed to make Ranger feel better. But, Montana June, I'm afraid—"

"I know, Mom. Just…not yet. I'll take him home and we'll spend some time together and I'll see how he is. I know the decision's coming, but not yet."

That evening, Montana June realized what Maura wanted her to see. Ranger's movements were much slower than before. For the first time, he couldn't get all the way to the stream. He struggled for each breath, coughing and choking. Back at the house after the aborted walk, Ranger collapsed on his bed by the fireplace, lying on his side, and looked up at June. His ribcage couldn't expand enough to pull in the air he needed. Worse, there was no joy in his eyes and this broke June's heart. She resigned herself to calling the vet tomorrow, to make the appointment for Ranger's last trip.

THE SUN HID behind clouds the next morning. June's night had been disrupted, and she awakened too early. She stretched long in bed, reaching her arms far above her, listening. Ranger was asleep, but his breath was labored as he worked to pull in each lungful. June scooted to the end of the bed, and lay on her tummy to pet her old friend awake.

"Hey, Ranger." She caressed his warm side. He opened his eyes and looked at her without lifting his head. No sweet doggy grin this morning. "How you doing? Need to go outside for a pee?"

Ranger struggled to his chest, getting his legs under him. He lifted his front end first, and then, with effort, his back. His tail tucked close and his head hung down as June put on her robe and slippers. She kept her hand on his shoulders as they walked out into the backyard. It was cool and cloudy. The maple leaves were falling, the flowers in the beds dried to brown. Ranger took a few steps into the yard, squatted to pee, then came back to June and leaned against her legs.

"Ah, my friend. You don't feel well, do you? How about some good canned food for your breakfast, would that help?"

June and Ranger went into the house to face their day.

Later, it took June three times before she completed the phone call to the vet. The first two attempts she began speaking, then put the phone down. She couldn't make herself say the words. When at last she got them out, she discovered Doc Ben couldn't come all the way to Missoula to allow Ranger to die in his own yard; the doctor's schedule was too full. But if June could bring Ranger to the clinic, there was time at the end of the day.

June got Ranger comfortable on his bed. To occupy herself, she cleaned house and worked outside. When she came back in and sat next to him, Ranger awakened, his breath a ragged and torturous sound. June got up to get a pen and her journal. She wrote:

"Ranger, my friend~
I sat down beside you and you rolled over onto my feet, a warm, comforting,
and loving hug. I got up for my journal because I wanted to write to you,
now, while you are still alive. But by moving, I caused you to move. The walk
from your place on the floor to your bed brought such choking and coughing
that I know I'm doing the right thing. Come visit me, my friend. Come to me
in my dreams. Run with joy, run with Logan. Logan and you are precious,
a part of my forever.
He will greet you, I know.
You're the best dog in the world.
I will love you and miss you always.
Go in Peace. No Pain."

June put aside her journal, lay down behind him, wrapped her arms around him, and cried.

Sometime later, June pulled a tissue from her pocket. She was so tired. It'd come home to her completely this past year that grieving is hard work, and again, her sadness took every ounce of energy. This was all she wanted to do. Lie here with Ranger until it was time to leave.

THE LAKE SPARKLED in the spring sun. Squiggles of sunlight danced on the water, squinting June's eyes as she lay, belly-down, on the dock. More joy than her heart could hold flooded her soul; of all the blessings in the world, after the massive grief of this past year, June could reach out her hand and touch Logan, right *here* beside her. She turned her head—looked into his beautiful eyes—stroked his dark brown hair.

"Well, hi there. I thought you were gonna sleep all afternoon. I've missed you, sweetheart Junebug girl." Logan's voice was deep and warm as always; she reveled in the sound. Logan reached out his hand, running his fingers through her long hair. "Want to walk? Ranger's up on the shore, chasing squirrels. Let's go find him."

June allowed Logan to help her stand. She laughed as he grabbed her into his arms and danced her to the end of the dock, as they'd danced on their honeymoon. Logan's smile rivaled the sun for brightness. His face, his dear precious face was so beautiful. June touched his cheek. Logan leaned down, kissing her deeply.

Ranger ran back from the hillside, barking with joy. He jumped up and put his front feet on the couple in their embrace. Logan laughed.

"Hey, old friend, come on in here. Let's make a sandwich hug." Logan released one hand from June and put it around Ranger's shoulders. The hug lasted a long time.

June's heart swelled with tremendous joy. After all this time she was back in the arms of her beloved. She closed her eyes and inhaled Logan's personal scent. The warm smell of the back of his neck, the good clean male aroma. She hugged—hugged—hugged. Such joy might burst her heart.

A CHILL PASSED over Montana June and the hard floor under her hastened the waking process. Her arm was around Ranger and she hugged him close, letting the intense joy of the dream wash over her again.

She listened for Ranger's breathing. Maybe the dream had helped him, too, because there wasn't that deep exhausted rattle that'd been there when she lay down behind him. She petted his ear; it was cold. Putting her hand flat on his chest, she felt no movement, no heartbeat, no breath. Ranger no longer struggled.

She clasped his body to her chest and let the waves of emotion flow over her. The intense, deep joy of seeing and holding Logan, of being with him again melded with the visceral knowledge that Logan had visited her to help Ranger, and now they were together. The joy of the dream mixed with relief that Ranger was no longer suffering, and with a deep aching grief that she, once again, was going to have to learn how to live without one of her best friends. She wanted with all her heart to return to the dream and have Logan take her, too.

Who will I be without Ranger? I've never lived totally alone. Gulping, gasping sobs shook June's body as grief overtook her.

22

Pace Pacinski's truck pulled up in the drive a week later. Montana June knew he didn't realize she could see him lean his forehead on the steering wheel before he opened the cab door, hesitated, and got out. His hand remained on the roof of the truck long moments as he looked across the yard, then he reached back into the front seat and pulled out a brown paper sack, medium-sized but with heft. June saw his shoulders rise as he took a deep breath, then turned to face the house. His steps were slow and deliberate. June got out of the green chair and went to greet him.

"June. Ah, damn it.... Whole yard feels different without his energy flowing out of the house." Pace took June into a long, gentle hug.

"You know, Pace, though I'm sad and so lonesome without him, I feel as if both he and Logan gave me a gift. I didn't have to take Ranger to Doc for his last appointment. I told you about my dream, didn't I? My brain and memory seem all wonky right now."

"Yes. You did. A good dream. Here, I brought you something. Um, 'fraid a brown paper bag is the best I can do in wrapping gifts." He handed her the bag.

"Thank you. That's sweet. Come on in. It's too cool to sit outside, but we can see the autumn color from the living room. I'll get us something to drink before I open this." June put the gift on the coffee table and went to the kitchen.

After they'd settled themselves with a beer and a glass of wine, and June'd turned on some music, she asked Pace about his trip. He told her all about New Mexico and the Fish, Wildlife, and Parks conference. She figured Pace knew she needed this time to gather strength to tell him about the rest of Helena's visit and Ranger's death.

Pace's voice was soothing and calm, and as always, quiet. "So, that's it about my trip. Sorry to've missed the rest of Helena's visit….How'd it go?"

June sat on the floor, leaning against the hearth with a pillow and her wine. "Well, thanks again for being understanding about her going off on you that way." She explained about what happened, and told Pace about the rest of the week, finishing up by saying, "We bonded as we haven't done since I was a teenager. We had such a good time at Flathead. It turned a stressful week into something special."

"Glad things turned out okay, and that she didn't have more… uh…incidents. Everyone deals with stress in different ways…even me." Pace gave a wry smile, then swigged the last of his beer. "Got another one of these in the fridge?"

"Sure. I'll get it for you."

"No, let me. How about turning on the fire, now the light's gone outside? Be right back."

June turned on the large gas fireplace and drew the drapes. An old romantic song came on that'd been a favorite when Logan was alive. She stood watching the flames, swaying to the gentle rolling chords: "*Oh, my love...*"

"June, hope you don't mind. Looks to me as if...well, if this isn't right, tell me." Pace came up behind her and put his arms around her, while piano arpeggios played in the background. June leaned against him and they stood still until the song ended.

"Thank you. That was nice. That was one of our favorite songs, and I miss being held." She took a deep breath and turned to look at Pace.

The cd ended with a soft click. He said, "Do you want to tell me about Ranger?"

She closed her eyes. "I think you'd be surprised at how fast he declined. It almost seemed like he'd been trying to stay with me through the first anniversary of Logan's death. When I came back from Flathead it was as if his light and energy had gone." June's voice broke. "I know he was in such pain, but I want him back."

"Here. Sit down." Pace guided her into the green tufted chair and sat with her, holding her next to him. She put her head on his shoulder, her sobs deep.

After a couple minutes when her tears were subsiding, Pace handed her his handkerchief. "Here. It's even clean...uh, maybe."

June wiped her eyes and blew her nose. "I'm sorry. Seems like you're always taking care of me. I must look awful."

Pace lifted his hand and tucked a lock of hair behind her ear. "On the contrary, June. You're beautiful." He leaned forward and kissed her lips. "Been wanting to do that for months."

"Pace." June looked down as she struggled to find words. "I like you so much. You must know I do. But I'm not ready to take a very big step."

"No steps are necessary. Happy sitting here, holding you. In a minute, you might open your present...but then, gotta get home. Got work early tomorrow, and it's already ten. For now, though, just rest. Let me hold you, okay?"

A few minutes later, when June's tears had dried and the warmth between them was threatening June's resolve to not take any steps, Pace reached behind him and grabbed the brown paper bag.

"Here. Better open your present. When I saw it at the open-air market, I couldn't turn away. And now, maybe it'll be the right choice.... Hope so."

June ripped the bag open, uncovering a perfect wooden box about twice the size of an egg carton, dark chocolate in color, with brass filigree set into the surface.

"It's simply beautiful! I've never seen anything like it. I love it. Thank you. Oh—"

"What is it?"

"I just realized what I'll use it for." She choked up again. "I'll keep Ranger's ashes in it, what doesn't go to Logan's grave."

"Yes. When I heard about Ranger dying, hoped it might work." He looked at his watch. "Gotta leave. You gonna be okay?"

Pace stood, offering his hand to help June up as well.

"Of course. Thank you for coming...and for the gift." June walked him to the door, then leaned in to kiss him. Pace prolonged the kiss then released her.

"Good night, June. Sleep well."

After he drove away, June locked the door and turned off the fire. She took the box with her, putting it on her bedside table, next to her journal. Tomorrow she'd go to Doc Ben's clinic to pick up Ranger's ashes. Now she had a receptacle worthy of them.

23

Montana June's head hit the roof of the Jeep as it bounced out of a pothole on the lane leading to Doctor Ben's Veterinary Clinic. She slowed, then used her hand to dash away tears. Had she always been crying, on the verge of crying, or getting over crying?

Mighty banks of storm clouds gathered on the eastern horizon, stuck on the mountaintops. The sky darkened; the temperature plummeted.

The last time she'd driven this road, Ranger was next to her, his nervous-dog smell telling her everything she needed to know about her friend—that he was alive. At least she hadn't had to bring his dead body here for cremation. June had called the vet in a flood of tears telling him that, no, she wouldn't be there for euthanasia, but yes, Ranger was dead, and what in the world should she do now, Doctor Ben? He told her to not worry. He'd come that evening with his son to take care of Ranger. A blessing.

Now, June was picking up Ranger's ashes. Doc Ben agreed, with his usual kindness, to divide them, putting part into a plastic bag and the rest into the new box—a perfect receptacle—beautiful, elegant, and strong, as Ranger himself had been.

June told no one of her plans for the day. She left the clinic in the late afternoon and drove up the western mountainside to the private cemetery where Logan was buried, relieved to do this alone. Ranger had been Logan's pup first, but became the dog of June's heart; she didn't want to share this with anyone. The sky overhead was navy blue as June parked at the cemetery fence. Clouds churned. The wind rose. June zipped her coat. She picked up the plastic bag filled with gray dust and bone chips and walked toward the cemetery.

The century-old fence surrounding the graves had wrought-iron posts stained with lichen and rust—some bent, many of the fleur de lis finials missing. The gate creaked as June opened it, then slammed in the wind against the post. Angry storm clouds roiled and covered the sky.

June leaned into the wind. At Logan's grave, she knelt, tucking the plastic bag under her knee so it wouldn't blow way. She wiped the headstone, then took a trowel out of her pocket and dug a hole.

She spoke, words carried away by the storm. "Logan, you came back. I felt you. It was exactly like when we were at Georgetown Lake on our honeymoon. Touching you again, looking into your eyes. Holding you. Oh, my angel, thank you for taking Ranger, but I miss him and I miss you." June opened the plastic bag and upended it into the hole. There was a flat, thumbnail-sized chip of bone; she covered all the gray with soil, then patted it down.

Without warning, her skin moved, her head buzzed. Her arms lifted, feeling her long hair stuck straight out. The headstone in front of her glowed. The trowel on the ground bounced into the air. The air in her lungs collapsed. Her hands clapped her ears. A boom, an explosion in her body...*No*...

COLD RAIN POURED. June woke facedown on the grave, clutching the plastic bag. She pushed away from the wet grass. Through the torrents, June saw a tall figure in a rain slicker coming through the cemetery gate.

Richard Donner walked toward her. *Richard? What in the world?*

"Montana June. Come." Reaching under her arm, he lifted, helping her stand. "Let me take you to the house. You need a blanket and hot tea. Come."

June couldn't form words. Richard guided her, his arm at her waist, past the Jeep and into a grove of trees where a small house with lighted windows came into view.

He opened the door and let her in.

"Sit in this rocking chair by the fire. I have tea made." He handed her a quilt then turned into the tiny kitchen, returning with two mugs. He sat in an easy-chair and put his mug on an end table. "I see you are confused. Maura asked me if you and she could bury Logan here, in my own ancestral plot. Yes, this is my home, and that is my sacred ground." He sipped his tea. "Would you like honey?"

June shook her head. Still unable to speak, she cuddled in the quilt to listen and enjoy being warm.

"You must wonder how I knew you needed help. When you arrived, I saw the bag you carried and guessed your intent. The storm clouds worried me, as I know how quickly the weather can turn violent in late fall. I watched. When the fence around the cemetery started glowing, I knew you were in trouble. As I hurried, your hair started flashing sparks. And then, that tremendous bang. We are very lucky."

June cleared her throat to speak. She sipped her tea and tried again. "Richard. Thank you."

He nodded. "Thanks are unnecessary. Now. Is your tea finished? I will take you to Maura's house for the night. I am quite aware she is home and alone. She would want you with her after this. Shall I drive your Jeep?"

The rain was now only a drizzle, in that strange way of autumn mountain thunderstorms. Richard guided June to her Jeep, opened the passenger door and helped her in, then went around to the driver's side and asked for the key. Soon they were on their way.

ONCE AGAIN, AS many times before, June came to Maura's doorstep needing care. She thought about this as she lay on the couch with Mr. Mouser tucked next to her belly, an afghan wrapped around them both, Ranger's brown box within reach. The sun setting behind the mountain lit the whole valley below, and through the windows they could see raindrops sparkling on the grass. A double rainbow arched north to south over the distant mountains.

"It's almost unbelievable," Maura murmured as they watched the light-play, "that an hour ago it was dark as night with the horrible lightning and thunderstorm. And now we might be in the Garden of Eden, freshly washed and glowing. Richard, thank you for bringing my darling girl here. It's good you left me when you did, otherwise you wouldn't have been home in time." She poured a dram of whiskey into cut crystal glasses for each of them.

Richard's voice was soft. "I believe things happen for a reason. I have seen tremendous thunderstorms and loved them, believing that because of my name, Donner, I was born of thunder. In fact, I was born in a thunderstorm not unlike today's, have I told you that, dear one?" Richard caressed Maura's hand as he spoke. "But I keep a watchful eye when the weather turns. We are fragile beings. June, how are you faring?"

"I feel…to be honest, I feel oddly calm. A sense of…oh, I can't even put words to it. As if nature has somehow honored my loss and—"

"And thereby made you complete? I do not mean to put words in your mouth, and yet perhaps I might know," he said, in a low, deep timbre.

"Yes. That's exactly it, Richard. You were born in a thunderstorm? Will you tell us about it?"

"Certainly. It is not happy, in fact quite tragic. Perhaps the story begins before my own arrival, though. My father was one of those people of whom you might have heard, who seem to attract lightning. As a boy he survived a lightning strike not unlike yours today. He awakened from it under a shattered, smoking tree that took the direct hit. Another time, as I was told by my mother, she, my father, and elder brother had all been out fishing, the weather fine, the catch good. Clouds gathered quickly on the far side of the lake. A strong wind came up. My father started rowing the boat into shore. But too soon the storm hit. Dad told Mom and Willard to throw the tarp over their heads to keep them dry. Mom heard a huge bang of thunder and peeked out. My father's hair was like yours today, June, sticking straight out. He suffered only a burn on his hand. The lightning must have barely kissed him as it went into the water. Maura, my dear, is there more whiskey? Talking is thirsty work."

"Goodness, of course. June, would you also like a topper?"

"No, Mom. I'm fine. Any more, mixed with the lightning, I wouldn't be able to talk at all."

Richard sipped his whiskey and cleared his throat before he continued. "Expected, of course. Electricity is a word-shocking beast." He chuckled. "Now, to finish my story. Willard was seven years old when my parents learned of my imminent arrival. On the day I was to make my appearance, the weather was dire. Father went to collect Willard from school, instead of having him walk home as was usual. Mother worried about her young son walking in the storm. Unfortunately, the storm became a monster. Father was finally able to get Willard to the barn, but while battling his way to the house, he was struck by lightning and killed, right there in the yard while my mother lay giving birth to me. An auntie of Mother's was there to help with the birthing, so Mother was not alone. Willard had heard the mighty thunder and ran to our father, but he was already with the ancestors. By the time my brother made it into the house, so the story goes, Auntie had as much trouble reviving him as she had with me."

The light on the far mountains had faded by this time. The people in the room sat listening to the purr of the cat. Maura dabbed her eyes and blew her nose.

"Richard, my precious man. What a story. Your poor mother. To lose her husband and then have to raise two sons alone. Did she marry again?"

"No. But neither did she ever let her hardships change her joyful way of life. We had a blessed childhood, camping, fishing, and picking huckleberries. If we were poor in money, we were wealthy in love. Willard died in Korea at Pork Chop Hill. That was when my mother chose not to fight her sadness. She faded away. I lost her two years later."

As darkness fell, June petted Mr. Mouser and looked at these two dear people in front of her. Each of them overcame obstacles, yet continued to live with grace and strength. She had a great deal to learn from them. *Who would I be, if I were as strong as they?* Perhaps, with luck, she'd find out.

24

The phone was ringing. Montana June reached to her bedside table, hand searching. She knocked over a glass of water. Water? That's not where her glass should be. Where's the damn phone? Ringing. Ringing. Oh, of course. She wasn't in her own bed; she was at Maura's house, having turned in after Richard finished his story. The day of picking up Ranger's ashes, placing them at the cemetery, and then the lightning strike had taken all of her strength. An early night seemed mandatory. Sometime later Maura and Richard retired as well, to the room across the hall.

Maura's raised voice was coming from her kitchen. Obviously she'd gotten up to answer the landline.

"Richard, June! Wake up. Get up now!" Maura sounded panicked. June bounded out of bed and opened the door, meeting the others in the hall.

Maura words were sharp, clipped. "Get dressed. We've got to leave. I'll get Nanny and Kid. Where's Mouse? Forest fire. That was the fire marshal. The whole mountain's being evacuated to the grade school in Florence."

For a half hour, they rushed, gathering vital papers and necessities. Nanny and Kid were loaded onto the rubber mat on the back floor of the Jeep, perfect for slippery, sharp hooves. June got in the Jeep, with Richard riding shot-gun, holding Ranger's box. Mr. Mouser's kennel-crate fit into Baby's passenger seat. Maura started up, then jumped back out, yelling to them.

"Be right back!"

Within minutes, they were on their way to the school.

As they bounced down the dirt road June said, "Shouldn't we go to your house, Richard? You must need to pick up things, too."

"No. The fire marshal told Maura the hotspot is near there. It is of no consequence. Everything important to me now are in these two vehicles. All will be well."

"What a thing to say. After hearing your story last night, it seems totally unfair you have to go through this."

"As I said, June, I believe things happen for a reason. We may not know the endpoint, but we take it on faith this was meant to be." The parking lot at the school was crowded as they pulled in. "Good. They have a corral set up for the animals. Nanny and Kid will not have to remain in tight quarters."

It was nearing daybreak. June parked close to a temporary fence set up in the football field where already a number of livestock gathered around bales of hay. Together, they unloaded the goats. The gymnasium doors were open, and people were entering, many in their pajamas. Some children were running around the playground in their slippers and robes.

Inside the doors of the gym, the Red Cross had set up an official table so law enforcement could be certain who was off the mountain. While Maura signed them in, and Richard gathered information, June searched for coffee.

"What's the news, Richard?" June asked as she handed them each a Styrofoam cup.

"The fire started downhill from my house. Evidently the calm at your place, Maura, was not shared over the whole valley. Strong winds drove the fire, despite the rain. And then during the night, it exploded. The fire crowned, and of course, that is when it moves fast."

June said, "Well, you certainly don't have to stay here. Come home with me. It'd be good for me to take care of you for a change."

"Hmmm." Maura calculated options. "Not a bad plan. But I also need to get news quickly. What do you think, Richard?"

"It a good idea, though we might go in two stages. Could you take Nanny, Kid, and Mr. Mouser as your first guests, June? Then we will come later after we know the status of the fire. There will be news in Missoula, but I agree with Maura. It is better to be close."

Having agreed to a plan, the three returned to the makeshift corral. In the short time they'd been inside, many other animals had joined the motley crew. Nanny's voice topped the noise. It was obvious she couldn't wait to get away.

With Nanny and Kid reinstalled in the back of the Jeep and Mr. Mouser's kennel-crate on the passenger seat, June was ready to drive back to Missoula.

"Call me when you can, okay?" June sniffed, then wrinkled her nose. "Holy Hannah, that acrid stink! Few smells are as frightening as a forest fire. Take care and please be safe!"

June gave Maura and Richard powerful hugs, then hopped in the Jeep and took off. Ash and cinders fell, visible in the air all around. These cinders were gray and cold, but June knew burning cinders could carry the fire anywhere wind might take them. Smoke smothered the valley. The day was dark.

AT HOME IN Missoula, June put the goats in the backyard. Kid was as big as his mom now, but not as well-behaved—though neither kept it secret they weren't happy with the accommodations. June realized she'd better call Animal Control to tell them she had two goats; with luck, they and the neighbors would understand the temporary need. She got big buckets of water for the goats. With the growing season past, whatever was left in the yard they were welcome to eat.

With the noisy ones taken care of, June turned to Mr. Mouser. She put his kennel-crate on the floor of the great room and opened it. The cat stepped out cautiously, looking around. His white-topped feet, spats to go with his tuxedo, glowed on the hardwood floor. He walked straight to Ranger's bed and gave it a thorough sniff. June put the filigreed brown box with Ranger's ashes on the hearth, right above his bed.

"Oh, Mouse. He'd be happy for you to use his bed. You were great pals, weren't you?" June said as she petted his black head. He rubbed up against her legs, purring. She poured his food brought from Maura's and water into bowls. "Now. I'd better get to work. Lots to do before your mom gets here."

By late afternoon everything was done, and there was still no news. Clean sheets were on her bed and her cot readied; groceries were bought, wine chilling, and a large pot of stew bubbled on the stove.

The goats seemed happy to eat their way through the backyard, trimming the flower stalks and grass to the ground. June was grateful they'd become used to their new digs and were now quiet. Little would be gained from irritating the behind-the-fence neighbors.

June texted the news to Pace, inviting him to come over for a dinner of stew and stories. While she waited, she sat in front of the fireplace and reflected on the last couple days. Her experience with lightning was profound and needed thought. Richard had said it might've made her feel complete; oddly, that felt very accurate. Since Logan died, there'd been an emptiness in her, but the fact that the lightning strike occurred right over Logan's grave seemed like a sign. She imagined what Logan would tell her, could even hear his voice saying "Bury your dead, Montana June. Don't let your loss define you. You'll never get over it, but you need to get past it." June swallowed the lump in her throat. This was hard work, healing. It wasn't all that long ago he died. She wasn't, would never be ready to give him up. She stood and stretched, took a deep breath, then pushed her thoughts further. On the other hand, it was empowering to help others. For so long she'd been the recipient; now, being able to help Maura and Richard felt good. This must be a sign of healing, recovering from her loss, getting stronger.

Quite some time later, the first sound of an arrival was Pace's truck in the driveway.

"Hey, Montana June. Thanks for the invitation," Pace said as she opened the door. "Any news of the fire…your refugees?"

"None yet." June hugged him. "I'm getting worried. I could call Maura, just don't want to pester them. But I'm anxious."

Pace came in and took off his coat. "Okay, there'd be news on-line, but your friendly FWP guy'll call the office. They'll know the real stuff."

As he called, June got him a beer from the fridge. His uniform was wrinkled and he looked tired. She handed him the cold bottle as he disconnected.

He took a long swig. "Thanks, needed that." He wiped his mouth with the back of his hand. "Well, sounds like the area around Maura's house is safe so far. But, Richard's place...maybe that's why they're late."

Finally they heard a car pull up. Maura gave one little tap on Baby's horn, not the usual cheery "beeep." June and Pace went to greet them. Maura had been crying. Richard looked drawn.

June ran to them. "Oh, thank goodness you're here. I've been so worried. Come in! What's happened?"

"I can't bear it." Maura threw her coat on the couch. "It's so horrible."

"My precious one." Richard was calm as he rubbed Maura's arm. "Things don't matter. People do. Nothing was lost that cannot be replaced."

"What? Whatwhatwhat? What's happened?" June's voice raised a couple octaves trying to get an answer.

"Richard's house is gone. Burned to the ground. His truck's destroyed. Nothing's left," Maura said, crying in anguish. "The fire started downhill from there, and it blew up during the night. Had he not been with us, June, he might've died." She started to quake.

Richard took her in his arms. "Now, dear woman. We cannot know that. We are here, and safe. Your place is untouched. The animals are good." He placed one hand on Maura's cheek and gave her a brief kiss. "I was insured for any loss. It should all be covered." Changing focus, he looked to the younger woman. "Montana June, what you have cooking smells delicious. I am starving, and I think we could all do with some food. May I set the table?"

June picked up on his desire to de-escalate emotions. "Nope, all done. Why don't you two wash up—you're covered in soot. By the time you're clean, dinner'll be on the table." June guided them into the bedroom, pointing out towels and robes to change into.

Dinner was muted. Mr. Mouser sat on Maura's lap, and Richard told about their day. They'd spent most of the time at the school, waiting for the regular updates from the fire-line. When it was evident Richard's home was lost and the fire had turned away from Maura's area, they left. The mountain was off-limits, so they couldn't view the destruction. But, Richard said, they were grateful to have a place to come, as many of their neighbors were bunking in the gym overnight.

After dinner, all four went outside to check on the goats, who also seemed subdued. The sky above smothered in the heavy pall of smoke, roiling brown and ugly. To the southwest, billowing plumes from the fire glowed magenta as the blood-red sun set over this long day. Pace would be working tomorrow in the fire zone and promised to call with any news. He said goodbye to the saddened group with hugs, kissing June as he left.

Richard's eyes crinkled with a tiny smile. "He is a fine man, my dear. I appreciate the help he offers." The robe he wore had been Logan's, one June couldn't bear to give to Goodwill. It was long enough even for Richard.

June hugged him. "Will you two be okay tonight? Please wake me if there's anything you need." She turned to hug Maura.

"Darling girl, you've done all we need. Thank you." Maura was quiet, and her face showed her age as it hadn't since Logan's funeral. She wore the necklace Logan's father had made, the garnet teardrop she'd worn at their party the night of the Northern Lights.

"Is this what you raced back for, Mom?" June touched the garnet.

"Yes, and the earrings you wore. They're the only pieces of jewelry I have left from him. I can't imagine life without them. Perhaps it was reckless to go back, but I had to do it."

"Mom, you did just right. Rest well," June said as the two older people entered her bedroom. She turned to her cot. Lying down, she remembered she hadn't asked about the cemetery. She'd gone there with Ranger's ashes only yesterday, and now it was all burned.

Fire. Ashes. Was there no end to loss and death?

25

The next weeks were filled with waiting, followed by dirty, hard work. Maura and Richard stayed at Montana June's house another four days, during which they spent several hours at the mall buying Richard a complete new set of clothes. His one grief in clothing was that his favorite pair of White's boots was burned. He'd owned them for decades, and it was impossible to replace the quality and fit. Maura also bought enough clothes to see her through until it was safe to return to her little house on the mountainside.

Richard would move in with Maura. They'd already discussed it, and the destruction of Richard's home just pushed the date forward.

When the fire was at last contained and they could return to the mountain, the first trip to Maura's house entailed moving the goats. Though they'd managed on bales of hay and the remnants of the yard, June was happy to have Nanny back in her own domain, and also certain her neighbors were likewise relieved to be done with the happy bleating. Maura took advantage of the circumstances and sold Kid to a neighbor, delivering him on the way home. Mr. Mouser, content wherever Maura was, also seemed to enjoy being back home.

The trip to see Richard's place was depressingly sad. The smell of sour wood ash permeated the area. All trees were gone; the entire hillside above and below his house was nothing but blackened stumps and tortured remnants of fence posts with melted wire. The cemetery itself was almost unscathed since the fire burned fast through the dried grass. Richard discovered the place where the lightning strike that'd come close to killing June had in fact struck his great-grandfather's monument, leaving a broken corner and weird jagged markings in the stone.

The three all helped Richard clean up what was salvageable, but there was little of this. Most of his belongings were just—gone. In his gentle manner, Richard would shake his head and ponder his family's connections to lightning, and then say he was very lucky to have his Maura with him, and how grateful he was for the two young people. For June, it felt right that the work they did together strengthened the bond between them. Richard had no living family. Pace's father lived in Washington. The four-way friendship tightened.

This fire that'd been so devastating, was the last of the season. Blessed rains came. Halloween neared. Though it was a gut-punch every time, June slowly became used to the sadness of not having Ranger at home to greet her.

THE LATE OCTOBER chill had crisped all the fallen leaves on the ground. As Montana June walked around Greenough Park, she enjoyed scuffling her feet through the drifts of maple and cottonwood leaves blanketing the trail. Many berries hung on the mountain ash trees in bunches ready for winter birds to pick at. June began the climb up the hill. Deep inside her inner pocket, her cell phone chimed with Pace's ring-tone. By the time she dug the phone out, the call had gone to voice-mail.

"Hey, June?" Pace's voice on the phone was soft and tentative. "Hoped you'd come over for dinner. Uh, want to ask you something."

She called right back and accepted the invitation.

June hadn't spent much time at Pace's house, and she looked forward to the evening. Pace said this was payback; she was not to bring anything.

LATER, JUNE DROVE to his house, a little farther up the valley near the trailhead of the Rattlesnake Wilderness. The October evening had darkened early, and June was happy to know the way.

Pace'd prepared a marvelous meal, from hors d'oeuvres to chocolate mousse. He guided June to the tiny living room filled with the type of things she remembered from her college days: brick and board bookshelves, and an eclectic mix of Goodwill furniture. He offered her a place on the love-seat.

"Holy Hannah, Cowboy! What's all this about? Gotta give it to you. You sure know how to impress a girl," June said as she accepted a glass of champagne.

He sat next to her, holding his own glass. "Well, don't worry. Not going to propose. But, want to ask you something." He cleared his throat and leaned back against the cushions. "Now, or after dinner?"

"Oh, you'd better not wait, not with that lead-in. What's up?" She helped herself to a smoked oyster.

"Okay. Well, this's…hmm…difficult." Pace rubbed the back of his neck; his face reddened. "Guess you know…well, despite that about not proposing…oh, hell." His halting speech slowed further. "Why can't I be like other guys and throw you on the bed?" He put his head in his hands.

"Pace?" June moved closer to him on the love-seat. "It's really okay. Hey, you know, I love how you kiss me. Maybe now's a good time?"

A few minutes later, Pace pulled away from June and leaned back. He ran a hand through his hair. A smile tightened the corners of his eyes, but one corner of his mouth was turned down and he shook his head. "Shit. Should have this down. You'd think I could make a pass."

"Pace, maybe I can make it a little easier. Even though it's more than a year since Logan died, I still grieve for him. I have the normal physical urges of a woman my age, and I really miss the closeness. I'm making progress, and feel almost ready." June face was getting warm so she knew she was blushing. "*But*. I couldn't make any permanent commitment, not to you or anyone else." She squeezed his hand and looked in his eyes, sparkling her own. "But—"

"Okay." He cleared his throat. "I sure'd like to spend some more, uh, serious time with you. In fact, got a particular question to ask."

"I know. I'm dying to hear what it is. Pour us some more champagne and tell me."

Pace got the bottle from the refrigerator and brought back an envelope. He slapped it on his hand as he sat down.

"Okay. Well, here goes. You remember I qualified for the New York City Marathon. It's in two weeks."

"Is it that soon, already? I forgot, with the fire and all that mess. Once again, I got so darn self-centered. How in the world did you keep up with your training while you helped us?"

"I just fit it in, no problem. But here's the thing. Want to go with me to New York? It'd be great to have you there at the finish line...'Course, I'd understand if you don't want to. Too much trouble...no worries. Just forget it. So, steaks can go on the grill now. You ready for dinner?"

June threw a small pillow, hitting Pace on the head. "You goofball. No, I don't want dinner, and of course, I'd love to go with you. I've never been to New York. Yay!"

"You will? Hell...that's great news." Pace beamed. "Well, here, then. Guess you better open this." He handed June the envelope he'd been slapping on his hand.

June opened it. Inside were two airplane itineraries, a hotel pamphlet, and tickets to "The Lion King" on Broadway.

"You already bought tickets? What if I'd said no?" June's voice held her surprise.

"Well, s'pose I would've been out the money, then. Trying to tip the odds. Wanted to believe it'd happen, like a reward for getting this far. Glad it worked out." His voice softened as he leaned over to kiss her again. His lips were warm, enticing; June deepened the kiss.

"Pace." June's voice was husky and serious as she pulled away. "I would love to go with you. But there's only one way I'd even consider it. I'll pay my own way. I can afford it, and that is that. Besides, that'd give me the freedom I think I need, at least in my own head."

"You won't go otherwise?"

"Nope. Take it or leave it, Cowboy."

"Huh. Guess I'll take it. But...uh, 'fraid we're gonna share a bed. Nothing's available at this late date. 'Course I could sleep on the floor."

June cocked her head and gave him a look Logan would've recognized, one eyebrow raised. "Well, Cowboy, if you can take it on my terms, we'll see what those terms will be by then. Like I said, I'm making progress, and I surely do miss…"

Pace's eyes sparkled. "And I surely miss it, too. Got another of those kisses anywhere?"

Breaking contact some time later, Pace reached again for the envelope. "Uhh…'kay, then." He cleared his throat. "Well…hotel's a couple miles from the finish line in Central Park. Pretty sure after the race no cabs'll be available, good to be close enough to walk back to the hotel."

"And, of course, after running more than twenty-six miles, walking a few more won't be a problem. Are you nuts? How about Uber? Anything?"

"Well, this's one of the biggest races in the world, lots of people there—50,000 racers alone. No way we'll get a cab."

June's excitement rose as they talked about plans, Pace asking June to choose one thing she'd like to do in the short time they had. Since he'd been there before, he could make suggestions.

"Holy Hannah, Cowboy. I really can't wait. Just two weeks away! I better decide what to pack."

"Tomorrow, okay? Now, let's get dinner on the table. You toss the salad, I got the steaks."

THE NIGHT AT Pace's house ended soon after dinner, which made June feel oddly relieved and disappointed. The chocolate mousse was superb, surprising testament to Pace's cooking abilities. It was served with rich, silky-moist whipped cream. When Pace spent long minutes licking a dollop off her lips, June's body turned rich, silky-moist. Her resolve melted. She decided if he asked her to spend the night, she'd agree.

After they did the dishes, Pace took her in his arms. "June. So glad you'll come to New York with me. And I'd sure like you to stay to-night." He kissed her again, and the bulge pressed against June's thigh made it obvious there was no doubt he wanted her to stay. "But I gotta work extra hours this week for the vacation time. And you need time to decide if this's…uh, what you want. If you decide you aren't ready for, well, sex, we'll still go on the trip, and I really can sleep on the floor. But in any case…oh, shit. Guess it wouldn't be wise to start tonight."

"Pace, I've known one other man who was such a gentleman. And he is much in my thoughts, always. Thank you. I do want to travel with you. I think I want to go to bed with you, and maybe I'm getting ready for that step. My emotions are kind of a whirl right now."

"S'okay, June. See you next weekend. 'Til then," he said, and kissed her. Deep, long, with feeling. His hands were thorough, and their breathing was rough when he pulled away. "Whew. Better stop, if stopping's happening tonight. Drive safely, my June."

June sat in her Jeep for a moment, letting her breath settle. Her body felt made of chocolate mousse. A smile lifted the corners of her mouth as she started the engine, then turned onto the road toward home.

TWO DAYS LATER, Montana June and Maura sat in the Finn Restaurant by the large windows looking over the Clark Fork River to the campus of the University of Montana. Mount Sentinel rose up behind the campus, outlined by fluffy white clouds.

"Wow. What a difference a month makes, huh, darling girl? No smoke, no soot. Just blue sky and sparkling water. I'm so grateful that part of our life is over. Richard and I are getting along superbly. We make good room-mates, to say nothing of the other…mmm, joys…of having that wonderful man close to hand!" Maura's eyes sparkled, and her cheeks pinked a bit. "But it's delightful to have a girls' day out with you. I'm happy we could meet for lunch."

"It's a great idea, Mom. Thanks for the invitation. As it turns out, I've got news."

"You do? Fantastic, because I have news, too! Let's save it until after we order, though. I'm hungry."

Salads had been brought and tea poured, when Maura motioned, pointing behind June. "Don't look now, but your friend Cara just got up from her table. She isn't looking all that happy. I heard from Doris at Valley Drug that Cara and Ludwig got back from their cruise some weeks ago, but he's been seen with other women. Shh, she's coming this way." Maura stopped talking, turned to look out the window.

Cara had her cell phone to her ear. As she walked by their table, she glanced at June and Maura, but seemed unaware of them. They heard her as she passed. "Ludwig, I tell you I love you and you speak of the mountains. Sweetie, that's not what follows!" She strode away.

June and Maura looked at each other and burst out laughing.

Maura wiped her eyes and chuckled. "Oh, we are mean. That shouldn't be funny, but darn it, it just is. That poor girl. She's reaping what she's sown."

"I wonder if they're even still living together. You know, her husband is such a nice man. When she told me at lunch that day she wished he were dead, I realized she's probably always been superficial and mean. She seemed fun and funny when we were young. Now it's all so ludicrous it's sad."

"Ah, well. Too bad for Cara. At least she got her cruise. So, tell me your news."

June told Maura all about the night at Pace's house and the upcoming trip to New York. She shared, also, the odd mix of feelings at the way the evening turned out. Maura, in her typical way, saw the wisdom in how Pace had ended the date.

"Well, in my mind, he handled it perfectly. He made it obvious, I gather"—Maura looked at June's warming face for confirmation—"he wanted to make love to you. He's putting it in your hands, umm, so to speak. He's letting you choose the time and place. He didn't want you to think because he made dinner for you he expected you in his bed. I find that very refreshing and old-fashioned. Good for him. And how exciting you're going to New York."

"I can't wait. But I should probably take one exciting thing at a time. Maybe I'll invite him to dinner on Friday, and we'll take that *first* big step. Oh, God. I can't believe I'm saying this to my mother-in-law."

"Remember what Logan wanted you to do. Remember the words on your bracelet?"

June touched her gold bracelet again as she said, "Yes. But it may be more than a year, but sometimes I don't feel ready to move on. I miss him so much."

"Of course you do. Of course. Take it slowly, but do take it. Step by step. This is a big step, undeniably. And just because you take it doesn't mean you have to marry the guy. Which brings up what I wanted to tell you when you're ready."

June blew her nose and took a sip of her tea. She looked out over the river and breathed. As the words sunk in, it dawned on her what Maura's news might be. Turning back to her mother-in-law and seeing her big grin, June said, "Wait a minute. What? Whatwhatwhat? What're you saying?"

"Darling girl, just this: I wanted to ask you to be my bridesmaid. Richard and I have decided to make this room-mate thing more official. We're getting married Christmas Eve."

"Holy Hannah!" June jumped up, hurried to Maura's side of the table, and hugged her. "That's wonderful news. Hurray! What a marvelous thing. Waiter, we need a bottle of champagne," June said as the waiter put their lunch plates in front of them.

"Oh, no, we don't. I still have to drive back up the Valley. But we can order dessert to celebrate. I'm glad you're pleased."

"Pleased? I'm absolutely thrilled. Of course I'll be your bridesmaid. A Christmas wedding. Tell me all about it!"

The lunch at the riverside restaurant lasted a long time. Maura and June discussed wedding plans, choosing and discarding ideas until they came up with an elegant, perfect way to celebrate the nuptials. After dessert, Maura insisted she had to leave in order to make it home before the late autumn light faded.

Montana June walked the short mile back to her own home, enjoying the rustling leaves and the Halloween decorations on her neighbors' porches. Halloween was a few days away, and excitement was in the air as she walked toward home. Children were shouting in the park; a sharp spicy smell drifted up as she kicked the rustling leaves on the sidewalk. At home, she took off her coat and sat in front of her fire in the green tufted chair, reflecting on how much had changed. Again, her thoughts turned to Logan.

With her hand caressing her bracelet, June thought about how excited he'd be that his mother was getting married. She would've loved to witness a friendship between Logan and Richard, two strong, wise and gentle men. June inhaled and rubbed her eyes. She was moving away from Logan, couldn't remember how he smelled, what his hair felt like. In her heart, she searched for a feeling she craved, knowledge that he would support her decision to continue with Pace. This was a leap off a cliff.

June leaned her head back against the green leather and listened to the wind. Darkness had fallen and the fire's light danced on the walls. She had told Maura she'd invite Pace to spend the night this weekend. Halloween was Friday night. A good night for company. She picked up her phone and called.

26

On Halloween, Pace arrived at Montana June's house bearing a pumpkin.

"Always loved carving jack-o-lanterns. Against the law for macho single guys to do this alone." Pace's smile went from ear to ear after he kissed June in greeting. "So, kinda hoped to do a little punkin carving this evening. Whatcha think?"

"Oh, yes. I adore the smell of jack-o-lanterns with a candle burning inside. And you've chosen a perfect one. It's tiny and do-able." June caressed the cantaloupe-sized pumpkin.

"Well, he ain't alone. Had to see if you're a willing punkin chopper before you met the others." June laughed to see his bouncy walk as he returned to his truck and opened the tailgate. He waved June over and handed her a pumpkin much larger than the first, then reached back inside for a monster one.

"Prize winners!" Pace put the huge pumpkin on the ground so he could close the tailgate. "Soon'll be a whole family of jack-o-lanterns, all with big goofy grins. Unless you insist on scary ones. 'Course, you get to choose. Your house, your rules."

"Let's get them inside. I always thought each jack reveals his own face, it just takes looking at him a little." She hoisted one to get a better view. "Oof. He's heavy. I'll lay down some newspaper."

When the area in front of the fireplace was covered in paper, and spoons and carving tools were ready, June poured them each a mug of hot spiced cider then put on some music. Pace was sitting on the floor with the medium-sized pumpkin in his lap.

"Hope you don't mind about these, June. Kinda spur of the moment idea at the market. But it's been so long…sounded like fun."

"I love it—it's the perfect way to start our evening. I have some great candles to go inside. And, besides, it'll make this whole part of the great room easier to be in. This was Ranger's favorite space. He loved being by the fire." June stopped to take a breath. "Okay, so. What do you think this little one wants to look like?" She held the smallest pumpkin next to her own face and grimaced at Pace.

"Yikes! That lil' guy needs to be happy, not scary. Give him here."

"Oh, no you don't. He's mine. And I'll make him cute. Just like you." June picked up the carving tool, and got to work.

By the time all three jack-o-lanterns were carved and sitting on the sideboard with candles flickering inside, June and Pace were covered with slimy "punkin guts" as Pace called it and were verging on uncontrolled hilarity. They gathered up the wet, fragrant newspapers and while Pace took them out to the trash bin in the garage, June washed her hands, then took the baking dish out of the oven.

Pace joined her in the kitchen. "Damn, that smells good!" He rubbed his belly. "I'll wash up and help you." Returning with his sleeves rolled back down, Pace came behind June and put his arms around her.

"Montana June. Thanks for humoring this Halloween-lovin' guy. Not every woman would be so spontaneous. Now, what smells yummy?"

June had set the table and finished the prep before his arrival, so all she had to do was take the salad out of the refrigerator and pour the wine.

"Well, it's stuffed pork chops from the grocery store, and some baked squash. Hot comfort food. Would you bring the jack-o-lanterns in to act as our candlelight?"

They settled themselves at the table, poured wine, and dished up. After several minutes of silent eating, Pace took a sip of his wine then looked at his companion.

"You're beautiful tonight, my June. Different…calmer. A sense of—"

She inserted, "Maybe joyful anticipation? I had lunch with Maura a couple days ago, and she gave her blessing to this, well, to our relationship. To be honest, she gave an exuberant and whole-hearted blessing to it!"

Pace choked, then took another big drink of wine. "What? Holy shit, June, umm…didn't think our possible sex life'd be a topic of general conversation. Glad she approves. You ask the mayor, too?" He smiled a tiny, wry smile.

"You're turning red! Goodness, who'da thunk?" June grinned. "I thought you knew there's little I wouldn't share with Maura. By the way, Maura invited you to their wedding on Christmas Eve and that was the main topic of conversation, not you and me. In fact, I think Richard will be calling you about it."

"Oh, yeah? A wedding in the family! How great is that? Be there with bells on." He took a big bite of squash.

"Also, Pace, you need to know I spent a lot of time thinking about Logan, too. In my heart I'm sure I have his blessing. There shouldn't be three of us in bed, and I had to get past the fact it's been years since I've made love to anyone but him. I imagine I'll never stop missing him, but if you can accept that, I'm ready to…ready to…" June's voice faded and she said, "Oh, shit. Sorry." She got up and ran to the bathroom.

By the time she came out, Pace had cleared the dishes and was standing in the great room by the fire. His back was lean and straight as she came up behind him. She put her arms around his waist and leaned her head on his tightened shoulder.

"Forgive me. Usually I can tell when tears are coming, after so many months of practice, and those times are farther and farther apart. And Pace, I told you the truth. I am ready to move on. I want it to be with you."

Pace was silent for many long moments. Finally, June felt the muscles in his back relax and his head leaned forward a little. He turned inside the circle of her arms and placed his own around her shoulders.

"My June. No forgiveness needed. Been in love with you awhile, seems to me." June swallowed her gasp, but couldn't control her eyes widening. Pace noticed. "Yeah, your eyes show those words surprise you. Wouldn't ask this—" he motioned with his head and eyes to the bedroom—"if I didn't love you. If you can make the leap to move on, I guess being patient's my job. Now, perhaps, for a minute, we can stop talking."

Pace leaned in toward June. His lips were soft and warm and tasted of cinnamon from the baked squash. June snuggled closer. She reached up and brushed the white streak of hair, tucking it behind his ear. She said, "Perhaps we might be more comfortable in bed. Just let me turn off the fire. Will you blow out the jack-o-lanterns?"

By the time Pace came to the bed, June was already in, leaning on one elbow with the sheets pulled barely over her breasts. A warm glow came from bedside candles. June focused on the man coming toward her, using her internal strength to put all memories and other longings aside. Pace lay down on the bed, turned to June, and smiled.

"My June. You are very beautiful."

He reached over to touch her hair, pulling a long blond lock out from behind her neck, letting it dangle over the cleavage showing at the edge of the sheet. He leaned in to kiss her, and this time there needed to be no ending. There was no time constraint, no job to rush off to, no inner turmoil putting on the brakes. Pace may have been shy and halting earlier, but all that disappeared in the flickering candlelight.

SOMETIME LATER, AFTER the candles had burned down, Pace pulled the blankets up to cover them both. With one finger, he stroked June's cheek.

"Look at me, my June. Open your eyes. See *me*."

June opened her eyes. There was a tiny crease between Pace's eyebrows; his eyes seemed sad. It was not Logan's face, not Logan's dark hair falling toward her. She swallowed and pushed his memory out of her mind, and breathed in the scent of Pace. She looked into his eyes, and felt a connection. Maybe this could be a new home.

"Ah," he said. "Hoped you weren't sleeping yet."

"No, not sleeping. Relishing. Thank you, Pace. That was amazing. You are a gentle and exquisite lover." June reached toward him. "You look worried. Something wrong?"

"Hmm. No…at least…there was a minute before, well, before we came, you were gone. Thought maybe it wasn't me you were making love to. Guess I gotta get used to that."

"Pace. Did I think of Logan? Yes. But briefly. Believe me. I was here, with you. *With you*. I promise." She touched his hair again.

"My June, thank you. You need me to leave now?"

"No, please don't. Stay with me. Breakfast is all planned. But right now, would you just hold me?" June scooted down and put her head on his shoulder. They made themselves comfortable. Pace reached over and snuffed out the candles.

June lay still, listening as Pace's breathing deepened and slowed. She waited until he sounded asleep before she retreated into her thoughts. The last time she'd made love to a man for the first time had been with Logan, many years ago. She'd been young, then, slender and tight in her body. She had the world by the tail. Now she was not as confident. Her body had softened; she was older. But it seemed Pace didn't mind, and for that, she was grateful. Pace snored and rolled over in his sleep.

His body was different, too, from the one she was used to loving. Logan had been a big man, six four, with broad shoulders to match his height, and muscular. He also had the beginnings of a paunch, which June had relished. Pace had a runner's body. He was shorter than Logan, five nine or so, and his muscles were long, lean ones, meant to eat up miles on the road, not lift heavy loads. The differences were disconcerting at first, but it wasn't long before they made *no* difference. June's orgasm had followed Pace's, full and deep, feeling as if the crests of the waves were falling off the edge of the world. Almost as the best times had always been with Logan.

Sometime later, long after Pace had stirred, gotten up to use the bathroom and returned, and June thought he'd gone back to sleep, she allowed her tears to fall. *Logan, my angel. It's been more than a year. I'll never have you again, and I don't know who I am without you. Oh, God, my sweet husband, please help me begin again.*

27

The roar of jet engines filled Montana June's ears. Her excitement soared. Pace raised the arm-rest between them; their hands clasped.

"We're off! Know anyone else on this plane, Cowboy?"

He looked around. "Uh, maybe four members of Run Wild Missoula. But they won't be with us in New York. Just us, my June." He lifted her hand and kissed her knuckles.

June thought back to their first night together. They'd made love again in the morning, then Pace left shortly after breakfast. Being with him was fine; not what she craved, but good.

Now, it was all happening. June examined the map of Manhattan she'd bought before leaving Missoula.

"So, my June, you choose something else to do in the Big Apple? Wish we could stay longer, but we'll get some good food, and 'course the theater," Pace said, trying to lean his seat back.

"Well, how about the Museum of Natural History? Or, if not, just walk around the city."

"Oh, girl. We'll do plenty of walking. Museum's a great idea for Monday, right across the street from where we need to be that morning, anyway. Gotta buy my official New York City Marathon jacket at the Finishers' Expo, there in Central Park. We'll catch dinner at a fancy restaurant on the way back to the hotel. Tuesday's our last day, get in more sight-seeing, then the Minskoff Theatre, for 'Lion King.' Busy few days." Pace's excitement showed. June noticed, too, as they'd gotten closer his speech became more even. This trip was deepening their relationship.

The flight attendant came by with drinks. When he'd gone, Pace told her what he'd learned from his friends, rehearsing the race out loud.

June snuggled under his arm. "I'm proud of you, Pace. Thanks for inviting me."

"Not much fun without you, my June."

WHEN THE PLANE landed at JFK, the Missoula runners shared a hired minivan to get into Manhattan. Montana June embraced her role of tourist, keeping her face pressed to the window for most of the forty-five-minute drive. Against the night sky, the big city blazed. The lighted bridges looked like strings of diamonds to June, who'd never been to such a metropolis before. Pace and June's hotel was second on the route; they were let out in front of the Wyndham Hotel on Thirty-sixth Street. Pace got their bags from the luggage rack, tipped the driver, and waved goodbye to the rest of the runners.

The hotel was unlike any June had seen. She supposed it must be typical in a city where each square foot of ground was exceedingly valuable. The footprint of the place was tiny. The compact ground floor had no lobby to speak of—as they entered the elevators were before them, the front desk to the right. Pace joined the line to check in while June explored. She walked left, then behind the elevators, around to the entry of a small restaurant. Continuing on past the maitre d' stand and making a full circle back toward the front desk, June discovered a tiny in-house deli. Then, she was back to Pace, who'd moved up in line to the desk.

After checking in, they found only two closet-sized elevators, to serve all the floors above. June eyed the many folks sardined with them, speaking languages from around the world. Their gear showed they were runners, too, bubbling with energy, ready to run the New York City Marathon.

Opening their door on the tenth floor, June was astonished. "Holy Hannah, Cowboy, will we fit?" It had all the usual hotel furniture, but the floorspace was minimal—just room enough to inch around the bed. "Good thing you *don't* have to sleep on the floor. You'd be standing up." As they unpacked, June scooted by Pace and parted the drapes.

This was the city that never sleeps, even this late. June looked through windows across the narrow street into what appeared to be a clothing factory. People worked at tilted tables, sketching. Racks of dresses crowded everywhere. Lights blazed. Next to the factory was an apartment building with a rooftop patio strung with globe lights; potted trees and shrubs stood next to small tables. Each detail seemed fascinating.

Pace came up behind her and wrapped his arms around her waist. "How you doin', my June? Tired? Hungry?"

"Hungry, I think. Too excited to be tired."

"Let's go find something to eat, perhaps a drink. Then bed. Tomorrow we go to Javits Center, pick up my packet. Then Central Park, check out the finish line. But now, let's go forage."

The restaurant downstairs was closing, but they could order a drink and bowl of soup. Perfect. Neither spoke much. Later, upstairs, they discovered making love in the big city was just as exciting as back in Missoula. Only the sounds differed. Car horns and sirens floated up to the tenth floor—not the owls and train whistle that serenaded them back home.

THE MORNING OF their first day in New York, Pace's excitement exploded. No way would he let June take time for breakfast in the restaurant.

"Come *on*, gotta start walking. We'll find some street food. This place's known for that, right? Grab the map. Gotta get to the Javits Center early. Ready?" Pace bounced up and down.

"Jeez, Cowboy! Yeah, I'm ready. Let me put my jacket on." Montana June grabbed his jacket, too, as he was already at the doorway, batting the door back and forth.

At the elevator around the corner, five people waited in line.

"Damn! Should've started earlier. Come on, June, gotta catch this elevator or we'll be here all day."

"Coming!"

Out on the sidewalk, Pace checked the map again and headed in the direction of the Javits Center, where all the racers had to sign in. A block down the street, June saw a bodega and decided if she wanted breakfast, she'd better take charge.

"Okay, Cowboy. Slow down. Once we get to the Center, we'll no doubt be in line a while. We need fuel, you especially. I'll go in here and get us some breakfast. Don't worry, I'll be back out soon as I can, okay?" She kissed Pace and smiled as he continued to bounce in place. His grin and excitement were infectious.

Inside the little corner market, she was amazed at the number of people—one big difference between New York and her hometown. Here, everywhere she looked were people upon people. June had to line up to snag enough to fill their bellies, then wait in line again to pay. By the time she got outside, Pace was pacing, looking at his watch.

As she neared him, he glanced up, grinned and said, "Super, let's go!"

Close to Javits were many indications this was one very big deal. Banners hung from every light post. Streams of people channeled from all directions into the front doors. Inside, huge two-story windows enclosed the large central area. Volunteers directed racers to join numerous lines snaking back and forth, divided by their estimated finishing time. Pace found his line and they stepped to the end of it. None of the lines moved.

A burly volunteer in a New York Road Runners jacket herded people, using his arms like a snow-plow, yelling "Six abreast. Come on. Close ranks. Six abreast, people. Move it!" The volunteer pushed toward Pace and June.

"Hey, what's up?" Pace asked him. "How come nothing's moving?"

"Not time yet. Don't you worry 'bout it. We handle crowds like nobody's bid'ness." He turned away, continuing to herd the huge crowd.

Before long, a loud buzzer sounded, and the snakes of lines all started moving at once. Soon Pace had his race packet and bib number and was standing in front of the big map of one of the most famous marathons in the world.

"Now what?" June said, jostling through the crowd to stay next to him.

"Let's go into the Expo Area. Need some souvenirs. Then we're outta here."

June had already had enough of crowds and spotted a place near the exit where she could wait. She pointed it out to him, made her way through the throng, climbed a couple steps, and settled in to do some people-watching.

Montana June felt like a sea anemone, tentacles waving in the current of sound. She'd never experienced such a mass of bodies; the roar of decibels was palpable against her skin. She heard unfamiliar languages, saw many skin colors and body shapes. Though this race was a premier event, not all the runners were elite. Some were shaped liked June, some even bigger. She admired them for tackling this race. It must take a great deal of motivation to put one's self out there to this extent, to be willing to participate in a race with the best runners in the world. Where did they get their nerve?

June saw many people with T-shirts naming charities. There were racers for the Christopher Reeve Foundation, and June remembered Ellen Painter was one of their number. Ellen had told her that it was through charity work regular folks could run a race of this caliber without running fast enough in a qualifying race. *That's* how ordinary people found the motivation to do this: they were passionate about a cause that needed money and jumped to help.

She saw a woman wearing an "I Run for Prostate Cancer Research" T-shirt and hailed her. "Here. I'm from Montana," June said, handing the woman a bill, "please add this to your donations." June turned away as the woman unfolded the money to see a hundred dollars.

The woman gasped. "Oh, wow! Thank you!" June turned back, hugged her fiercely, and then they were separated by the crowd. *Sometimes, you gotta go with your gut.*

Before long, Pace arrived carrying shopping bags, looking exuberant but tired. They decided to go back to the hotel for a rest before walking to Central Park. They needed a break from the unbelievable crowds of raw humanity.

Though they'd started the day as early as possible, it was noon when they got back to the room. Pace took his bags to the bed and stretched out, pulling pillows up behind him. June tossed her jacket on the mini-bar counter and joined him.

"Whatcha got, there? Can I see?" She picked up a bag and started to open it.

"Hey, gimme that. You can't have that one now." Pace had a twinkle in his eye as he retrieved the bag and tucked it under his knee. "Here, let's look at the program. This one'll have route maps."

June cuddled up to him and looked at a smaller handbook as he flipped through the program. His race bib slipped out, and she picked it up. "Hey, your number is 6-395. Handbook says your starting time is going to be 9:40. You're in the first wave. It says you have to find the right corral. Like cows, Cowboy."

Pace stretched his legs. "Yup. Good to start early. You said I start at 9:40? Probably finish about 12:30 at the earliest. Jeez. This time tomorrow, it's all over."

"Well, are you too excited to nap? I might be able to come up with a way to relax." June's eyebrow raised and she ran her hand down his chest.

"Hmmm…be gentle, my June. Gotta save energy. Damn, that's good." Pace turned on his side, reaching for her. The pamphlets, mag-azines, and bags slipped to the floor.

SOMETIME LATER, JUNE woke and opened her eyes to find Pace looking at her.

"Love watching you sleep. Your hair's like gold, here on your breast." With his finger, he released the sweat-sticky hair. Leaning in to kiss her, he smiled. "Bought you something. I wanted a special time to give it to you." He handed her the bag she'd tried to open earlier.

"Ooh, I love presents." June kissed him back, then reached in and withdrew a long-sleeved blue T-shirt. "Great color. Thanks! What does it say? 'To Hell and Back'?"

"It's a reference to Hell's Kitchen, a neighborhood a few blocks away. But it made me think of you 'cause of what you've gone through this year. To hell and back—that's you. Can't even imagine what it must've been like to lose Logan, not let it kill you, too. You've been through hell and survived, my June."

June's eyes brimmed with tears. She swallowed and sniffed. The tears fell anyway. "Thank you so much. To hear you say that means the world to me. It *has* been hell. Pure and horrible. More pain than I thought I could bear. Frankly, I didn't think I'd live through it. And yet, here I am with you now. You know, sometimes it's like I'm living in two worlds. I'm drawn backwards. I still talk to Logan, dream of him. He'll always be my first love. Can you handle that?"

"My June. I fell in love with you as you are now. Comes a time you're wholly mine, guess I'll share any part of you that remembers Logan. It'd be an honor to take care of what he loved most."

June cupped his head with her hands and kissed his forehead. Her voice became very soft. "Excuse me. I'll be back in a minute."

Montana June slipped out of bed and stepped to the bathroom. She closed the door, turned on the tap, put a hand-towel to her face, and sat down. And cried.

After a few minutes, June decided a shower was in order. Tears, several thousand people, a few miles of walking, and the air in this big city all had made her grungy and damp. Her heart in her throat at Pace's kindness and her own memories, June let the hot water flow over her body, washing away all thoughts of sadness.

June used the solitude to think about her deepening connection to Pace. If she'd stayed home, she would've missed this chance to further their relationship, all at once vital to her, a step in her healing.

She felt stronger now—certainly since Logan died. But. Maybe even stronger, better than ever before. She was now a woman making her own choices, building her own future. In coming here, she had turned a page in her story.

But this was Pace's weekend. June decided there would be no more tears—only happiness the rest of the trip.

28

Leaving the Wyndham the next morning at 10:00, Montana June thought she had plenty of time to walk the distance to the finish line. It wasn't too far, but in unfamiliar surroundings there was no telling how long it would take, and June didn't want to risk missing Pace cross the finish line. The day was cool, perfect for running and walking.

As June worked her way toward Central Park, she passed many tiny, grungy shops. Hurrying past, she tried to not make eye contact with the hucksters outside, but was fascinated with their very explicit signs. Closer to Central Park, the crowds got bigger. Masses of people, all going her direction, filled the sidewalk. Constant car horns. Shouting drivers leaned out their windows. Sirens. People with folding tables selling knock-offs. Hot dog stands. Food trucks. People. People. People.

For someone who'd lived all her life in a state with five people per square mile, this was a different world entirely. *Who would I be if I lived here?*

It took June a full hour to slog the two miles to the area near the finish line. Sometimes the crowds were so dense she had to wait to find a hole to dive through. When she reached the area Pace said he'd look for her, she found a large boulder and sat down. At least an hour remained before he'd be by, plenty of time to people-watch.

June wore the new shirt Pace had given her: "To Hell and Back." It overwhelmed her that he'd chosen this particular shirt. It had been, most assuredly, hell. Twenty months since Logan had been diagnosed. Sometimes it felt like a lifetime ago; sometimes it seemed like yesterday. The darkest times she couldn't even remember without panic rising again. The day of Logan's death wasn't the worst, because real, physical shock kept most of the anguish away. The most horrible were the days, weeks, months, when Ranger was the only thing that kept her alive. What June remembered, though, about the day Logan died was how *physical* the pain was. Weight, heavier than all these buildings surrounding her now, sat on her chest, crushed her heart. But, she was recovering. By thinking back, she could chart her progress. June remembered her birthday, the first one without Logan. She remembered killing the dead-end sign. She remembered the near-rape. In each case, she'd used her own strength to survive, and also the help of friends: Maura, Pace, and Ranger. Then, of course, Ranger died. "To Hell and Back" indeed.

She touched her gold bracelet and promised Logan she would continue to honor his love of her, continue to honor her friends by living this new normal. Day by day. Step by step in the right direction. And Pace was becoming the right direction for her.

June's butt on the rock was getting sore. That simple fact brought her out of her reverie. She glanced at her watch.

Holy Hannah. I might've already missed Pace.

She jumped up and walked closer to the barricades, eyeing the racers coming by. The time-clock at the finish line read 3:01:07. How could she have been so involved with her own thoughts that she'd ignored this roar of noise and excitement? June joined the mass of cheering on-lookers, standing on tiptoes to see these serious runners, trying to make good finish times, their goal in sight. Each face showed exuberance and joy, effort and exhaustion. June cheered for each racer who passed.

As the time-clock ticked further past the three-hour mark, though, June became more unsettled. At 3:30:00, she was very worried. She pushed closer to the barricade. Had she already missed him? Where the hell was he? The time-clock ticked on. More minutes. As she started to turn away and search for him in the finishers' section, June caught a glimpse of the white patch of hair. His head was down, unlike the other racers running by, and he was struggling.

"Pace!" she called. He looked up. His mouth stretched into a pained grin and he pumped his fist. "You made it! GO PACE!" June screamed as he passed her, now yards from the finish line. He had bandages on his knees. Both hands were clenched, but it seemed they were bandaged, too.

She turned away from the barricade and worked her way through the crowd, trying to get closer to the finishers' exit. She knew Pace would be given his medal and water, be monitored by a volunteer, and then would come through the gates by the street. June craned her neck, waiting. Ten minutes later she saw his distinctive hair bobbing through the sea of heads.

"Pace," she yelled, "I'm here!"

He scanned the crowd, spotted her, and adjusted his trajectory. June tried to run, dodging people in her way.

"My June! Knowing you'd be here…got me here…running to you." Pace grabbed her; his weight sagged onto her shoulders.

"What in the world happened? Look at your hands—your legs! Oh, you poor thing. But you did it, you finished! But what happened?" Worry and excitement fought to come out first.

"Well, gimme a minute. Gotta sit down, okay? Holy shit, not my best race."

Montana June grabbed his wrist above the bandage and looked around. Her body wedged through the crowd as she hollered, "Excuse me. Sorry. Need to get through here." She spotted a bench two people were vacating, made a bee-line for it, and was able to sit down just before it was taken by three teenagers. Her expression made them turn away though she did hear "bitch" from the one with purple spiked hair.

"They think they're original. Those fashions went out of date in the eighties. Okay, my wonderful Cowboy. Tell me what happened. Here, I brought chocolate milk." She pulled the bottle out of her purse, cracked the seal and opened it.

Pace reached for it with both bandaged hands, then chugged without stopping. "Thanks. Needed that. Shit, good to sit down. Gotta breathe a minute." He stretched his legs, wincing as the bandages on his knees wrinkled, and leaned back, his face in the sun. "Better…. Good news or bad?"

June cuffed his bicep. "Tell me about the bandages, you jerk. What happened?"

"Well, okay…whole route's lined with folks cheering, right? Near the Water Station Mile 23, this little kid jumped in front of me to get a high-five. Didn't see him 'til it was too late. Had to dive right, took a header. Kid screamed, and an ambulance guy got me up and taken care of. Sure slowed me down. Last three miles, totally lost my push. Great before that."

"Oh, you poor thing. Here, you want your jacket?" June pulled it out of her bag and put it around his shoulders.

"Better start walking....Don't wanna freeze up."

At first, Pace walked gingerly, stretching, reaching his arms up, twisting his lower back. They headed toward the hotel with June as pointman, spotting holes in the crowds, keeping them going straight on the sidewalk. She linked her arm through Pace's—several times he lurched and stumbled. June watched for a taxi, but all the ones passing, even the pedicab rickshaws, had occupants. It was now mid-afternoon, and with the time change, close to dusk. Towering buildings blocked the sun.

Back in the hotel room, Pace showered, saying he wished there was a tub to soak in. June called the front desk for first aid items. She used the salve, gauze and tape to cover his wounds before getting him settled on the bed with plastic bags filled with ice from the machine down the hall. She threw the blanket over him and kissed him, then went down to get dinner. June ordered a range of things she thought would sound good to a tired runner: hamburgers, asparagus, french fries, easy finger-food. As she passed the in-house deli with her bag from the restaurant, she also grabbed beers, a bottle of red wine, and a small chocolate cake made for two.

Sometime later, the wrappings of the meal in the trash, and the plate of cake balanced between them on the bed, Pace reached for his glass of wine and said, "Holy shit, my June. Feast for a king. Great choices."

"Well, good. Now, do you have the energy to tell me about the rest of your race?"

"Yeah. I'm pretty waxed, but too excited to sleep….As expected, crossing the Verrazano Bridge, they had Sinatra's 'New York, New York' on the loud speakers. Way cool! Fireboats spraying, perfect day. Great beginning for a race. Then going through Williamsburg…uh, Hasidic Jewish neighborhood, men all wear wide-brimmed hats, women dress like the 1950s? Not to be disrespectful, but it's like they didn't want us there, even turned their backs to us. Only place people weren't cheering. Weird. Like we weren't even there…thousands of runners. Real Twilight Zone."

June swallowed a bit of cake. "That's so bizarre. I wonder why they'd do that."

"No clue. That's maybe Mile Ten. Lots of bridges, but no worries there for a Montana mountain boy. Bands playing. Just before my crash, there's a great salsa band—lead singer yelled 'Welcome to Spanish Harlem.' Farther on, there's a bar called 'the Banshee Pub.' Looked pretty inviting, might've quit hadn't been for you." He stretched and groaned. "Got to Central Park and thought the end was close, got my hopes up, but then you gotta run all the way down the Park, around the end, partway back up." His words were softer, a bit slurred. He yawned. "Not fun. Never hit the wall like that before. Right now, can't imagine doing another marathon." Pace drained his wine glass and motioned for a refill.

June got up and poured, then sidled to the window. "You've had one big day, Cowboy. It's dark already. I don't suppose I'll ever get back here again. Oh, hey! The people across the street are having a marathon party on their roof-top! A big banner facing us says 'Congratulations, Runners!' How cool is that?"

June turned and saw Pace was in danger of dropping his wine glass. Just that fast he'd started to doze. She took the glass from his hand.

"Hmm? Whuzat?"

"Nothing at all. I'm going to take a shower. Want to brush your teeth before you sleep?" June realized he was past hearing. She tucked the blanket in around him and turned off the bedside lamp.

June came out of the shower wrapped in a large towel, her hair up in its bun and wet tendrils escaping. Pace's snores were quiet. His bandaged left hand lay on the pillow near his white patch. She pulled the blanket up again, smoothed his hair.

June poured herself more wine. Pace'd had a couple beers with his hamburger, and then wine with the cake, saying he couldn't seem to get enough calories into him to make his head feel right. This race, complicated by the fall, had depleted him. Tomorrow he'd be more sore than he was this evening. June realized there'd have to be adjustments in their plans the next few days. She sat, tucking her feet under her, in the easy chair where she could see Pace but also look at the city nightscape. She'd done a good job caring for him today. It felt fine to once again be able to lavish attention on someone else. This, she realized, was another new step for her, taking it further than when Maura and Richard had stayed with her after the fire. For so long, others had taken care of her, and now she was strong enough to return the favor. Growth and healing came in many forms. She wasn't there, yet, but she was making progress.

Grief is, almost by definition, a solitary and self-centered emotion. *Big grief,* the achingly complete suction of joy caused by the death of someone as dear as Logan, brings the whole world down to one spot of immense weight. A black hole of pain. It had taken these last months to realize that maybe life might be worth living again. She sipped her wine. Yes, she did want to live, in great part due to this man right here beside her. *Logan? Is this a good thing?* Remembering his last letter to her, she touched her bracelet, and looking out the window to the lights of the city, thought of the stars of home.

29

Gentle morning light, diffuse and fragile. Without moving, Montana June focused her attention on the man behind her, listening. Was he close to waking? No snores. She rolled to her back and turned her head to see. His eyes were open; he smiled.

" 'Morning, my June."

"Hmmm." June stretched, pointing her toes and reaching her arms over her head. "Good morning to you, Cowboy! How're the wounds and muscles?"

"Don't know yet. Gotta take a leak, didn't want to wake you. Hope I can hobble that far." Pace used his elbows to prop himself up, holding his hands away from the bed. He swung his legs over the edge. "So far, so good. But…can the mighty runner stand?" With careful movements he did so, then took a tentative step. "Guess the bathroom's possible."

Pace gave a wry smile as he passed the foot of the bed. Each slow step looked painful. "Hey, I'm starving here, but don't want to go downstairs. How 'bout calling room service? Order us a big breakfast, whatever you want. Lots and lots of coffee, for sure. No," he said, holding up a bandaged hand in the face of June's imminent argument, " 'course you could go get it. For once, let's splurge. And this's definitely on me."

Taking him at his word, June ordered plenty of protein and carbs. Hearing the shower going, June dressed in her comfortable sweatshirt and jeans, brushed her hair, and used her cold cream to clean her face. By the time Pace came out, she was almost ready for the day.

"So, how do you feel? I see you found the rest of the bandages." She hugged him, then looked in his eyes to see for herself how he fared.

"Better n' I deserve, my June. Breakfast'll help, but not bad, considering. Even shaved!" He slapped his cheeks.

A knock at the door announced the arrival of breakfast. The waiter scooted chairs around, set the dishes on the wide window ledge, then left. Fast.

"Coffee, nectar of the gods!" Pace poured their cups. "Could get used to such service. Only thing missing is a couple aspirin after there's something in my belly."

"You sound better, Cowboy," June said as she put marmalade on a piece of toast. "So, what's on for today? You fit for going back to Central Park and then the museum?"

"Hell, yeah. Gotta get my finisher's jacket. And no way can you miss the blue whale and the elephants at the museum. But maybe we'll snag a cab. Walking that far? Nope. Take it slow. Do what we want, but no more. Sound good?"

SITTING ON THE airplane two mornings later, June reflected on the days in the Big Apple. They'd been able to find cabs when they needed, walked when they wanted. The weather was lovely; and with the right attitude, the lines at the Expo and museum had been a fun, people-watching experience. Dinner at Trattoria Dell'Arte was a wonderful splurge. The restaurant was at the end of Central Park near Columbus Circle, right on their way back to the hotel. Stepping into the restaurant, great aromas enveloped them. They'd never forget the exquisite food nor the intriguing, fun ambience. A large white nose hung on one wall, a huge pair of white lips on another. Coming out of the place afterward, they faced a brass statue that delighted them both: a perfect human butt, a magnificent brass ass, shining on the cheeks where generations of people had given it a good-luck caress. The next day, seeing the "Lion King" had been tremendous fun, with marvelous costumes and music making June's heart sing. A perfect culmination to the trip, doing what Pace said: "what we want, but no more."

Now they were going home. The house would be emptier than ever before, with no canine friend there, but soon it would be the holiday season: Thanksgiving (so different from the devastating pain last year), the wedding, Christmas.

Montana June turned to look at Pace, already sleeping in the seat next to her. He wore his "New York City Marathon Finisher" jacket. Band-aids had replaced the bandages. With his head propped against the window, he seemed to be as comfortable as possible in the cramped seat. June laid her head on his shoulder, closed her eyes and slept.

ARRIVING HOME IN Montana was a literal breath of fresh air. Though June had loved the visit to New York City, she wouldn't ever get used to that many people. Pace's truck was in long-term parking, so they were soon on the freeway then back in the 'Snake again. Heaven. Fun to travel; pure heaven to come home.

Pulling up in the driveway at June's house, Pace jumped out and carried her bag to the door. He walked around to check that all was safe and sound. Assured everything was as it should be, Pace put his hands on June's shoulders and looked in her eyes.

"My June. Thank you…for going along, for caring for me after the race, for being such a sweetheart. I love you." He leaned in, eyes open as his lips touched hers. Gentle, sweet nibbles, then more forceful, more passion. His breath came faster, as did hers. "Hmmm. Better stop there. Honor our promise to give each other time to adjust to being home." He gave another brief kiss and stepped back. "Gotta work tomorrow. Call you in the evening."

She cupped her hand around his cheek. "Thank you for an amazing trip. I never would've experienced all those things without you, and I honestly feel very different from the person who left here, just days ago. I'm going to see Maura tomorrow, since we have wedding plans to talk about, maybe stay the night. See you soon, Cowboy. Thank you."

They hugged again, and Pace left, turning to wave as he walked down the drive to his truck.

Montana June stood in her doorway until his tail-lights disappeared around the bend. It'd been a long day since waking up in the Wyndham that morning—the cab ride to JFK—the flights. What an incredible, exhausting week.

She turned on the gas fireplace. Curling up in the green tufted chair, she leaned back. Unexpected tears started. The day *had* been exhausting, but more than that, there was no sweet Ranger here. She reflected on how much life had changed. After some minutes, she dried her tears, then touched her gold bracelet and imagined Logan's arms around her, comforting and consoling her. June imagined him telling her she was becoming stronger, more resilient, and more compassionate. She was very grateful.

GRATITUDE WAS FOREFRONT in June's mind the next six weeks. Thanksgiving was quiet, with Maura and Richard, Pace and Montana June celebrating at the little house on the mountainside where the elder couple now lived together. The trees still festooned with the handmade wind-chimes clicked and tinkled. Richard's native tools and toys were outside and in. He demonstrated the traditional Indian stick game to the other three, and soon all were laughing as they worked off turkey. The four-way friendship was becoming family.

The weather turned cold enough to make ice luminarias for the wedding. Using buckets of water and weighted bottles that were then removed, they froze large cylindrical blocks of ice, each with an empty core. At the ceremony, bright flickering battery candles in each center would glow, adding more sparkle to the night.

On a series of days when June knew Pace was working, she decided to put up her Christmas tree. She needed plenty of time; there would be lots of memories and, most likely, tears. Logan and June'd loved doing this, and always celebrated finishing by making love next to the lighted tree, with old Crosby or Sinatra Christmas music playing. June needed time alone with these memories.

This year, with snow falling like goose feathers and the fireplace glowing, June set up the tree she'd bought at the Lions Club sales, and attached the fairy lights. The next day came the ornaments. Each one brought memories. June went through a box of tissues, but she realized these tears were not of sadness, rather ones of memory. Her heart was full, not heavy.

Finished, June stepped back. The past was there, but so was the future. She called Pace and asked him to come over to see her finished tree. She put a blanket on the floor near the lowest branches, put on some instrumental holiday music, and waited for her beau to ring the doorbell.

30

Snow fell steadily for three days, stopping mid-afternoon on Christmas Eve day. Friends of the groom from the Lewis and Clark volunteers had shoveled. They'd hung lights on the trees and set plenty of firewood near the fire pit. Inside, tables held heaping platters and an elegant wedding cake. Christmas trees with white lights lined the dance floor. Myriad candles flickered. Montana June gave a final inspection, then went to attend the bride dressing in the yurt next door. The two women spoke little, hearts full. As they dressed and brushed their hair, June kept her ear tuned to activity outside.

All-wheel drive vehicles and trucks were arriving; voices raised in greeting. So soon after the Winter Solstice, it was already dusk. Evening deepened as the guests gathered by the fire. The musicians wielding a guitar, banjo, fiddle, and bodhran—a handheld Celtic drum—had tuned up. Music began.

Time neared. June stood in the open door of the darkened yurt looking at the group by the fire. Many friends had come, even though it was Christmas Eve, a testament to the good people being married this day. June looked from the fire to the sky as the first star of evening twinkled above the mountains to the east. *Logan, bring your blessings and your presence here tonight.*

June watched Richard Donner step from an RV and walk toward the fire. He wore jeans, cowboy boots, and a leather jacket over a wool vest and flannel shirt. At his neck was a bolo tie with a slide of elk ivories, an early wedding present from his bride. He walked with a straight back, his white hair shining in the glow of firelight. As he neared the fire, the guests stopped talking and musicians increased their volume, finishing the last notes of the song. Pace stepped forward to shake Richard's hand and stand beside him.

In the silence that remained after the bodhran and fiddle riffed to climax, the fire crackled. Above, the sky was the color of a dusky plum; more stars sparkled. The woman playing the bodhran started a steady, slow thrumming, like a beating heart.

This was the signal. Montana June began the slow walk to the fire, through the aisle lined with ice luminarias. Pace told her later that his breath caught in his throat—he'd never seen her so beautiful. Her hair, braided to dry then brushed out, lay over her shoulders like a rippling mantle of gold. Her denim skirt brushed her boots; she wore a shawl of evening colors: gold, white, purple, teal and midnight blue. She held a fir branch coupled with red berries, tied with a long golden ribbon. June stepped to the fire, then turned back to face uphill. The door of the yurt opened again and all eyes went to the bride.

Maura walked as if she were a goddess. She was covered head to toe with a cape of swirling gold and white, its large hood over her hair. She walked with slow, regal steps toward Richard between the flickering vases of ice; her face glowed with love and joy. The fire paled in comparison.

The bodhran increased its tempo; the fiddle joined in. Richard took Maura's arm and they turned to the officiant. The music trilled, rose, and ended in a triumphant descant.

Darkness deepened as the vows were spoken. Flames from the fire danced. When the rings were exchanged and Richard leaned in to kiss his bride, the musicians began again, this time with Beethoven's "Ode to Joy." As Richard increased his kiss, Maura's hood fell off the back of her head, uncovering her long auburn hair sparkling in the firelight as if stars had fallen into it. The guests burst into applause. June cheered—cried—touched her gold bracelet and looked up at the sky.

Richard and Maura broke their embrace to include June and Pace, and then all the guests. When the communal hug broke, the crowd moved to the waiting warmth of the Center. The wedding feast began.

MUSIC FLOURISHED AND Pace pulled June closer, finishing the dance's last twirl. The six couples on the dance floor all stopped and clapped, beamed at each other and the musicians.

"Holy Hannah!" June wiped her face with one of Helena's hankies. "My feet maybe never touched the floor. You, Cowboy, are a fantastic dancer."

Pace bowed. "My June…one of many hidden talents. Now, how 'bout a beer and a sit-down?" He guided June to their table, then went to the keg of KettleHouse Coldsmoke. As Pace returned, handing June her beer, Richard took the microphone from the musicians and tapped its surface, calling attention to himself.

"My friends. Your presence here, on this happiest of all my days, is a true gift. That you gave up your holiday traditions to join us tonight speaks to our hearts. Please know, if you choose to leave now, we cherish your gift of time. If you stay until dawn, be aware this bridal couple will long be…enjoying…our bed by that time." He raised an eyebrow, pausing for the laughter. "Allow me to say this: if any of you think because this groom is ancient and his beautiful bride a woman of a certain age, the fires of spring do not burn within, I can only wish you the joy and passion with which we face our marriage." Cheers interrupted Richard. He bowed toward Maura, who, in her simple ivory gown, curtsied in return.

"Now, one more thing we have not shared even with closest family. We will be spending New Year's Eve, a short week away, on our honeymoon, traveling in South America. We plan to be gone a full year. Tonight is our farewell party. Keeping this secret was not Maura's choice. I have reasons for the odd farewell." His glance swept every person in the room. "So, family of my heart. Dance, celebrate, eat, and when it is time, drive with care to your warm Christmas houses. Hold our love, as we will yours, until our safe return."

With these last words, Maura joined Richard at the mic, kissed him, then turned to the musicians and raised her hands. They broke into a reprisal of "Ode to Joy" and again the crowd cheered.

Maura and Richard walked straight to Montana June and Pace. June knew she was staring open-mouthed, but couldn't close it.

Maura reached June and hugged her hard. "Darling girl. I see you are simply gobsmacked with our news. And small wonder. Do you hate us for not telling you in private?"

June swallowed, gulping down a sob. "Mom. I'll miss you terribly. When did you get this idea? Why didn't you tell us?"

Richard's soft voice wasn't audible over the music and dancers. He gestured to a far corner, where an old-fashioned settee and chairs made up a frontier-type living space. With the women settled on the couch, Richard and Pace took the easy chairs.

Richard spoke. "Montana June, the blame is mine. Maura and I have spoken of this for some months now, and she wanted to include you in the plans. But I believed with you just coming out of your grief, Maura's leaving would cause you sadness. I wanted you to rejoice with us in our wedding, no cloud over it. Forgive me."

June, recovering, reached over and squeezed Richard's knotted fingers. "Richard. Of course. Where'd the idea come from?"

"I believe the current term is 'bucket list.' With the companionship of my bride,"—Richard nodded at the glowing woman—"I will finally pursue this life-long dream. Together we will see the Amazon and volunteer in a village in Chile, while we still have the ability."

Maura hugged June's shoulders, then leaned forward, resting her forearms on her knees. She looked at the men, then turned to June. "To be honest, it's something I've always wanted to do, too, even with Logan's father, but never followed through on. Now I'm excited to be going with Richard. The worst of it is, for the first months, we'll be pretty off-grid. But I wouldn't have agreed to go if I wasn't confident that you're now strong in your heart. I can leave knowing you'll be okay."

Pace chimed in. "You can leave with no worries. June's good; she's not alone."

June was too emotional to speak. She smiled, blinking away tears, then lay her head on Maura's shoulder.

They sat this way for a few moments, then Maura patted June's knee. "Goodness." She laughed. "Let's rejoin the party! We aren't leaving for several days. Lots of time to talk. Let's dance!" She kissed June's head, then stood up grabbing Richard's hand. The groom's long legs made short work of the distance to the dance floor, the bride skipping to keep up. They bowed to the musicians and joined the waltz, Maura's gusseted skirt swirling in the turns.

Pace joined June on the couch. They watched the dancers while June collected her emotions. Eventually she said, "Well, this's the end of an era. I hope it'll go well and they'll be home soon. But Maura's right. It's time I took care of myself."

"You aren't alone, my June."

Pace took June into his arms. They sat there, enjoying the music and dancers, while the Christmas lights twinkled.

Sometime later, June became aware enough to notice most of the guests had departed; a group was still putting on coats and hugging the bridal couple. June stood and stretched.

"Well, Cowboy, I guess we'd better start the clean-up. Shall we make a pass through with the garbage bag?"

As they entered the dining area, though, they saw the work was finished. While they'd rested, other guests had seen to the clean-up, a blessing indeed, as a wave of exhaustion engulfed June

Pace walked from tree to tree unplugging lights while the musicians packed their instruments and gathered their coats.

June walked to Maura and embraced her. "Oh! I just remembered. What'll you do with Mr. Mouser? Shall I take him for the year?"

"No, Montana June. But thanks. Richard's asked a friend who needed a place to stay to house-sit for us for the year. Mr. Mouser's already met him and the two hit it off famously. Best for my old pussy-cat if he can remain at home, to say nothing of Nanny. With your permission, I'll give Seth, the house-sitter, your phone number in case anything happens, but there shouldn't be any problems." Maura stretched her arms over her head and let a soft groan escape. "Oh, my. What a marvelous day! Thank you, darling girl, for being my maid of honor. Hasn't it been fun? You must promise, if another wedding's in the works, you'll wait until we return."

"Mom, certainly—but nothing of the sort has even been mentioned. Will I see you before you leave?"

"Of course! Now, where's my groom? It's time for bed. One more hug." Pace and Richard joined the women, and Maura hugged Pace as well. "Drive safely, Pace, and take good care of my girl. We'll see you this week. Merry Christmas!"

Richard kissed June and hugged Pace in farewell.

The four people, parkas over dress clothes, crunched through snow to their vehicles. They beeped their horns in goodbye, turning in opposite directions at the highway.

Relaxed in the passenger's seat of Pace's pickup, June reflected on this Christmas Eve. It'd been a most wonderful wedding, a gorgeous day filled with joy and love. The stars shone overhead. June noticed on the dashboard clock that it was Christmas.

"Merry Christmas, Pace," she said, then looked out the window. *Merry Christmas, my angel.* The black velvet night sky took her words and echoed back only love.

CHRISTMAS DAY, MONTANA June and Pace slept in after the late night before. June had timed the automatic coffeemaker appropriately, so the aroma of coffee awakened her. She stretched and gave a groan of contentment, then opened her eyes to see Pace already awake.

"Good morning, my June. Love watching you sleep." He kissed her.

June lengthened the kiss. "Merry Christmas, Cowboy. Hmmm, that coffee smells good. Let's have a cup in bed. I'll get it." She donned a robe as she padded into the great room, where she turned on the tree lights before going into the kitchen to pour coffee into Santa mugs. This one day, she decided, she wouldn't think of the announcement following the wedding. Nothing would cloud Christmas with Pace.

On the flight from New York, they'd decided presents this year would be limited to help compensate for the expense of the trip; three each and total cost couldn't exceed $30. This tight budget required creative thinking and handwork, but June was pleased with her choices for Pace. She was dying to discover what her presents from him were. All were wrapped, under the tree.

Coffee in bed—leaning against the pillows, with soft light from the muted sky, and tree lights from the great room—felt decadent. Mugs empty, they scooted back under the blankets.

"Well, Cowboy." A smile crinkled the corners of June's eyes. "If it wouldn't go against our agreement, one more present? The only cost'd be a little energy. You up to the task?"

"Hmmm…let's see," he said, nipping a tiny bite on her earlobe, "perhaps." He leaned over, placed his mouth on her nipple and buzzed. She giggled.

When it was time to open the *other* presents, June was fully awake and content. "I'll get the cinnamon rolls and coffee. Meet you in the great room."

Pace put on Christmas music then pulled a square, flat package from under the tree. True to form, Pace had wrapped the package in a brown paper bag. He put it handy by the green tufted chair, and then organized the rest of the packages. "How do you want to start?" he asked as June brought in breakfast.

"Just grab any of them. You first."

Pace opened a large box, which contained a pair of slippers June had knitted for him of a hardy, deep teal yarn. He put them on over his socks, stuck out his legs and admired the slippers. "Gorgeous! Your skills continue to amaze."

June opened hers and was thrilled to discover a photograph of the two of them at the Fourth of July picnic. She didn't remember it being taken. One of Pace's friends had snapped the shot when they were watching the fireworks, and both Pace and June were staring up at the sky, smiling, eyes glowing—a perfect photo in a simple frame.

The next present Pace opened was a copy of the Little Golden Book, *The Poky Little Puppy*. He started laughing so hard coffee came out his nose."How'd you know….my favorite book as a kid?"

June, laughing too, said, "Just a happy coincidence I guess. But I figured it'd be a way to celebrate your name. You didn't get named Pace by being poky." Her voice settled. "Well, except when I want you to be, like earlier today in the sack." June winked.

The next gift June unwrapped was an ornament Pace purchased in New York. A big red apple in the center of a gold ring soon hung on the tree in a place of honor right at center front.

Oddly, the last gifts were both hand-drawn certificates. June's allowed Pace to choose his favorite treat, and Pace's entitled June to a full personal massage.

Pace wiggled his eyebrows, sparkled his eyes. "How 'bout we combine these, my June?"

"Mmm." Montana June purred, stretching. "I love massages. The base of the Christmas tree, right after I put the ham in the oven? This'd be a great time for you to practice that Poky Little Puppy thing you're so good at, okay, Cowboy?"

This Christmas ended up being quite satisfactory.

31

The holidays were over. It'd been a whirlwind getting Maura and Richard off on their adventure. Montana June met Seth, the house-sitter, finding him a likable, responsible young man, one of the few paid employees at the Lewis and Clark Travelers' Rest. He was a new-comer to the area, and he and Richard had hit it off. For Seth's hiring process a thorough background check had been done, and Richard felt confident in him.

Now the newlyweds were on their way to their senior tour of the Amazon, followed by their volunteer placement in Chile. June tried to reconcile herself to life without frequent contact with her mother-in-law and friend.

Pace'd spent the nights between Christmas and New Year's with June, but his job was starting earlier in the morning, so he decided to sleep at his own house. June found this to be both a small relief to have time alone again and also somewhat disconcerting. It'd been sweet to share coffee and small talk, the ins and outs of each day.

After taking down the tree—always a tiring chore—June rested with a glass of wine.

Pace was coming over the next day. He'd called while she was packing ornaments, saying there was something he wanted to discuss. June's heart was on a rollercoaster because she *knew* what it would be. During the trip to New York they'd become a couple. Thanksgiving, then the wedding and Christmas—all were happy, romantic, so very beautiful. Each passing day June felt a little more in love with Pace. He was gentle and strong, and obviously loved her; the fact that he'd known Logan made it all seem right. If, as she suspected, Pace proposed, June had decided to accept. She leaned back in the chair and watched the fire dance, content in the thought that soon she wouldn't be alone.

Soon I won't be alone. June allowed that thought to expand. Her craving for children had waned after Logan's death, but a family wasn't impossible. June smiled, then took a sip of her coffee. Pace would be a good father. She spent the rest of the evening, cuddled in her chair, imagining what life would be like with Pace and children.

The next morning, feeling at odds with a small sadness at seeing her newly undecorated house and happy nerves of what was coming, June decided she needed a morale-booster. She called a salon and was able to get right in for a facial and hair appointment, a rare indulgence. The joy of being pampered, the luxury of hot towels relaxing her face, and the new hair trim and style increased June's sense of well-being, of joy and contentment.

THE WIND WAS stronger and the temperature plummeting by the time Pace was due to arrive. He said he'd be coming straight from work, so June had a pot of stew ready to serve him. She sang as she set the table and put a loaf of crusty bread in the oven to warm. The fireplace was on, some quiet piano music playing; June walked around the house lighting candles in each room. As she began to worry he'd been held up, his truck rolled into the drive-way. Glancing in the mirror she fluffed her hair, then opened the door.

"Hey, there, Cowboy! I've missed you. Come out of the storm." June hugged him, cold parka and all. "Hmmm, you smell good, all outdoorsy." Pace took off his coat; his uniform was rumpled from the day's work.

"Speaking of smelling good, whatever's on the stove smells wonderful, my June." He held June away so he could look at her. His smile was tired. "You look different....Hair cut?"

"Hmm-hmm," June murmured. "You hungry?"

"Hell yes...always. Didn't expect you to cook tonight, though. Something we need to talk about."

Her voice held a smile. "Cowboy, time enough for that later. Let's get some hot stew into you."

While they ate, she kept up a patter of small talk. Pace appeared quite distracted. He ate faster than usual, then jumped up and started to take care of the dishes.

"Oh, leave those, Pace. I'll do them later. Are you staying tonight? Let's take a glass of wine into the great room and sit by the fire," June said, putting her bowl in the sink.

"No wine for me, June. You have some though....Listen, let's go sit...this's been hanging over my head, driving me crazy all day."

That sounded ominous, not at all like a marriage proposal. She followed him in and sat in the green tufted chair while he stood in front of the fire.

"Ah, hell," Pace said, facing away from her. "June, I've got bad news….Better say it and be done with it." But then he stopped talking. He ran his hands through his hair and turned his back to the fire. His eyes looked sad. His face was drawn.

"Well, whatever it is we can work it through together." Ice ran through June's veins. Her first thought was that he was ill; she didn't know if she could face that again. "Please, just tell me."

"My June." Pace squatted down in front of her chair and took her hands in his. "Last night Cindy called."

"Cindy? Who's that?"

"Cindy…you know, my ex. She's been in prison, right? Well, last fall, during the FWP conference in New Mexico, I went there. Hadn't seen her in years. Guess I was curious to see how she was in prison. Shouldn't have done that. She's just been released. They sprung her early for some god-forsaken reason. Stupid….Anyway, she called, desperate, wants me to go help her. Feel kinda obligated."

"Wait. I don't understand." June pushed his hands away. "She's your *ex*-wife, right? For how many years now? And you saw her and didn't tell me?"

"Well, the divorce was finalized five years ago. Haven't lived together for more than ten years, but…damn it…I might've implied we'd been divorced that long. And last fall, well…you and I weren't really together yet, remember? Anyway, she's out of prison and needs some help. She's got no friends."

"You are not serious. You can't be ready to run to her. How about the jerk she ran off with? Why didn't she call him?"

"He's in prison, too, for the mess they got into, and not getting out anytime soon."

June's breath came faster as her temper flared. She jumped up from the chair, pushing past him. He lost his balance from his squatting position and fell backward onto his butt. June stalked from the fireplace to the kitchen wall and back again as Pace clambered to his feet.

"Are you still in love with her? That's why you're running to her aid?" Her fist clenched.

"Ah, shit. No, June. I told you, all that was over long ago." He reached his hands toward June. "But, feel a responsibility to help her… get her on her feet somehow."

"Are you bringing her back here? I don't want to meet her. No way in hell." June's voice was tight and low. With her fist she punched her forehead, punched the sideboard. She strode back and forth across the floor.

"No, 'course I wouldn't bring her back here. That's why it'll take a while. Gotta get her settled, help her find an apartment, maybe a job. She's in Albuquerque now, and that's where I'm going."

"When? When, Pace?"

"Have to work through this week. Gotta take unpaid leave since all my vacation's used up. I'll leave Saturday. My boss promised he'll save my job. Truck's ready. Don't know how long it'll be, but…I'll call you every day."

June's marginal grasp on self-control shattered. "Call me? You'll *call* me? When you're back with your ex, taking care of her, and what, living with her while you do it? Oh, please don't bother about me. There's no need to call. Not every day. Not ever. You better leave."

"My June—" he began.

"Don't call me that! I am not your June. Here I had my hair done and got all pretty for you because I thought, oh, shit, stupid me, I thought you were coming over to propose tonight!" Incandescent rage made her voice ugly. "Leave. Just leave."

"Oh, God. June….So, so sorry." Pace's voice cracked. "Listen…it shouldn't happen this way."

Tears streamed down June's hot face. She thrust his parka at him, pushing it into his chest with each word. "I. Do not. Want. To see you. GET OUT!"

Pace opened the door. The wind pushed it, banging it against the frame. Outside a blizzard howled. He turned around, reached a hand back to June.

"GET OUT NOW!" She slammed the door in his face and locked it, then turned to run to bed, but was stopped by a burning smell coming from the kitchen. The stew had been left on the stove, scorching to the bottom of the pot. She pushed it off the burner, yelping at the heat. Pivoting to the sink to douse her hand with cold water, she picked up a bowl with the other hand to put it in the dishwasher, but it slipped and fell to the floor, shattering. June screamed. Pounded her hands on her head. Jerked the knob to turn off the stove. Slapped the light switch. Ran to her bed and collapsed, tears taking over.

Such a fool, she thought over and over. *Such a fool. How could I be such a bloody fool.*

OVER THE NEXT couple days, Pace left multiple voice-mail messages, none of which June returned. She listened and deleted them. The messages started out being apologetic: Pace was sorry he'd mishandled the announcement of his upcoming trip; he told her all would be well, she shouldn't worry. But as time went on, the messages got more terse, less self-deprecatory. His last message said it was obvious June was angry at him, but she shouldn't be. He wasn't going back to Cindy, he was simply helping her get on her feet. He'd return.

On Friday evening, he stopped by. June opened the door to his knock, but though it was quite cold out, she didn't invite him in. She stood in the doorway, arms crossed.

Pace's forehead wrinkled and his eyes looked sad when he saw her. He sighed. "June, couldn't leave town without seeing you again, try one last time. Maybe you got a right to be angry and hurt. Just wish you'd see reason. I promise you I'll be back. Okay," he said when he saw her scowl, "okay, then I promise myself. But know...I love you."

He reached and touched her arm. The touch was enough to marginally soften June's resolve, and she moved forward to give him a quick hug before stepping back.

Her voice was hard, biting off words. "Pace, I am, as you say, angry. No, I'm pissed off as all hell. And I'm hurt. Worse, I'm crushed. I don't understand why you need to go to a woman who treated you like shit, but you obviously do. I won't hold you. Do what you need to do."

With that, June stepped back and closed the door. She leaned her head on the door and added, "And remember that I love you, too."

32

For Montana June, January had always been difficult. With the holidays over, the winter seemed to drag on forever—no end in sight. This year, record-breaking snow fell, and June shoveled her long sidewalk and driveway several times each day. Every snowfall, every lonely dawn, every solitary evening weighed heavily. Many days passed when she saw no one.

She received a postcard from Maura and Richard saying they'd arrived in-country and had headed off-grid. Seeing Maura's handwriting sank her further into melancholy. Tears. Still tears. Crying hadn't yet fixed a thing and didn't now.

June called Helena, hoping a long talk would help. Helena filled her in on improvements with Arno; her store had blossomed, keeping her so busy her weight was dropping; Toby's affair fizzled and he'd apologized to Helena, giving her the upper-hand for a while which she made the most of. In fact, she was planning their 25th anniversary cruise. "Have to rush, Juney, late for Helena Teacup. Byee!" Helena sounded very happy. Hurray for her.

That evening, June opened a bottle of wine. She sat by the fire, near Ranger's empty bed, holding her journal, hoping to start writing again; she hadn't since the dark days after Logan died. Now, the darkness was back, but no words flowed.

One thing to write about was Pace leaving just when she'd fallen in love and begun thinking again about having children.

And she wanted to write about missing Logan. She poured another glass of wine and opened her journal and began to read. Before she knew it, the bottle was empty.

(excerpt from Montana June's journal)
I dreamed of Logan. This time he was
crying, and I held him, trying to comfort him.
All I could say was, "Don't cry, baby. Please
don't cry." Is he grieving too? Does he
remember his beautiful Montana and cry
for me being alone in it?
I just don't have it in me to go on anymore
without Logan. Sometimes
the thought of drifting off to sleep and
never waking up is so tempting.

THE NEXT MORNING, June awoke with a headache, furious to find another four inches of snow had fallen overnight. "God damn it. I'm so over this snow." Once, long ago, she'd been glad to have Ranger to talk to, since talking to yourself seemed flat-out crazy. She didn't worry about sounding crazy anymore. She took aspirin, downed a couple cups of coffee, and went outside to shovel. Yet again.

Soon the driveway was done, and she got into the work, moving faster, hefting shovels of snow, even singing. She moved to the sidewalk, speeding up. Suddenly, without warning her feet were in the air. Her shovel went flying, shoulders downward. June fell hard. Her head was in the street, her back jacked on the edge of the curb. Excruciating pain. *Holy shit, did I break my back?* For a long time, moving wasn't possible. After catching her breath, she made assessments, wiggling one foot, the other. *Okay, back isn't broken...how do I get up?* She managed to roll over and—grasping the shovel—leverage herself up. The shovel became a crutch as she hobbled to the house.

Gasping in sharp, almost silent shrieks—*shit! Shitshitshit*—she snaked out of her wet coat and boots, pain slowing the process. "Okay. Back to bed. Rest," she mumbled. In tiny movements she reached the bed—lowered herself down—closed her eyes.

Waking a couple hours later, she knew she'd have to go to the doctor. *Pace, where are you? Oh, God, Cowboy, this would be so much easier if you were here.* She wished she could call him for help, like in the old days. No one, now, to call.

With her back seizing in pain, standing took forever. She managed to get her coat over her shoulders, but boots weren't feasible; she slipped her feet into scuffs and shuffled outside, gasping. *'Least I shoveled this first. Couldn't get through snow in scuffs.* Her Jeep was in the garage, but its high seat seemed inaccessible. Thinking through the pain, she nudged an upside-down bucket over and used it as a step. Once inside, she backed out, then turned onto the street. Thank goodness,

NowCare was close. She inched the 4-wheel drive through unplowed streets. Any accident at this stage would be disastrous.

HOURS LATER, HOME again, June was utterly exhausted. After X-rays, the doctor had told her no bones were broken, but it'd take many days for the assaulted soft tissue to heal. He prescribed heavy-duty pain pills. She downed one, got an ice pack per the doc's orders, and sat in the green tufted chair.

The medication worked like magic. June loved the floaty feeling. She knew her back was damaged; pain was somewhere in the distance, but she just didn't care. A spiderweb glistened in the corner of the window, and she imagined being a spider, climbing each tiny thread. Her hiccuping giggles seemed to echo in the empty room. And that was funnier still.

Ice packs weren't June's idea of fun. The doc had said keep one on the damaged area for fifteen minutes, take it off for a while. Repeat. June'd bought three ice packs at the drugstore when she got her pain meds, so she alternated them to always have one ready. But dang it, they were cold. The fireplace and a cup of hot spiced wine counteracted the chill.

The night after her fall, June screamed awake, her heart pounding. Jeb Murdoch—huge, more powerful than he'd been in life—yanked his belt around her waist, cutting her in two. Her screams echoed (were they only in her dream?) and she gasped, trying to get enough oxygen. The pain in her back, where nightmareJeb had been squeezing, screamed, too. Moaning, she released her death-grip on the sheets.

Breath wasn't coming. *Okay, Juney, Pace once said to concentrate on breathing out slowly.* As she imagined her exhales become a visible trickle, she relaxed enough to get oxygen in. Her heart slowed, but her back was agonizing. She reached to the bedside table and opened the pain meds. One in, a swig of water. Soon she'd have to get up to pee, but right now that wasn't possible. Pain retreated under the pharmaceutical fog. Sometime later, June could roll to her side and gingerly sit on the edge of the bed before standing.

Over the next several days, Montana June fell into a routine that, if not quite what the doctor ordered, helped keep the pain at bay. She kept her back iced and her feet close to the fireplace. In the mid-afternoons, she'd make a mug of hot spiced wine. Not only did that help the pain meds work, but the warmth and aroma were soothing. With no Ranger to take care of, no Pace or Maura to talk to, and certainly no Logan by her side, she'd doze the afternoon away. By evening, another mug or two of mulled wine allowed her to trudge to bed and sleep.

The days melted together. One midmorning, June had to turn on the TV to see what the date was. "When's the last time I knew? Doesn't matter, I guess," she said aloud, giggling as she changed the channel.

Waking later from a nap, she mumbled, "Hmmm, hunger. Interesting sensation." She left the TV on and shuffled toward the kitchen. Her image reflected in the big mirror on the wall of the great room was almost unrecognizable. Her long braid had loosened. She tried to re-braid it, but the nasty smelling rat's nest wouldn't untangle. In the kitchen, June dumped scuzzy water out of a pan in the sink and sluiced it cleaner. She grabbed the first can she saw in the cabinet, cream of chicken soup. While the soup heated, June scratched at her scalp. The phone rang. She listened as it went to voice mail. Pace, again. His calls had become less frequent, down from one a day at first to one every several days. The messages were similar.

"Hey June? Hope you're at least listening to these messages. All's okay but I miss you. Sure wish you'd call. Goodbye, my June."

June didn't notice her tears until one hissed, landing on the burner. She used her grubby bathrobe sleeve to wipe her face, then poured the soup into a mug, swallowed another pain pill, and lumbered back to the TV.

"So, Pace's doing okay. Good for him. But he's far, far away. If he's not going to be here, I wish he'd—just—fucking—stop—calling." Every call pulled the scab off all over again. In her chair with her mug of gloppy soup, June thought about the call. Pace said "all's okay" there with Cindy. Cinders. Cinders start fires. *Cindycindycinders*. It became a nursery rhyme in her head, and she waved her mug along with it. *Cindycindycinders, ashes ashes we all fall down.*

THE NEXT DAY, Missoula experienced a weather inversion, upper-level air pressure keeping deep cold temperature and dense fog packed into the valley. June couldn't see to the street, let alone the mountain. Her back wasn't healing. In frustration, she searched for the ice packs, finding one in the blankets on her bed, another in the chair by the TV, but had no idea at all where the third one was. She put the soft ice packs in the freezer, took two pain pills, and went back to bed. The phone rang, but she didn't bother listening to the message: Helena, Pace, whoever. She moaned. "Just stop. Leave me the fuck alone." She pulled the blanket over her head and disappeared into the haze of medication.

The next time she woke, it must've been a Saturday, because she discovered a "Marathon Weekend!" of her favorite old crime scene show. June downed a pain pill with wine straight from the bottle and settled in to binge-watch. "What a lucky girl I am! Three marathons in one year. Who'da thunk?" she told the TV. She cackled each time the screen read "Marathon Weekend!" Her last marathon weekend she'd been with Pace in New York City. From masses of people to not one in her life. She woke up sometime in the night in front of the TV, her back screaming, the TV blaring. She jabbed the clicker off and tried to stand. Nope. She slid off the green chair to her knees, then used her forearms for leverage up. Hunched like an old woman, holding on to furniture as she passed, she made her way to the kitchen for a pain pill. None left. *Damn.* The wine bottle was on its side, empty. June grabbed an ice pack from the freezer and shuffled to bed.

The next morning, June called the pharmacy to get the prescription refilled, but they said they couldn't do it without doctor's orders. *Shit.*

COLD. EXCRUCIATING COLD.

Leaden sky matched her mood.

Another day—one after another after so many days—of no light. Unending inversion kept out sun, kept in cold. A slow death, smothering in gray. At least she was outside, the first time in so long. Pain meds had sapped all desire to move; she'd felt bound in quilt batting knowing pain hovered outside the wrappings. When the pills were gone, and the wine was gone, she slept. A long time. Could've been forever.

But now she stood, outdoors. Her back was healing. With no drugs or alcohol in her system, every minute detail of sight and sound scraped her raw senses.

She headed down the path she'd walked each day with Ranger, back when she'd begun to feel vibrant again, when birds sang with a fervor she'd all but forgotten. Now, paltry winter birds huddled in tired bunches, trying to escape the cold. Crusty snow tramped into dirty ice covered the ground. June's soul plummeted. She trudged on.

The path turned near Rattlesnake Creek. The water's force kept open a center channel, with ice hard and deep at the far bank. Constant roiling wavelets under the ice tasseled the edge. Upstream was frozen bank to bank into the clear pastel green of an old Coca-Cola bottle, a sparkling sheen of water flowing over it. Downstream, the creek poured through an ice cave where constricted banks deepened the water. It raised and receded, waves lapping under the shelf of ice.

June struggled to sit on the steep bank of the stream's edge; listened to the siren song of the water. The constant rush. *How long would it take to drown here? Or would the cold kill you first?*

The dark ice cave sucked the roiling water in.

Oblivion—enticing—entrancing. Nothing left to live for.

Churning water gurgled under the ice. Deep. Clear. So very cold. Easy to slide down into the stream. No more crushing grief. No pain. Her boot-heel slipped on the bank, pushing ice chunks into the water. Fascinated, June watched them swirl and turn in the current, get sucked into the ice cave. And then—gone. Just like that. Easy.

She could join them.

Yes.

June's butt froze. Her nose ran, an irritating tickle. She tried—couldn't—reach her pocket for a handkerchief. Scooted back from the bank's edge to stand, found a tissue, blew her nose hard. Attention distracted, suddenly her feet slipped and she was down. Sliding uncontrolled. Her right boot hit the icy water. Hands grabbed snow, found no hold.

Her left leg dug at the bank, boot hooking an embedded tree root, stopping her slide.

Butt on the creek edge; one leg dry, one wet. Brain not comprehending.

The sound of rushing water brought her eyes to the ice cave where the current still sucked in. Montana June's breath exploded in a sob.

Her right foot ached, freezing in her boot. She stood, stomping out what water she could. Her back hurt. Movement now was mandatory. She scrambled up the bank, not looking back at the roaring water. Her body was thoroughly chilled, leg soaked, butt wet, head not focusing.

She started down the path, blood returning to her veins and brain with each step.

The path narrowed. Thorny shrubs—wild roses, a delight in the spring—reached for June's coat and snagged her scarf. The creek's sound was swallowed by dense tangles of briars and fallen limbs. Above, skeletons of cottonwoods in colors of smoke and charcoal used their boney trunks to hold up the lowering sky. In this winter-scape of grays and blacks, patches of red showed through branches where the mountain ash trees still held their berries. June saw them as smears of blood on gray flesh. Fallen berries were drops of crimson—berries of blood. The smothered sound of the stream echoed the pounding of blood in her ears. Her breath came ragged. Blood. Blood. Blood. A crow screamed. Her nerve shattered.

In terror, she ran. The icy path was no sure footing. Fog obscured her way. She escaped the park. Careened across the street to her house. At her door, she struggled, but the door wouldn't open, wouldn't open, wouldn't open. *Shit, where's the key?* On its chain at her neck. She tore through her scarf and zipper. Found the key. Wouldn't fit. Again. Again. Wrong key. Wrong lock. Wrong door. Nightmare. Try once more. At last the door opened; she fell through, slamming it behind her.

June ran to the green tufted chair by the fireplace and collapsed into it, pulled her hood over her face. Tears covered her cheeks. Her breath slowed. She was home. Warm. Empty, but warm.

June came to sometime later; it was full dark outside. A bath, perhaps.

Water burbling into the tub mimicked the siren song June had heard in the frozen stream, the call to succumb to icy death. She stepped into the steaming water, knowing her decision to kill herself changed when the nightmare-slide toward the creek became a pull of death and push of fear. But she grieved for the lost opportunity. *It's not over, yet. I can still do it.*

When June had last thought of suicide, coming home from the aborted lunch with Cara, she imagined driving off the road into the Bitterroot. Then, the thought of Ranger at home had been enough to keep her from spinning the steering wheel. Now, Ranger was dead. Maura and Richard were gone. Pace was gone. Logan was still and always dead. Death was the place where all comfort lay. June didn't have the strength to fight.

Life was pain.

Slipping beneath the surface of the water in the tub would be easy.

Tears streamed down her cheeks, over her breasts into the water. Even this decision took too much energy. She put her head back against the edge of the tub as the hot water relaxed her body. *Tomorrow I'll decide.*

When the water cooled, Montana June dried herself off and climbed into bed. She didn't talk to Logan; she did *not* want to hear what he would answer. Logan would want her to be strong, keep going, live to fight another day. June had to decide on her own.

33

When Montana June awoke, the light through her closed eyelids was so bright she thought she *had* died. Unearthly pure brilliance. She opened her eyes and looked up at the window; no, not heaven—Mount Jumbo bathed in sunshine reflecting on snow, brighter than summer.

The inversion had lifted.

June stood so she could see the backyard. Everything was coated in hoarfrost—diamonds might've fallen from the sky. She walked from window to window, staring first at spruce branches, then Oregon grape leaves, the trellis, the window frames. The whole world sparkled.

"What on earth?" Montana June's voice cracked as she continued to wander and gaze. "Logan? Is this from you?" From the shocking despair of yesterday to this. Though she wouldn't speak to Logan last night, he must've had something to say to her today. June put her hand flat against an icy window. The frost melted and ran to the sill; drops pooled and she wiped them away. Water yesterday had offered an escape. Now, outside, crystalized water displayed a different option. *Okay, Logan, I hear you. I'll try to take the bad with the good, for a while. For you. For as long as I can.* She touched her gold bracelet, stared out to the wonder-scene for another moment, then turned to her closet and dressed. At the door she added coat, boots and scarf, and ran outside. The air danced with ice crystals.

It was—simply—beautiful. Though white at first glance, she could see blues, greens, deep reds, and bright yellows in the crystalline ice that coated each needle of the ponderosa, each twig, every bush. June stretched her arms wide and turned in a circle, mesmerized by the shimmering ice show. She wandered into the park, down the path that last night she had run from in terror. The mountain ash berries that looked like droplets of blood mere hours ago now shone like miniature candy apples, each in a clear frozen coating. Up on Mount Jumbo she saw the elk herd near the summit, soaking up the sun's energy.

Too soon, June became cold. The beauty was profound, but the temperature was close to zero; time to go in.

As she turned to the house, from nowhere a dog ran toward her. The dog stopped, saw something in the bushes, became a stealth missile. In the shrubs near June's feet a cat hissed, then arched, hair out in a desperate attempt at making itself look bigger. As June watched in horror, the dog lunged into the shrub, grabbed the cat by its neck, gave two violent shakes, and then tossed the now limp body to the snow. June screamed but was far too late to save the cat. In the distance, a man called for the dog. Finished, the dog picked up his head at his owner's voice and took off down the path. The silence of the attack was chilling.

"Hey, jerk!" June yelled. "Your dog just killed a cat. You better come quick!" Her voice caught. The man didn't respond. *Bastard!* She was alone to deal with this. She fell to her knees in the snow and reached out her hand. The cat was obviously feral and very skinny, except for a swollen belly. As June watched, the swollen belly moved.

"Oh, no. You poor little mama." As June watched, the almost dead cat gave birth to one tiny wet kitten. *Shit. What should I do?*

June, with tender care, picked up the tiny wet body still in its birth-sac, and the now dead mother cat. Her body was still warm, might offer help to this new kitten. June put both cats inside her own coat, and using one finger to rub away the amnion sac, placed the baby at the scrawny teats and hurried home.

She knew there was a veterinarian in the strip mall a half mile away. She didn't take time to call; just clambered with the dead cat and living, mewling newborn into the Jeep and tore off down the street.

Slamming through the door at the vet's office, June got immediate attention. The vet techs called to the back and the veterinarian appeared, all three gathering around June. The vet was tall and very thin, his voice gentle as he took the bundle of coat and cats from June and went into the backroom. The vet tech asked June to sit and wait; soon there would be an answer one way or another.

Later, June was shown back to the surgery. Dr. Marcus told June the kitten was alive, quite a fighter. If June wanted to take it on, he would show her how to feed the female infant. It would take constant attention to do well, feeding every hour or so. Was she devoted enough? Adopting a motherless newborn was an all-encompassing task, one few could handle.

Montana June inhaled, held it, and looked out at Mount Jumbo shining in the winter sun.. Yesterday there'd been no reason to live, nothing in her heart but grief and pain. Now, here was a tiny life she might be able to save. She exhaled and turned to the veterinarian. His kind face seemed full of understanding, whichever option she chose.

"Yes," June told him, "please show me how to take care of this little one. I think she might be my own lifeline."

Dr. Marcus smiled and began the list of instructions.

BACK HOME WITH the tiny new bundle fed by dropper, wrapped in a warm blanket and settled near the fire, Montana June made herself a cup of rose-hip tea from hips she'd harvested in late August. She sat in the green tufted chair, cupping the mug of deep orangey-red liquid, and enjoyed the summer-scented steam. Her new feline charge slept in its nest. June was content in a way she hadn't been since just after New Year's.

A tiny "mew mew" from the blankets on the hearth caught June's attention. She got up and prepared another dropper of kitten formula. Miniscule claws stretched and pulled as the kitten blindly nursed the dropper. She'd need 2 ml of formula at least every two hours for the first several days, then the amount of formula and the time between feedings could both increase. The vet had showed June how to, after each feeding, stroke the kitten's tummy and hindquarters to motivate the little one to eliminate. Then June cleaned her up and continued to pet her. Her white fur was as pure and spiky as the crystals of frost had been this morning.

"Hey, Frosty! Is that your name? Frosty the Snow Kitten? Are we a team, baby girl? All right, I hear you. 'Quit with the talk, Mom, and give me more formula.' Okay, my Frosty girl." June touched the tiny white head, busy at the dropper. With her tummy full, the kitten was again asleep. June realized she should also nap often. Feeding this baby would require setting the alarm clock. Not much solid sleep for a good long while.

June's heart was happy. One tiny life depended on her. She relaxed and drifted off.

34

The snowfalls had slowed to a stop, much to Montana June's relief. Winter was ending. It was March.

The past month had brought profound change. She'd learned to function on little sleep since Frosty needed to be dropper-fed very often. The intervals between feedings lengthened; now June could sleep several hours straight, giving her energy for chores in the day. While she tackled the first of these, a thorough housecleaning, June decided to drop all prescription drugs. Anti-depressants, intended to help her get through the dark times after giving up the pain pills, also clouded the bright times. She'd always be haunted by the darkest day when the icy stream had beckoned—the agonizing loneliness, the desperate sadness that froze her bones and soul—but she knew if she wanted to heal it would be through her own strength, not pharmaceuticals. And no alcohol, for the time being.

June also started writing again. Her journal now overflowed with descriptions and drawings of her new kitten. Frosty was the perfect medicine. The little ball of white fluff needed June, and her heart grabbed onto that with joy. When Frosty's eyes opened about ten days after her arrival, June's excitement felt uncontrollable. She called her sister, going on until Helena cried uncle and said, "Okay, doll, I get it! You're thrilled with that new baby. When you have a human one, then I'll listen. Now I gotta run, 'kay? Byee!"

Frosty's eyes were bright blue, and Dr. Marcus said even though all kittens' eyes start out blue, this kitten's might remain blue, since she was very white. When Frosty was three weeks old, June started mixing the formula with canned kitten food. Frosty licked the warm mixture right off her finger. Bit by bit, Frosty the Snow Kitten was developing the skills to become more independent.

Each time June left the house, Frosty was tucked inside her little kennel-crate, nested in towels. Someday the kitten could wander the house at will, but not yet. She had the heart of a lion and the curiosity of, well, a cat, but was still too tiny.

The early March sun was weak overhead, barely enough at noon to poke through the clouds. June decided she better take advantage of the marginal weather to get to the grocery store. Glancing in the mirror as she put on her coat, June was pleased to see herself looking happy and sparkly. She smiled at the reflection, then turned to capture Frosty, climbing on the hearth.

"Okay, Frostygirl," June said, securing the kennel-crate, "I'll be back soon."

June walked down the sidewalk toward the strip mall that held both the grocery store and Frosty's vet. The day was chilly and gray, but something gave a hope of spring. *What is it? Birds. That's it.* Birds singing their hearts out. Something else too—June's deep breaths brought in a faint, pungent smell of green things; under all the dead leaves and brown grass, new sprouts were forming, ready to jump up at the first hint of sun.

A neighbor's mountain ash tree appeared oddly misshapen. As June walked past, hundreds of bohemian waxwings erupted from the branches. She stopped to watch. They flew in a huge, ever-changing mass. She hadn't seen any yet this year, and she stood in complete awe, watching as—without audible communication—the birds flew their intricate, choreographed dance, now in circles and ribbons, now in smokey mists changing to dark tight bundles. They swooped and soared, then descended, engulfing a another tree full of berries. June turned to look at the last: not one berry remained.

Montana June resumed her walk toward the grocery store, knowing she'd witnessed one of nature's wonders.

At the grocery store, June gathered her necessary items, pushing her cart up and down the aisles. Walking to the store had two purposes. It involved more exercise, but also limited the quantity of purchases: no heavy bottles of wine. She picked up a new journal, kale, chicken breasts. Some eggs. As she wandered up the dairy aisle, she saw a woman in front of her who looked almost familiar. No, it couldn't be. It was.

"Cara! How are you?" June said as she neared. Cara'd changed since June saw her at the riverside restaurant last fall. Then, Cara's hair had been bright brown spikes, her make-up and clothes too youthful. Now, her longer hair was coming in gray. Her face looked gray and drawn, too. She wore sweats.

"Oh. Hi, June. Yeah. Um, I'm fine. How're you?" She pushed her hair away from her face with the back of her hand.

"I'm really okay. I live in the 'Snake now, did you know? Tell me about you though. What's up? How was your cruise?"

"Oh, the cruise was fun. You know, I'd moved in with Ludwig, and things were going fantastic. At least, I thought they were. But, shit, June, Ludwig ended up being a real prick. He dumped me for some young slut. When we got back from the cruise, and by the way, I paid his airfare, he hooked up with this bitch and I'm out on my own. Can't believe it. After all I went through, leaving my husband for him and everything."

June reached toward Cara's arm, stopping as Cara jerked back. "I'm so sorry. Are you back with Peter then? You two were such a great couple."

"No, Peter moved on. I called him after Ludwig the Dudwig dropped me, but Peter said I'd hurt him too badly. Our divorce was final just before the cruise, when I thought it was the right thing to do. How could I've been so stupid."

The last words weren't a question. Cara dug a tissue from her sweatshirt pouch and blew her nose. "I saw you and Maura, you know, in that restaurant. I just didn't want to talk. Things weren't so peachy then. Shouldn't have wasted any more energy on the Dud." She shook her head sharply. Her mouth pulled back into a brittle smile. "I'm moving to California. Yeah, a new start! Moving in with my mother in her adults-only retirement village. I'll be one of the younger women! Won't be an old bag, like the Dud called me, the bastard." Her face collapsed. She sucked in a sob. "Gotta go, June."

Cara jerked her shopping cart away. June managed to say, "Goodbye, good luck. Call if you want to talk," before Cara turned the corner. June shook her head at her one-time friend's misfortune. Cara had thought she could grab on to youth by trying to be something she no longer was. Poor Cara. June sighed as she went to the check-out counter.

THE LATE WINTER sun lit the floor with a welcome warmth. June sat in a sunbeam while Frosty the Snow Kitten jumped over her legs, attacking her toes. Frosty was now four weeks old and had just learned how to play. Her white fur and shocking blue eyes made June chuckle.

June's cell phone rang with Helena's ring-tone.

"Hiya, Sis! What's up in the great warm south?" June asked.

"Well, not all that much, doll, so I thought I'd give you a call. How's things with you?"

"Absolutely adorable, at least this little kitten is. You get the photos I sent to you?"

"Yep. You'd think she was a human baby the way you go on, but I'm glad something's making you happy. You sound great."

"Yeah, I feel tons better, getting lots of exercise. So, what's up?"

"June-doll, I'm glad you're doing well. But you've had one catastrophe after another, and one hell of a bad winter, right after the worst winter of your life. I've been thinking, and you may not like what I have to say."

June changed the phone to her other hand. This sounded serious.

Helena continued. "Okay, so here's the deal, Juney. When I came to Montana, you pushed me past my emotional block with my family. I figured Toby was having an affair—and I knew Arno was turning into a little shit. I was using those things as an excuse to start a nasty slide into problem drinking. And you, doll, stopped that cold. You helped me when I didn't want help."

"Yeah. I remember, believe me. But so?"

"Well, turn-about's fair play. You're probably not going to want help either, but I've got an idea. You remember Sarah's club she and her friend started called Matrix Table?"

Helena reminded June about the club Grandpa Max's Sarah started. She was the main push for it back in the 1950s when housewives' focus was truly the *house*; intellectually stimulating work was available but rare. In that era, wages for women were far below those of men, and women were often treated as second-class citizens. The main goal of the organization was to gather women from all walks of life who wanted more. Each time they gathered, they'd dress to the nines, for fun, but also to reinforce that dress, comportment, and the way they treated each other were important. At the yearly banquet, only women were invited, and a well-known female motivational speaker was always on the docket. It was Sarah's idea to call this club Matrix Table, saying it was the perfect name for two reasons. First, "matrix" was a Latin term connected to the word "matron," and they were all that, women of a certain age with families who depended on them. But more importantly, a matrix is a support system, a scaffolding upon which something is built. In this case, the matrix supported each of them toward the betterment of all women. It was a cause Sarah had supported until her death.

June let Helena finish, then said, "Yeah, I remember seeing her all dressed up on her way to Matrix Table. Got a box of her records from it downstairs."

"So, doll. I keep in contact with someone who knew Sarah—that's who I visited that afternoon I was on my own in Missoula. And guess what? Matrix Table is still going! In fact, they've joined with a regional group that's getting ready for the Northwest Convention of Business Women. So, here's the deal. They're looking for speakers for the April convention. I suggested you. You'd be perfect. The theme for this year's convention is 'From Tragedy to Strength.' Right up your alley."

"I can't believe you did that! No. Won't do it. Can't. I haven't given a speech since I quit teaching. Unh-unh. Nope."

"Now, just do me a favor and think about it. They like the idea of a local speaker. That'd be you, doll. I'll give you the name and number of my contact there." Helena insisted June get a piece of paper and write the info down. "Okay, now I've planted the seed, I gotta run. I'm late for Helena Teacup. Talk to you soon. Byee!" and Helena was gone.

Frosty jumped at June's chest. June picked up the ball of fur and held her in front of her own face. "Frosty? Could I do it? Whatcha think?"

The idea of speaking in front of an audience was scary, but exciting. June walked around the house, fiddling with pillows, dusting, thinking. After some time, she got her journal and wrote the title "From Tragedy to Strength" at the top of a page. She started jotting down notes of things she'd learned since Logan's diagnosis. As she wrote, she began to realize perhaps she did have some thoughts worth sharing. By the time she ran out of ideas, she'd covered the front and back of a page. It was time to feed the little white monster.

After Frosty was fed and tucked in for another nap, June donned her coat and went for a walk. The weather was bright. Spring was teasing, coming close.

June walked up the valley, past where she and Maura had walked in the race last August. She hiked uphill toward the mountains of the Rattlesnake Wilderness. As it got steeper, she slowed, conscious of a minor twinge in her back. *Oh, God. Who am I kidding? I'm a wreck. Nothing I have is worth saying.*

June thought about all that'd happened this past year. Only a matter of months after Logan's death, when she'd just started to enter back into some type of social activity she experienced the near-rape, which still caused nightmares. Compared to that, the incident with Helena's drinking was minor. Right after the anniversary of Logan's death, Ranger died. Then the lightning strike. The forest fire. Things seemed to improve with the wedding and Christmas, but then Maura and Richard left. Pace abandoned her. She nearly destroyed her back. She spiraled so far into depression that suicide seemed an option.

Her steps slowed further as each memory made her sadder. Continuing to think along these lines would set her right back into that depression. *Who am I to speak to others about strength?* She stopped and leaned her forehead against the rough trunk of a ponderosa. She swallowed the threatening tears and inhaled. A scent of vanilla came from the jigsaw bark on the tree and brought back a shred of memory. Years ago, Logan had used his Montana-made knife to pry off an especially beautiful chunk of bark for her. June mentioned how the two colors in the bark were like the variegated colors in the knife blade.

"See, Junebug," Logan had said, "here's how they make the knives. Bars of two kinds of steel are pounded flat together, heated in a forge, folded, pounded, heated, folded, over and over again. And then they're pounded thin, cut and sharpened. All this rough treatment turns the two types of steel into one, makes the blades harder than either metal had been alone, turns it into some of the best knives around."

She inhaled the vanilla scent again, then pushed away from the tree, turned and looked across the valley. *Is this what's happened to me?*

I've taken the worst times with some good times, been pounded and blasted, heated and honed. Maybe now I'm stronger—sharper—better than before. The bad and good parts became one. Has it been worth it? Sure can't change it, so I guess it's gotta be worth it. From now on…stronger, sharper, better.

She took a deep breath, thinking about her speech. Could she take her notes and turn it all into something worth saying? Yes. She decided to talk to the woman Helena had mentioned. If they still wanted her, Montana June would do it.

An hour later, June returned home. Her legs were tired, and she was cold. Frosty the Snow Kitten heard the key in the door and was mewing and scratching, anxious to be released from her crate.

"Okay, okay, little button. I'm home. Let me get a drink of water and then I'll feed you, you cute little monster."

With Frosty fed and curled up in her lap, June saw she'd missed a call on her cell. The message made the hair on June's neck raise. A familiar voice, tight with stress.

Richard.

35

The message was brief: "Montana June, it's Richard. I called as soon as possible, so if you see the news you would know we are safe. Do not worry. We survived the earthquake and are coming home. Maura sends her love, as do I. I will call again soon."

June looked at the clock and saw the evening news would soon air, so she turned on her TV. The lead story was about a huge earthquake in Chile. The images showed devastating destruction. Many bodies were being uncovered. June's eyes filled with tears as she watched; she was very grateful Richard had called before she saw this broadcast. At least her two people were safe and on their way home.

June didn't sleep well that night. News images kept running through her memory, into her dreams.

The next morning, June had poured her coffee and set down Frosty's food when her cell rang again. She snatched it up. Richard's soft, deep voice was exactly what she needed.

"My dear. I hope I haven't called too early."

"Richard! Anytime—I'm so worried. Please, what's happening, where are you, are you both okay?"

"Yes. We survived. Most of the news will wait until we are together, but for now, we are out of country and coming home. May we stay with you again, will you pick us up at the airport?"

"Of *course*. When?"

Richard gave a time the very next day. A late evening flight; June would be there. All the stories would wait until they were on home ground.

After Richard disconnected, June called Seth, the house-sitter. Richard would want to honor the full year agreement, but Seth deserved to know about the change in circumstances. And of course Maura would need Mr. Mouser with her.

Seth was horrified at the news, but relieved they were safe and coming home. As it turned out, Seth had a new lady friend in Hamilton. He assured June he'd be happy to move, willing to help.

The next evening, as Montana June drove toward the airport, the western sky held the last hint of sunset; the night was clear, perfect for flying. June had spent the day buying groceries and treats with which to comfort the refugees. This time, at least, they wouldn't have to deal with the goats, unlike during the fire.

June waited, leaning against the same wall as when Helena came, but she couldn't stand still. As arrival time neared, she started pacing.

The jittery feeling—a craving to hold Maura safe in her arms—was almost unbearable. The plane's landing was announced. Long minutes later, passengers started coming down the stairs. No familiar faces. June waited, the urge to break through the security doors profound. She clenched her fists and watched the clock. The rush of arriving passengers slowed to a dribble then stopped. Had they missed the flight?

Minutes passed. June saw two old people, one with a head bandage and using a crutch, turning the corner from the elevator on the far side of the glass wall. Maybe Richard had stayed to help these elderly ones deplane. But then the one with the bandage raised her head and June realized these tiny, tottery old folks were in fact Maura and Richard themselves, pale shadows of the dramatic, strong newlyweds who'd departed three months ago. June rushed forward and hugged them as they exited.

"You poor things! Here, give me that bag, Richard. We'll get you to a bench. Good lord, you're injured, Mom." June swung Richard's carry-on onto her own shoulder and guided them through to the baggage area. "Here, sit down. I think I'll recognize your luggage, and we can head home."

Maura's face was ashen, drawn, almost unrecognizable; her eyes under the bandage nearly closed with fatigue. She wore no coat, only an airline blanket around her shoulders. It was evident she saw June, but there was no sparkle. Richard appeared close to falling. His shoulders hunched and for the first time, he looked his age. His white hair, usually pristine and shiny, lay in yellowed clumps.

Richard spoke even quieter than usual, voice cracking. "June, we are grateful. Our last vestige of energy. But there is no luggage. We lost everything except what is here."

June hugged them again, making sounds of sympathy. There were no words yet, and no understanding. Instead, she said, "I'll bring the Jeep to the curb. Can you make it outside by yourselves? Look, here's a wheelchair."

"Yes, good," Richard said, getting Maura settled in the chair with her crutch at her side.

June ran to the parking lot, disturbed that Maura hadn't said a word. She didn't smile, seemed only vaguely aware of being home.

The single necessity now was to get these dear ones to the house, safe and sound. June drove out of the parking lot to the front of the terminal where Richard leaned on Maura's wheelchair as if a breath of wind might knock him over. June jumped out and helped him get Maura to the front seat.

Finally Maura spoke, whispered, as June latched the seatbelt. "Thank you. Thank God for you, darling girl."

June hugged her again, then helped Richard into a makeshift back-seat. "Okay, everyone set? We'll be home in two shakes. And heads up, I have a new house-mate, but I'm sure you'll approve." June tried to keep up a mild chatter as they drove to the freeway. Soon, though, she realized they weren't listening. Their eyes were closed, faces slack. At least they didn't have the long drive to Maura's place in the Bitterroot. Five minutes they'd be there. Even that seemed too much.

At home, June pulled up front. Richard helped Maura out as June got the house door unlocked. She hurried to put her arm around Maura's waist, then guided them in. "Let's get you settled in the bedroom. I've set out the same robes you wore the last time. I'll make a hot drink. A toddy? Tea?"

Richard answered for both of them. "Tea, perhaps. Hot and sweet. If we had a toddy, we might not make it to bed. We will come out to the great room as soon as we can, my dear." As Maura crutched into the bedroom, he pulled June aside. "June, Maura's appearance is shocking, I know. The emergency doctors at the aid station in Chile said she would be safe to travel, and I will take her to her own doctor tomorrow. In the morning, I will tell you the full story. But for now, my dear girl, can you bear waiting? We are simply too tired to explain."

Montana June hugged him. "As long as you believe Mom is safe for the night, I trust your instincts, Richard. I can wait."

"Bless you, dear one."

June went to the kitchen and made a pot of tea. She put it, along with some cookies and cups, on the coffee table in the great room by the fire. She set Frosty's kennel-crate near her chair. Soon, the door to the bedroom opened. Richard helped Maura to the couch.

He sighed. "Such heaven, Montana June. You have no idea what this means to us, being here safe with you."

June gave them each a cup of tea and offered cookies.

Maura sipped her tea, then leaned back against the couch. "Did you mention a house-mate, darling girl? I've seen no one else here." Her voice was a paper-thin, not even an echo of her usual deep chuckle.

June leaned over to open the kennel-crate. "Oh, yes. May I introduce my little life saver? This is Frosty the Snow Kitten."

Richard and Maura flowered when June put Frosty on the couch between them. She began investigating, making the new-comers smile at her antics. June told them a bare-bones story of the young kitten, withholding the darkness of before Frosty's birth. If she ever told them about her own winter, it'd be long after they recovered.

The two refugees didn't last long after tea and cookies. They were drained beyond words. One would sometimes reach over to pat the other's hand; they'd turn to look at each other through fathoms of emotions. Once a car backfired on the street outside and Maura dove down to the couch; Richard covered her with his body as if to protect her. They sat up, gave matching deep sighs, then Maura put her face in her hands as Richard stroked her bandaged head. June watched without speaking. Time enough for questions another day. Now, rest was required. They hobbled toward the bedroom, leaning against each other for support. They kissed June. They would see her in the morning. Until then, that was all she knew.

With the fire turned off and Frosty tucked in her kennel-crate, June lay on her cot with a book she wouldn't read. Her mind raced, trying to imagine what'd happened to make such vibrant, beautiful people turn into these little, gray, elderly crusts.

If sleep were to come, June needed to change her focus. She walked outside to look at the ancient stars that had already witnessed everything. It was not quite midnight. The clouds had cleared; the moon was hours from rising and the constellations blazed. June turned in her heart to Logan. Though she didn't speak to him anymore, she thought of him and listened, hoping to garner wisdom she needed for the coming day. Before many minutes passed, June returned to her cot by the fire.

IN THE MORNING, though not up as early as usual, June had her coffee long before her house-guests awoke. She ate some yogurt and readied things to make a hot breakfast for them. In time, she heard rustlings and soft voices, the toilet flushing. Richard came out of the bedroom.

June took his face between her hands and said, "Richard. I'm glad you're here." She intended to say more, but tears threatened, so instead, she held him.

"My dear. Thank you again. Is there coffee? I will not be good for much until I have a cup."

June got Richard settled in the sitting room with a throw over his knees and brought him coffee, then sat on the floor by his legs. Frosty rustled through the folds of the throw, walking over the tops of Richard's socks.

"Frosty, you rascal, leave the poor man alone." June put the kitten on her own lap. "Richard, everything can wait until you're ready, but if you need to talk, I'm here."

He looked outward, as if at a far horizon. "Montana June, I am sure you see Maura is very fragile. What she witnessed was shattering, to say nothing of her physical injuries. We will recover, I believe. But when I think of what happened to that wonderful woman—" At this, Richard's voice broke. He put his face in his hands, shoulders shaking.

June stood and wrapped her arms around him. "Richard. You're here and safe. There are no worries now. All is well, and we'll get Mom the help she needs." She held him as he cried.

Minutes later, Richard used his napkin to blow his nose. "Thank you. I am humbled to grieve in front of you."

Montana June returned to the coffeepot to give Richard some space. "Do you want to talk about it now, or wait until later? Whatever you choose." She poured herself another cup.

"I think Maura will rest for another hour or so, and it would be best for me to tell you a small part of what we witnessed before she rises. We may never be able to recount the whole story, but you deserve to hear the bare facts." He rewrapped the throw around his legs and tucked the robe closer to his chest, then took a swig of the coffee. "You make fine, strong coffee." He set his cup down. "Now. We have good memories, too."

Richard started at the beginning. The first weeks they played tourist. They explored, rested, ate marvelous food. They joined a senior tour of the Amazon, and reveled in seeing the animals, the mighty river, immense forest. After leaving the tour group, they headed to Chile, to the village in which they'd scheduled two months of volunteer work. They were living there when the earthquake hit. Richard said the sound of the earth moving was a thunder from which he would never recover, "the soul-shattering cataclysm of Mother Earth tearing herself apart." The quake hit at night. He and Maura held each other while the house collapsed around them. Timbers fell on them, one angled over Maura's body. They knew they would die. In daylight, they heard people trying to dig them out. Richard made enough noise for the rescuers to find them, but it took hours for the debris to be lifted, and by that time they were hypothermic and dehydrated. Maura was in shock, Richard thought, as her demeanor was flat and her skin-tone ashen. Her head, no longer bleeding, was injured and swelling. Her leg had been damaged by the timber. Their neighbor, her three young children, and elderly in-laws had been killed by the quake. While Maura and Richard were being rescued, they saw the broken, bloodied bodies of the children, and the mother crushed trying to protect them. As they watched, the bereft husband tried to crawl back into the wreckage to die.

Richard and Maura were treated in a makeshift hospital by people they'd worked with as volunteers. So many deaths happened in the village that bodies were still being discovered in the rubble, even as the two were finally moved to the larger city from where they could get a flight home. There Richard called June.

"As I sit here, Montana June, in your warm and safe house—" Richard's voice broke again, and his shoulders quivered, "I think of what I nearly lost. I might have been crawling back into the wreckage to find Maura. At our wedding, I had the gall to feel young and strong rather than this old man before you. When I *found* the love of my life, I was almost three times older than my mother was when my father was *killed*. She was only twenty-six when she lost her life's love by that thunderous lightning strike. I am now many years older than she was when she died…decades older than my brother Willard was when he died in Korea. I have had decades to live that they did not. And yet, I quake at the thought of what I could have lost. Such unforgivable hubris." Again, Richard put his face in his hands and cried.

The area around them was covered in crumpled tissues, which Frosty tore into little pieces. Richard's voice had weakened to nothing. June put her head on his knees and they rested, allowing the warmth and safety of the little house to begin the process of healing the memories of death.

MAURA SLEPT UNTIL noon. The sound of the shower in the en suite announced she had awakened. The water ran a very long time. When she came out, the ends of her hair were wet, draped over her shoulders like a shawl of red and gray. The bandage, dry but dirty, must've been covered with a shower cap. Her face was pale as marble; no smile reached her eyes. She walked with her crutch to June. The two women stood supporting each other for many long moments.

"Mom. Thank God you're here. I'll make you breakfast. We've both eaten, but we'll sit with you. Nothing to be done right now except rest. Later, we'll call Seth and talk to him about Mr. Mouser and your house. There's good news there. I'll call your doctor, make sure he'll see you today. But for now, sit. I'll get you fed."

The quiet day progressed. There was, as June said, nothing to be done except rest and heal. The week passed in the same fashion. By the time Maura and Richard were somewhat stronger, Seth was ready to move to Hamilton to join his girlfriend, and Maura's home was once more available. They brought their boxes out of storage and returned to their mountain to continue the long process of recovery.

36

Spring had well and truly sprung. Daffodils, dandelions, tulips and buttercups, many sparks of color brightened the fresh new green of lawns, fields, pastures. The run-off of mountain snowmelt brought Rattlesnake Creek close to flood-stage—strong enough to rumble boulders—but the banks held. Montana June enjoyed the sound of the noisy water. The sun warmed her shoulders as she walked around the park.

She breathed in, walking fast, filling her lungs with the fragrance of blossoms, and thought about Maura. Richard had called yesterday to say they were making slow progress. The brain MRI had shown shadows that would be watched. Maura hadn't regained her confident, assertive demeanor; she was quiet and withdrawn, seeking to stay near Richard as they puttered in the garden. She had horrible headaches, which sometimes led to nausea and loss of vision.

Last year, Maura had been June's stalwart guide, her mainstay in their unwanted journey through grief. This year, Maura forgot June's birthday in March, an additional sign all was not well. June didn't even mention the passing of another year; rather, she spent a quiet day working on her upcoming speech.

She tried not to worry. Maura believed all she needed was rest, calm and the presence of her Richard, and he made sure Maura was never alone.

The Regional Conference for Women was scheduled for the coming Friday. June had revised her speech enough to be confident it was the best she could make it. She vacillated between feeling thrilled and ready, or *knowing* she couldn't present. She fantasized getting laryngitis or strep throat. In short, she was terrified. She hadn't spoken in front of a group of adults for years. Why had she ever agreed to do such a thing?

June'd be one of several break-out speakers during the day; a nationally known woman would give the keynote address following dinner. Maura, if no headaches arose, would come. Richard would stay at June's house and take Maura home the next day. All was planned. Now June just needed a shot of self-confidence.

Her walking route took her up the North Hills overlooking Missoula. The incline became steeper. Wildflowers dotted both sides of the trail, all ground-hugging in this dry landscape. In one area, bitterroots bloomed in a thick mat enthralling June at their unusual sight. As she rested she turned, hands on hips, and looked out over the valley. Few clouds floated in the dazzling sky; the many trees lining the streets of Missoula were bunches of chartreuse lace. The steeple of the Catholic church glistened in the sun, and beyond, the Clark Fork River sparkled as it rushed on its way west.

Having caught her breath, June turned again to her climb. She didn't want to lose her impetus. She had miles to go before her rest, and plenty of time to practice her speech. The route continued uphill a long way, some parts steeper than others. By the time the trail turned down to join the road, June was relieved to be heading home.

At Greenough Park, she was weary. June slowed her pace, deepened her breath, let her arms hang. Her shirt was sweaty. She sipped from her water bottle.

Through the trees she could see a truck parked on the street. Someone was by the creek, near June's favorite log, the one she'd come to so often with Ranger. A man crouched on his haunches, forearms on his thighs, facing downstream, the top of his head barely visible as she walked by on the pine-needle-strewn path. A muttered "damn" as he rose to stand. A streak of white hair, over his left ear.

Pace.

His head was down as he climbed up the bank. He wiped his sleeve across his eyes and slapped his other hand against his leg, brushing off the duff. He gained the top of the slope, straightened, then startled to see her.

"June! Didn't see you there. Thought…hell. Been waiting more than an hour…thought…I'd missed you. Was gonna leave." His hands reached toward her, then fell to his side. A smile came and went, and he took one step closer.

June used all her strength not to run to him. She wasn't sure why he was here, couldn't know how long he would stay. But he looked so good standing there. She'd forgotten how beautiful his eyes were. His face glowed, even in the shade of the trees.

"Pace. You're back?"

"Yes, my June. I am…back."

She reached a hand to him and he bounded the rest of the way, taking her in his arms. The kiss was long—long and deep. Then June pulled away. "Um, Pace? I hate to say this, but I've just come back from a long walk, and, well…I really have to pee!"

Pace smiled, released the hug, and let her run across the street to her house. He followed. As he neared the door, Montana June called back, "Come on in. I'll be right out."

A few minutes later, June came from the bedroom, having brushed her hair from the ponytail, washed her face, and changed her sweaty T-shirt for a clean one. While freshening up, June thought, *It's April. Almost four months since I've seen him. I never returned any of his calls. It should be over, but, holy* lovin' *Hannah, what a kiss!* Part of her wanted to run and hug him. Part of her wanted to slug him in the face for leaving. She couldn't imagine what Pace thought. She found him standing on the patio, scene of so many good times and two very bad times. He was looking up at Mount Jumbo, arms crossed on his chest.

"Pace? Would you like a glass of iced tea? A beer? Some water?" June's voice was quiet as she slid open the screen door.

"No…thanks." He turned to her, his head tilted down, voice soft. "What I gotta do now, is just…talk. Uh, at least, if you…well, shit. You never took my calls. Knew you're really mad and hurt. Hell, I couldn't blame you. But, well, now…need to clear things up. That is, if you have time."

June cleared her throat, took time answering. When she did, the words were spaced, emphasized. "Oh, yes. I have time. Let's sit." They angled their chairs toward each other. When she continued, the edge in her voice became more pronounced. "I *could* apologize for not returning your calls. I listened to your messages, most of them. But you were with Cindy and I couldn't reconcile that in my heart. I took to calling her 'Cinders' because she turned my world to ashes. You were with Cinders."

"Yes, but not…uh, in the biblical sense. She was so messed up when she got released…guess prison'll do that, even if you're not messed up going in. Found her an apartment, started in a job. 'Course the half-way folks helped there, too, but it took longer than anyone expected, 'cause she's really a basket case. Up to her, now. Honestly, I was like a big brother or something, trying to get her to grow up. May not stick, but she knows…onetime deal. I won't go back. All that time, helping get her feet on the ground, all I thought about was you. Knew I'd screwed up badly by leaving. Wasn't sure you'd be here, and well, may-be you aren't still my girl. But…had to see you again to check."

June watched him, keeping her expression closed. She wouldn't give him immediate peace. "I don't know, Pace. It's good to see you. But so much has happened since you left. And there's a great deal of anger in me still. Why didn't you at least *talk* to me about it before you made your decision? We had such a wonderful Christmas, and then, you just—left!"

He reached to her, but seeing her face, pulled back. "You're right. Shit, should've talked to you beforehand. Done a lot of thinking on it. See, June…been a loner all my life. Only child. On the track team, racing even against my own teammates. I run alone, train alone. My work with FWP is solitary. *Always* made decisions by myself, never learned otherwise. Should've talked to you about it, but it wasn't your deal, your mess. See?" Pace's voice faded to almost nothing. "I…felt some responsibility to Cindy. Can't really explain. Stupid after the way she treated me, but I…just had to go." He was struggling: head tipped down, arms wrapped around his gut. "Can you forgive me?"

June gave a sharp exhale. "It was a bad—no, a terribly dangerous winter for me. I was alone, and I almost didn't survive. No." June saw Pace's face as he looked up in shock, "No, I don't want to tell you about it now. There are parts I may never tell you. Can we maybe take it step by step? Can you be okay with me saying I'm happy to see you again?"

Pace's eyes closed as he inhaled. His head tipped back, and his face seemed to relax. "Yes, okay. That's good, my June, uh…if it's okay to call you that. Well, um…take you out to dinner?"

"No, but how about that beer now? I'd like one, too. I haven't had any recently, but there's some of Richard's stashed in back." As she said this, Frosty scratched at the screen door. "Oh, hey! That's right. I have a new roomie you haven't met. She isn't allowed outside, so let's have our beers inside, okay?"

"You bet. Aw, what a cutie." Pace opened the door for June, then, bending down, put one finger toward Frosty, adding, "Who's this little ball of fluff then?"

"Pace Pacinski, meet Frosty the Snow Kitten, my lifesaver. She was born in January, the day after one of the worst days of my life. Without her, I'm pretty sure I wouldn't still be here. And no, that's not a story you're going to hear yet. I'll get the beers, you two go on into the great room."

As June busied herself in the kitchen getting out crackers and cheese to go with the beer, Pace sat on the floor to play with the kitten. "Hey, June," he called, "where're Maura and Richard now? You hear from them at all? Bet they're having a great time. Sure'd like to hear all their stories."

June carried the tray in and set it on the coffee table. "Well, I do know where they are, as a matter of fact. And their stories *are* something." June looked at her watch, noted the time. "Hmm. It's Thursday afternoon. Three o'clock. Richard's working his volunteer shift at Travelers' Rest. Seth is with Maura. No doubt they're weeding her garden and trying to keep Nanny out of the new greens."

Her sad eyes belied her smile at his look of shock. Then, with deliberation, she told the story of the earthquake and their abrupt return to Montana. She didn't pull any punches about how terrifying or dangerous their experiences were. She told Pace that Maura wasn't coming out of the panic and insecurity the tragedy caused, of the massive headaches Maura had, and how sometimes she couldn't find the right words.

"So, Pace, there're good reasons I need to take your return slowly. This winter was every bit as bad for me and mine as last winter when the loss of Logan was new and raw. You need to understand it's only through luck that Maura, Richard, and I are even alive. And yes, I've held a good bit of anger in my heart that you weren't here to help."

Pace, cross-legged on the floor, put his head in his hands. Frosty climbed up his back and June reached over to disengage the sharp little claws from his shirt; his shoulders shuddered as he tried to control his tears.

"So very sorry....Should've been here." His voice came ragged through his hands.

"Pace," June said to his quaking back, "all winter while I was so angry at you, part of me realized my anger wasn't founded. I knew—in my heart, if not my head—you were being the white-hat cowboy you can't avoid being, helping out someone who needed you. Because of your previous relationship with Cindy, I couldn't accept that. I hated you being with her. Part of my anger, I've come to understand, was because I'd started seeing us as partners; I'd allowed my inner teenager to get the better of me. Maura and Richard's wedding was so romantic, I'd begun to imagine another one in the future. I shouldn't have made that assumption. If I wasn't actually borrowing happiness, I was at the very least trying to use other people's happiness as a magnet to draw it to me. And, I could've trusted you more. You can't be every place at all times. But now, you're here. That's all that counts. Well, I guess, that counts if you're here to stay." June pressed on his shoulder so he would turn to her. She took him in her arms, dried his tears and then let him sink his head onto her shoulder as he continued to cry.

"So…damned…grateful to you. So glad to be back, my June. I love you; missed you every day. Please forgive me. I wasn't here when you needed me."

"Day by day, Cowboy. Day by day." She held him. In time, they scooted over to lean against the couch. As June re-accustomed herself to being with Pace, enjoying again the scent of his skin and the touch of his hands, she felt as if, with Pace's return, perhaps it was she who had come home.

37

Montana June and Maura Donner sat at the front of the conference room in the hotel near the river in downtown Missoula. They'd arrived earlier in the day and attended one break-out section themselves, but June's nervous energy wouldn't let her sit any longer. She needed to walk and rehearse. Though she'd hoped to walk outside, rain was coming down in buckets, so she walked the hallways of the hotel. The urge to run away was almost irresistible, but after all, the focus of the conference was "Tragedy to Strength." It wouldn't show much strength if she backed out now.

There was a half hour between the early afternoon session and the one in which June was scheduled. June'd walked to the bathroom twice, stood and sat multiple times, then closed her eyes and tried to use deep breathing to calm her nerves. Maura patted her hand and whispered, "You'll do fine, darling girl. Pretend these people are your students. No worries."

June heard voices of the women entering to hear her talk. The rustle of noise as they met friends and took off raincoats—the aroma coming from the coffee cart—all were comforting. A woman rose and walked to the microphone at the lectern; June was flattered by her introduction and the welcoming applause. She took another large breath, then faced the audience. She saw several people she knew, including Ellen Painter. Every seat in the room was taken, with women standing at the back of the room as well. June was surprised at a standing-room only crowd for her little talk. She began.

"Thank you for your presence today. I'm honored to be among the speakers for such a valuable, important topic. Tragedy to Strength. Yes, indeed—the title about says it all, doesn't it? In fact, you know as well as I do that every woman in this room could be up here speaking. Each of us has lived through tragedy. Once, I believed I had my full share of tragedy when my parents died in a car wreck when I was fifteen. My sister did a good job of stepping in to raise me, but what fifteen-year-old doesn't need her mother and father? I thought I'd paid my dues. I married a wonderful man, had a blessed life with him for ten years. Life was good until he died eighteen months ago from prostate cancer. If you ask me how it felt, living without him, I'll tell you it was like having half my body and mind and soul torn away, then being told to go on living with the bloody stumps. But as I said, I'm not the only woman here who's lived through tragedy, experienced loss. Here today are many who've lost husbands; one I'm close to also lost her son and then lived through an earthquake that killed many of her friends. With us today are women who are doing the most important job

in the world, raising children alone, as single moms. In the audience are survivors of rape, incest, domestic abuse, other violence. Women who deal with physical injuries and illnesses that affect them every day. Women who deal with cancer. A woman here is in chemo right now, and may I say, the wig looks very natural?"

June paused to allow the light laughter to bubble through the room, since the woman to whom June referred wore a Cruella de Ville wig, half-white hair, half-black. The woman stood and bowed to the applause of the room.

"Women are here who've been walked over by men reaching for the jobs better filled by the women, women who've given their all to a society that sometimes marginalizes them, mistreats them, pats them on the head, and says, 'Why don't you stay home with the kiddies where you belong?'

"I know I'm not the only one in this room who has contemplated or attempted suicide and lived to tell the tale. Women are here who've lost people they couldn't bear to lose. To suicide. To cancer. To accidents. To drunk drivers. To war.

"And, of course, there are losses and tragedies represented here today that I'm not aware of. I don't want to minimize anyone's experience. We intend to honor all of us. We cannot quantify or put degrees on loss. Each of us feels pain and loss differently. One size does not fit all.

"Yes, we've all lived through tragedy—loss—pain. We've lived through dark days we did not *believe we could survive. And how did we? How did we survive when we thought we could not? How did we find the strength to face just one more day, one more day, and step by step live to come here today?* Damned *good question."*

Again, June paused while people chuckled. She took a drink from the glass of water below the lectern and also used a tissue to blow her nose. She noticed there were other women in the audience blowing their noses, too.

"Yes, I didn't come here today to cry in front of you, but figured I might. If anyone needs a tissue, I'm happy to share. Got a whole box.

"I've thought much about how we live through tragedy and come out stronger. I believe there are three points integral to our success.

"For the first point, I want to draw a mental picture. I live across the street from Greenough Park, about a mile from here. Local folks know the city's bound by law to keep half the park in as natural a state as possible, so little is done in terms of landscaping. Just down the street from my house are two trees that've been in a particular juxtaposition for many years. One of the trees was once a mighty cottonwood, perhaps thirty-six inches in diameter. This huge tree fell, as cottonwoods are wont to do, but instead of falling all the way down, it was caught and held by a slender, young maple. The maple, now these many years later, is still only six inches in diameter. This all happened so long ago that the base of the cottonwood is almost rotted away, with one tiny peg of itself remaining on the ground. The entire weight of the cottonwood rests on this patient young maple that's borne the weight almost all its life. Now, I wouldn't want this to happen, but imagine the city came through and cleared out all these trees. Took away the dead cottonwood. Cut down the young maple and the other maples of the same size right next to it. I'd be willing to bet a cross-section of our little maple would show the very cells of it are different from its neighbors. Having to bear the weight of that cottonwood all its life has changed the cellular structure, made it stronger. Because it grew up bearing the weight. Day by day.

"Putting this in human terms, maybe it happens like this. For the luckiest of us, we lose our favorite blanket when we're toddlers, and can't sleep for weeks. Then our dog dies and our hearts break again. The boy we *have a crush on doesn't invite us to the prom. Bit by bit, we learn how to deal with sadness, with heartbreak. For the less lucky of us, we lose parents, we develop cancer, we go to war, we come home broken in body or mind or heart. So…I think one way we turn tragedy into strength is that our cells, our hearts, our souls, and our minds change with each loss; and loss, large or small, is a part of life. Each time we bear the weight, we get stronger. I'm stronger now than I've ever been because of my past. That strength allowed me to save my own life. Life is a marathon. We take it step by step, day by day, loss by loss, and each iteration makes us stronger."*

June stepped back, took a drink from her water, cleared her throat, and continued.

"The second checkpoint on my list is somewhat lighter. Women, well, most of us anyway, deal with life with a healthy sense of humor. I had to modify that statement because this week I saw on the internet an article and picture of a woman who simply boggles my mind. The photo of her shows an attractive—if serious-looking—woman. It was the write-up that floored me. You see, this woman is proud of the fact that she hasn't once, not one time in the last forty years, smiled. Nope. Not even one tiny little grin. Guess why. Because she believes smiling causes wrinkles. WRINKLES! You heard me!"

June laughed as the women roared. It took a good minute for the laughter to settle down.

"Yes, for forty years, this woman hasn't smiled because she doesn't want to give herself wrinkles. Now, I love growing older. I hope, when I am a little old thing, my face will be crisscrossed with the wrinkles of a long life-time of smiling. I'd rather see a face with smile wrinkles; frown wrinkle; happy, sad, and emotional wrinkles of a life well lived than a face that's a perfect, unmarred surface of stone. But, despite this exception, women have

wonderful senses of humor. The fact that you all found that woman funny shows I'm right. We're strong because we laugh. And holy Hannah, a good laugh is pure medicine.

"So, we take tragedy to strength because we do it step by step and we do it with our innate sense of humor. What else?

"There've been many strong women who've thought about this question of how we live through times of trial. Eleanor Roosevelt was quoted as saying, 'A woman is like a tea bag. You don't know how strong she is until she gets in hot water.' Mother Teresa said, 'I know God won't give me anything I can't handle. I just wish He didn't trust me so much.' Here's another one, by an anonymous voice: 'You never know how strong you are until being strong is the only choice you have.' Perhaps a good one for today is from that all-wise, all-powerful woman with the truly mighty rack, Dolly Parton. She says, 'If you want a rainbow, you've got to put up with the rain.'

Again, June allowed the laughter a chance to settle. She looked at her watch and saw she was right on time.

"We put up with one heck of a lot of rain in our lives and we live through it. Floods of the stuff, right? But the question is, how do we come out the other end better than we started? How do we go from tragedy to STRENGTH? I think the answer is in our genes. Not our Levis, mind you; rather, our X chromosomes. Because we have, from the beginning of time, been the fire-keepers, the hearth keepers, the home-makers, the care-givers to the family, by our very definition, we turn to each other for strength. When one of us is in trouble, we know we can turn to the rest of us for help. We don't have to prove our manliness or muscles; we don't need to have the pissing contests it seems some of the male gender insist on. One of us becomes ill and others step in to help with the children. One of us loses a husband, and immediately, the casserole-bringers start delivering food. (Really. God

bless the casserole-bringers.) Even if we lose our mothers at an early age, as my sister and I did, someone steps in to fill that role. Thank you, Maura, mother-in-law from heaven. How was I ever so lucky as to have you?"

June blew a kiss to Maura, who stood and blew one back. June caught it and put it on her own cheek.

"One of the organizations that came together to put on this wonderful conference today was begun decades ago by another second mother to me, my own dear Sarah England. She and her friends started, back in the 1950s, the group still known as the Matrix Table. Perfect, perfect *name. Of course, a table is a gathering place. And then, matrix. WE, my friends, are the matrix. You and I together are the framework that holds society together. It's almost a chemical reaction, a crystalline structure. Put two women together and they form a bond so strong that others are drawn in. We get involved, we seek help, we offer help, we volunteer. The matrix grows stronger with each woman, and each woman grows stronger by her involvement in the matrix. You and me. Strong separately, strong together.*

"So, finally, I want to thank you. You lived through your tragedy. You brought your strength to the group. You became an integral part of the whole simply by being 'woman,' and isn't that the best? Together, we are better. Together, we are stronger. Together, we are saviors of the world.

"Tragedy to Strength. We hope we have less of the former, but we know we've all we need of the latter. Because together we are…"

June stepped away from the lectern, overwhelmed by the applause from the crowd of women. One by one the women in the audience stood in a standing ovation. The clapping didn't stop until June returned to the lectern and held up her hands. The women sat back down and June said, "Goodness. Thank you. That's extremely kind. But I know as well as do you, you weren't clapping for me. No—" June again stopped them, "no, you weren't, but thanks for that. You were clapping for yourselves and for each other. Women. We are so powerful together. One at a time we are pretty darn good, pretty darn strong, and tremendously sexy. But put us all together? Holy Hannah, girls, put us all together and you have the very matrix of the world. Put us all together and you've got a power that cannot be beaten. Again, thank you, and please, drive with care through the rain. Without the rain, we don't get the rainbow."

June stepped away and the women applauded again, then started gathering their coats and bags.

Maura walked up and gave June a tremendous hug. "Darling girl, what a testament to womanhood. Marvelous."

June took a big inhale and laughed, wiping her face with her hands. "Whew, thanks, Mom. I'm glad it went well."

A woman wearing a shapeless gray sweater, her hair scraped back into a tight ponytail, approached. She said, "Thank you, Montana June. You inspired me to stop being so sad. I lost my son last year and I couldn't break out of my grief to ask for help, but now I know I can. Maybe I'll volunteer at a grief clinic. By helping others, I'll help myself. Thank you."

June embraced her and said, "Oh, yes. Without the help of others, we have *no* hope. One by one we aren't strong enough, but together we are. I'm very sorry for your loss. It is a horrible thing, isn't it?" She gave a sad smile as the woman nodded. "The pain feels insurmountable and there are no short cuts. The only way through it is through it. Step by step in the right direction. Keep breathing until you feel like living again. That's all we can do. And, ask for help." June turned, including Maura. "This is my mother-in-law, Maura Donner. Would you like to get a cup of tea with us right now? You ask for help. We're here."

The woman shook her head. "Thank you, but I have a counselor's number I've been meaning to call and now I will. I've got to get home to the rest of my family and make dinner, but I'd love to visit sometime."

June shared her phone number, and the woman left.

Others came to congratulate June, hug her, thank her for the message she'd shared. Ellen smiled and waved as she left.

As June and Maura packed up their own bags and coats after the last woman left, June said, "You know, Mom, I didn't say anything new or different. This's something inside us, but we need to be reminded once in a while that we have each other to lean on. It was a good day." She stretched her back, and again took a deep breath. "I'm glad I didn't back out. And very glad it's over! I'm also relieved we decided to skip the formal dinner and speech. I'm done in. And how're you? How's your head?"

"It's fine, darling girl. You know Richard gave me a pill before we came. But I forget what's next."

"Now we meet Richard and Pace for dinner. I'm starved. It's good the restaurant is just down the street. Let's go."

38

The two women walked together so Montana June could hold Maura's umbrella in one hand while letting her mother-in-law link arms for the needed support. They hurried down the block and across the street to El Cazador on the corner. Richard and Pace were already seated, with beers in front of them. The men stood, hugged the women and took their raincoats and umbrella.

Richard looked at June's bright face and said, "Montana June. How was it? I assume it went well, since you are here with a smile."

Maura answered as he held her chair, guiding her safely. "Richard! You wouldn't believe June's speech. She blew their socks off, and they gave her a…oh, damn. You know, the audience stands? It was very inspiring."

Pace smiled. "A standing ovation? I knew you'd do it! Congratulations." He gave June a high five.

Maura touched June's shoulder. "So, Montana June. Now that you've given the speech, what's next on your...uh...agenda?" Frustration turned to relief as she recalled the correct word.

"Mom, I've been blessed in my life. But I've also been through hell and back. Even have the T-shirt!" June winked at Pace. "I can't continue to be a lady of leisure. I'm too young to retire. I want to contribute. You told me, some time back, that I'm a good writer, and it's something I enjoy doing."

Maura smiled. "You *are* good. Think of all you said today. That's you, writing."

"Yeah, and that's kind of where I'm going, I think. I've changed in the last two years. It almost seems when Logan was alive, I was a child pretending to be a working adult. Naive. I'd never lived alone. Never had to make my own decisions. People were always taking care of me. And now that's all different. Maybe I have something to say that might help others. I want to write a book...for young widows. And perhaps my speech today is a starting point."

Richard said, "Perfect."

Pace simply beamed.

Maura wiped tears from her eyes, but her smile was one of pride. "This will be desolate...oh, hell. That's not what I meant. But what I think is, it won't be easy."

"Yes. It *will* be difficult. And I suppose there'll be times writing will make me feel desolate, too. It'll probably be more revealing than I'll be comfortable with."

Just then, the waiter came and took their orders. Drinks arrived for both of the women. Inroads were made on the chips and salsa.

Pace said, "Montana June, continue about your book. I'd like to hear more."

"Well, this's been percolating for a while. I've learned so much from each of you. Good things, I mean," she said when she saw Pace's downcast eyes. She smiled when he looked up. "And I learned from Logan, from Ranger, from Helena. I even learned a thing or two from Cara, believe it or not."

"Oh goddess, spare us from that one!" Maura spurted, and they all laughed. The food arrived, and everyone dug into the steaming, spicy plates.

They talked as they ate. The discussion centered around June's book idea and her speaking experience.

As dinner drew to a close, Maura touched Richard's hand and said, "Sweetheart, could you say what we talked about last night? I remember the conversation, but can't put the bits in the right order."

"Of course. Last night Maura was anticipating your speech today. She was confident it would go well. Then she said, 'My darling girl was once a sweet child. She turned into a power-house. She will do marvelous things.' "

Maura said, "Exactly right. Thank you, sweet man. Now, Richard, I'm afraid I need to go home. Is the truck close by?" Her face was pale and deeply lined, showing her exhaustion.

"Yes, around the corner. And it appears the rain has stopped. It is good to go now. We will soon be in our mountain home." Richard rummaged in his pocket and brought out a prescription bottle. "But you should take one of your headache pills now. Perhaps you can sleep on the drive home."

As the two elder ones gathered rain gear, Pace turned to June. "My truck is nearby, too. If you want…I'd drop you off…maybe stay over?" he said, his voice rising in hope.

"Pace, thank you." She touched his cheek. "But after today, I want to be alone and have time to think. Since the rain's stopped, I'll walk. I'll call you tomorrow, though. It's really great to have you back."

Pace's shoulders slumped as he pushed in his chair. Lines appeared between his eyebrows and one corner of his mouth turned down. "Okay, Montana June….Thanks for including me this evening. "

The four walked out of the restaurant together. June hugged Maura hard and helped her into Richard's truck, then turned to him. "Thank you, Richard, for taking such good care of her. I'll see you both soon."

"Yes, of course. Again, remember the power-house we see in you." His rich voice held love and pride. He walked around to the driver's side. Soon they were on their way home.

June hugged Pace. He put his hands on her shoulders, looking into her eyes. "I'm proud of you, too. You've changed…grown. I look forward to…well, hope I get to know the new you."

June's eyes crinkled with her smile. "I'll see you soon, Cowboy." She left him there and started walking home.

AS MONTANA JUNE walked through the fresh rain-washed evening, down Higgins Avenue toward home, she was happy with her speech, but her thoughts centered on what she wanted to write, if in fact, she *could* write.

She'd learned much about herself in the last two years, and a great deal of it wasn't flattering. She'd lived through frightening times and come out stronger. *I used to wonder who I'd be in different situations. Instead, I'm learning who I am* now. *That's what's important. Whatever a person lives through, no matter how horrible, wonderful, or personal, those are the only tools we have. What we live is who we are; that will help me write.*

She caught her reflection in a shop window and paused. *Am I looking at a writer? If so, I'd better be more insightful than that. Everyone starts somewhere, but really, Juney.* She tried to dig deeper. Maura had made a Freudian slip when she said that writing would be desolate. June knew writing well meant stripping naked—further, even: she'd have to expose her soul; that terrified her. But, after all she'd gone through she damned well refused to be defeated by that fear. If she was victorious over her own fear, perhaps she could write a book to help other young widows. In any case, she'd give it her whole effort. A power-house effort.

June looked up and saw the rain clouds were gone; the evening light struck the North Hills, making the spring grass look almost fluorescent. It was a spectacular evening.

At the main intersection, June's progress was halted as the green light turned yellow, then red. Walking toward her on the cross street was a tall man. He turned to wait for the light, standing well away from her. They exchanged glances. His deep red hair brushed his shoulders; he had a well-trimmed mahogany-colored beard. A striking leather jacket accentuated his broad shoulders. He flashed a smile and nodded, causing a lock of hair to fall across his forehead.

"Excuse me." His voice was a deep bass. "I'm new in town and looking for a good restaurant. Any nearby you'd recommend?"

As June told him about her favorites, she was exceedingly aware of a shock of attraction striking her core. This was the exact feeling she'd had the first time she met Logan. She felt her face get warm. It was impossible to take her gaze away from his deep green eyes. As she spoke, they missed the light to cross.

"This's bold of me," he said, "but the Mexican place you mentioned sounded best. Would you join me for dinner? I don't know a soul here in Missoula."

"Well, honestly, I just finished dinner there." June gave him her best smile. "But it's right down this street. You can't miss it." She pointed back the way she'd come.

"Well, thanks. I hope I get to see you again."

"Oh, if you've moved here, there's no doubt we'll run into each other. For a city, Missoula's a pretty small-town kinda place. Enjoy your dinner." She smiled again and turned to catch the green light as the red-haired man went in the other direction. June chanced a look back at him and caught him looking over his shoulder. A big man with a big smile. Again that flash of electricity zinged deep inside her.

As she continued walking toward home, June had an added spring in her step. Confidence, that was it. A world—a whole sky—of new opportunities lay before her, exhilarating, and maybe a little scary. Though she'd never get over losing Logan, her spirit *was* recovering. She had family, a house of her own, and a future that held promise.

As she crossed the train tracks and entered Greenough Park, she remembered Frosty would be awaiting her dinner. June's step quickened. The sour-spicy aroma of rain-soaked cottonwoods was invigorating.

Rattlesnake Creek roared, full of new snowmelt. Looking up toward Mount Jumbo, Montana June saw a bright double rainbow stretching across the horizon. She no longer heard Logan's voice, so she had to say it herself: *Montana June, begin again.*

About the Author

KIMBERLY ELLEN DREDGER lives in Missoula, Montana; her childhood stomping grounds are the backdrop of this book. She currently resides with her husband, and a Scottish terrier, in the Rattlesnake Valley.

One year into her teaching career in western Montana, Kimberly's young husband of two years was killed. Living through that loss and beginning again seemed insurmountable, but in time she recognized that her story was not unique. Life and death go hand in hand; strength comes in learning that.

After Kimberly retired from teaching, she began training for long-distance walking. In her first year, she completed both the Missoula Marathon and the New York City Marathon. Though she still walks, distances no longer call to her. She spends her time reading, writing, and walking around the park with her husband and dog.

This is Kimberly's first novel.

Made in the USA
Monee, IL
27 April 2022